Somewhere Geese
Are Flying

Books by Gary Gildner

Poetry
The Bunker in the Parsley Fields 1997
Clackamas 1991
Blue Like the Heavens: New & Selected Poems 1984
The Runner 1978
Nails 1975
Digging for Indians 1971
First Practice 1969

Limited Editions
The Birthday Party 2000
The Swing 1996
Pavol Hudák, The Poet, Is Talking 1996
Jabón 1981
Letters from Vicksburg 1976
Eight Poems 1973

Fiction
Somewhere Geese Are Flying 2004
The Second Bridge 1987
A Week in South Dakota 1987
The Crush 1983

Memoir
My Grandfather's Book: Generations of an American Family 2003
The Warsaw Sparks 1990

Anthology
Out of This World: Poems from the Hawkeye State 1975

Somewhere Geese
Are Flying

New and Selected Stories

GARY GILDNER

Michigan State University Press
East Lansing

∞ The paper used in this publication meets the minimum requirements of
ANSI/NISO Z39.48–1992 (R 1997) (Permanence of Paper).

 Michigan State University Press
East Lansing, Michigan 48823–5245

Printed and bound in the United States of America.

10 09 08 07 06 05 04   1 2 3 4 5 6 7 8 9 10

LIBRARY OF CONGRESS CATALOGING-IN-PUBLICATION DATA

Gildner, Gary.
  Somewhere geese are flying / Gary Gildner.
  p. cm.
  ISBN 0-87013-733-6 (pbk. : alk. paper)
  I. Title.
  PS3557.I343S66 2004
  813'.54–dc22

                                        2004012332

Michigan State University Press is a member of the Green Press Initiative and is
committed to developing and encouraging ecologically responsible publishing
practices. For more information about the Green Press Initiative and the use of
recycled paper in book publishing, please visit www.greenpressinitiative.org.

Cover design by Heather Truelove Aiston
Book design by Sans Serif, Inc.

Visit Michigan State University Press on the World Wide Web at:
www.msupress.msu.edu

For Gretchen and Margaret
my daughters

Acknowledgments

Certain stories in this book first appeared in the following magazines: *Antaeus*, "Pavol Hudák, The Poet, Is Talking"; *The Georgia Review*, "Below the Gospels," "Sleepy Time Gal," "The Great Depression," "A Week in South Dakota," "The Inheritance," and "Somewhere Geese Are Flying"; *Grand Street*, "Tornadoes"; *The Kenyon Review*, "Come Sta? Come Va?"; *The North American Review*, "Genealogy" and "Leaving"; *Shenandoah*, "Something Special"; *Tendril*, "Burial"; *Western Humanities Review*, "A Million Dollar Story"; and *Witness*, "I Have Work To Do."

Six stories are reprinted from earlier collections: "Sleepy Time Gal" from *The Crush* (1983); "Tornadoes," "A Million Dollar Story," "A Week in South Dakota," "Somewhere Geese Are Flying," and "Burial" from *A Week in South Dakota* (1987).

Stories beginning on the pages indicated are dedicated to Pat Haugh (1), Jean Gildner (98), Judy Pim (193), Kathryn Terrill (217), and Ann Holman (234).

I owe special thanks to Shannon Ravenel and the late Stan Lindberg.

"Somewhere Geese Are Flying" received a National Magazine Award for Fiction and a Pushcart Prize in 1986. "A Week in South Dakata" and "Burial" (1985) and "A Million Dollar Story" (1988) are cited in the years shown among the Distinguished short stories in The Best American Short Stories series.

An Introduction

The oldest story here, "Sleepy Time Gal," was written at Yaddo in the summer of 1978. At breakfast one morning I told Richard Selzer a family anecdote I'd been carrying around for years, never thinking it was anything more than that, but he said I had better go type it up. A way to turn the anecdote into a story–the multiple point of view–came to me while typing it up–once–on my old portable Simth–Corona. "Sleepy Time Gal" is my only story composed like that; everything else I've written, including poems, novels, and memoirs, was first put on paper with a pencil and fussed over. *Somewhere Geese Are Flying* brings together five other previously collected stories with eleven new ones, including two that appear in print for the first time: "The Rock" and "The Roots of Western Civilization." These seventeen stories were written in many places–Michigan, Paris, Iowa, Slovakia, Oregon, Greece, Idaho, and on the Isle of Skye–and for a time I thought to call the book *Foreign Stories*. But the title I use, which had been waiting nearby all along, carries a sound I favor, a music both close and far-away, something like stories trying to connect in what seem the only ways available to us: love and loss and that inseparable hold.

Contents

Come Sta?
Come Va?

On the phone, with the husband, I thought the name was Tuttle. But it turned out he had trouble with his r's. The wife, when I arrived at their house, said she was Jane *Turtle*. The dog, a sad–looking springer spaniel who leaned into her legs, was Cleveland, she said. "He'd like you to shake his hand." I bent down and we shook. Cleveland was nine, she said. The parrot, Warren, was forty—her age actually, she said, taking me up to his cage.

"He enjoys sitting on our shoulders. If you wouldn't mind? In the evenings?"

"For how long?" I said.

"Oh," she said, "not long."

He was red and blue and sat on his swing hunched into himself like Uncle Sam with a hangover, and when I made eye contact I could swear he said, "Get lost."

Jane Turtle was tall and thin, in drab granny clothes, and she spoke as if we had already struck a deal and now I should pay attention. I followed her through the kitchen—which had baskets of laundry to get past, lumber on the counters, tools all around—and down to the cellar. The cellar had things more or less in the way, too. Empty aquariums, flowerpots, organ pipes, a wooden tiger from a carousel, at least four bicycle frames, a scooter, a rusty scythe, and I don't know how many cartons overflowing with papers and books.

"This started out to be the library," she said, "but it got away from us. No—that's not quite true. We had considered making this *part* of our library, then we found Daisy. Then we got Marilyn and Homer and, as you can see, the space has become theirs."

Daisy, Marilyn, and Homer were turtles. When Jane showed them to me, I said, intending a little joke, "Well, they found the right home."

"We think so," she said, not exactly smiling.

They lived in a pine box about two feet deep, four feet wide, and as long as a pool table. It sat on legs, flush to the wall, beside a window. A length of furnace tubing snaked from the box through the window, letting the turtles come and go between their inside and outside pens. The outside pen, I would see for myself later, had these stone turtles of different sizes and shapes that Daisy, Marilyn, and Homer could hide under or climb upon and sun themselves. I don't know why all this reminded me of the elaborate Lionel train setup my cousin Richie had when we were kids—turtles and toy trains don't have that much in common—but it did. So I kind of liked the place, messy as it was.

The cellar box was half full of dirt. Daisy, big as a football, was already preparing to bury herself, Jane said. "She was abandoned—simply left behind by the previous owners' children, in the garage. Go ahead, you may pet her. But when she's fully covered, of course, you must not disturb her—or the other two either." Marilyn and Homer were a third Daisy's size and sniffing—if that's the word—hunks of lettuce. Weeks later, after Jane and Evers, her husband, were abroad, picture postcards showing various kinds of turtles began arriving at the house, addressed individually to Daisy Turtle, Marilyn Turtle, and Homer Turtle—or just to "The

Turtles." Cute. The first card had a P.S. "We hope the Signor will tape up all your mail where you can see it." Cleveland and Warren got mail too, but nothing like the trio in the pine box.

According to the Turtles' ad in the paper, they wanted a house-and-pet-sitter. And when Jane and I came up from the cellar and were joined by Evers—who was another string bean, in very thick glasses—that's how we referred to the arrangement. But it soon developed they also wanted me to sign a lease and pay rent—six hundred bucks a month! For a house with sagging floors and probably poor insulation it was so old. *And* they expected me to buy Cleveland's food out of my own pocket. "Hey," I said, "I know rent in this town is outrageous—but dog food too?" Right away Evers, pushing the heavy specs up his nose, knocked a surprising two hundred off the rent. "Okay?" he said. I was doing some silent figuring of my finances, when he said, "Okay, how does three hundred sound?"

"Total?" I said.

"Sì," he said.

"What brand of food does Cleveland like?"

"It's up to you, amico." Then he said, "And we'll go a thousand in vet bills if he needs anything serious done." Evers pronounced it "seeweus."

I said, "What if something happens and it's a little more?" Everything in this world is always a little more.

They both sat down on the living room floor and got Cleveland between them, rubbing his muzzle, cleaning the goop from his eyes.

"Well," Evers finally said, pressing his forehead into the dog's neck, "he's had a good life. Haven't you, old friendo?" This came out "old fendo."

"A deal," I said. But to tell the truth, I felt funny about this thousand dollar business, especially with Cleveland looking at us. Not that a thousand didn't seem enough; it was the strict cut-off—bam.

They gave me the name of a friend, Ursula Sea, and her number. I should deliver my rent to her; also the lease, which Jane wrote up with a pencil on the back of a flyer for a "40th-Anniversary Party and Reading Honoring Allen Ginsberg's HOWL—Prizes for the Best Beat Poet Costumes—Must be 18 or Older." All the parrot food I'd need was already there, in a big gunny sack under the kitchen table (where Cleveland also had his rugs and toys); and as for the turtles, I should give them my veggie scraps.

"You *are* vegetarian?" Jane said. "Our ad stipulated . . ."

"Yes," I said. Which was sort of a lie.

"Ursula will make a Xerox of the lease for you. Just remind her," Jane said.

"And she's the one to ask if you have questions," Evers said.

Then they left. I thought they might clear away their breakfast stuff, do or say something about the lumber and tools in the kitchen, the huge bag of *peat moss*—at least take the clothes out of the washer I could hear running and pick up the bank statements and what looked like personal letters scattered around the place. But once I signed the lease they only gathered up some suitcases, called a taxi, and were out the door. I was still standing in the middle of their mess, Cleveland's head on my shoe, when the phone rang. It was Ursula Sea.

"Scotty D'Antoni, the sitter," I said.

"Thank God," she said.

"They just left. I've got the lease here."

"I'll be back in a few days. We'll get together."

"They didn't give me a key."

"Oh, they never lock the house. Well, my friend's waiting."

"Hold on—where are they going?"

"Poland. See you soon." And she hung up.

I had met odd ducks before, but no one like the Turtles. How many people leave a pot of oatmeal on the stove, on *low*, when they go to Poland for a year? Or their bank records— *and* a box of blank checks—out in the open? Or send post- cards in Italian to a guy they didn't know? Just because my name is Italian didn't meant I *am* Italian. The fact is, I am only half Italian for sure. I didn't know what my mother was, and the few times I can remember asking about her, after she died, my old man either hit the table, if he was sitting there, or cried. Or both. So they were irritating, those postcards. I should have said something when Evers started with the sì and amico stuff, but how was I to know he was just warming up? I showed the first card to Ursula Sea, and she only laughed. The rest I didn't bother trying to translate, just taped around the edge of the wobbly kitchen table for Cleveland— lots of churches, the Polish Pope, some lady called the Black Madonna. Come sta? Come va? to you too. And Jane and Evers, I learned from Ursula Sea, were professors of sociology! Wasn't sociology, if I remembered right, about being social?

Ursula Sea also taught at the college. She was in Theater. She designed sets. If the Turtles didn't seem to practice what they preached, she practiced her subject all the time. She built sets at the college, she built them at home. Her apartment was the entire top floor of an old warehouse, and every month or so it took on a new look. One time it's a desert, with Bedouin tents, real sand under them, next time it's filled with hobo shacks beside old railroad tracks made out of cardboard, next time it's the parking lot of a mall, ghost-like plaster of paris shoppers standing around loaded down with sacks. She owned two dinner plates, two forks, two wine glasses and, I have to say, great eyes. You felt, if you were not careful, you'd fall completely into them. She was originally from Amarillo, Texas, and that little bit of an accent she still had was some- thing else powerful about her. I didn't think her friend Boog appreciated her—or was even screwed in all the way. He owned the one decent deli in town, the Big Sammich, but what does he do there? He sits at the round table under the stereo speakers and plays games on his computer. And eats. Drop in almost anytime, there is Boog, the three-hundred-pound zombie, stuck to his puzzle. A perky number named Jake Kelly, who was part Puerto Rican, part black, really made the Big Sammich go—and built soups, I swear, you'd give up sex for. Except after you finished one you wished you had a warm body to tuck in with. Especially after winter started howling down from Canada.

Jake would dip her ladle in the day's special, and say, "Scotty, honey, tell the truth—how long's the train been gone?"

"Too long, Jake."

"You sleep okay?"

"Sometimes."

"You need a little help. We all need a little help."

She would fill my bowl to the absolute brim. If a drip ran down the side, she'd wipe it up with her finger, then lick her finger.

Ursula would say to me, "Boog's too heavy. It hurts, Scotty, it really hurts, to hear him breathe so fast. What can I do?" Then she'd look at me with those great eyes. Then she'd go back to hammering or painting or whatever she was in the middle of when I came by with the rent or just to say hello. "Help yourself to the fridge," she might say. "Try that real nasty garlicky avocado stuff—it'll give you ideas," she might say.

Like Jane Turtle, she was tall and thin—except in front. In front, Ursula was remarkable. Jake, too. I am not one to fixate on only part of a woman. When I was younger, yes, but once I got into sales work and had accumulated some insight into how to get along with people, I tried to study the entire individual. Nonetheless, I was, at that time in my life, lonely and, let's face it, horny a lot, and here were two women friendly to me with good working habits, sweet voices, warm eyes, and remarkable fronts.

What was it, about me, that Ursula or Jake might go for? This was the question.

I sold dumpsters. In a hard week I traveled a thousand miles over my territory, but I could always make it back home at night and save the motel money. That's why I picked Moscow as my base—it was centrally located. Actually, I worked with Burke. He didn't care to beat the bushes anymore, he was too old for that, so I'd go around to the fast food joints and hospitals and you-name-it and start the conversation. I'd get a signature myself often enough, but more often just a good maybe. That's when Burke would tool down from Spokane and seal the deal. He was a closer. Big, deepvoiced, direct, and the reconstruction job they'd done on his face years before really enhanced his presentation. He looked like a freshened-up Johnny Cash, like a man who had fought the bottle no-holds-barred through ashes and muck, then on his raw belly crawled up the Mountain of Opportunity, visited with the Almighty, and been told to stand tall and go back down there and put honest-to-God high grade carbon steel dumpsters in the hands of decent believers with trash to bear. That was his rap, and it worked. But if a customer was slow, he didn't mind describing the shotgun blast his Maker let happen that took off all the soft parts of his head one drunken night.

I had nothing about me to compare with Burke. I was barely five-eight, reached 130 pounds only after a heavy meal, had no special talent (unlike my cousin Richie), and was prematurely bald on top—right over the parietal bone. The rest of my hair, which was curly, shot up like a black bush around a half-buried stone. Often I was mistaken for Jewish.

In fact I had a serious girlfriend once who *was* Jewish, during my short college career back in Bloomington, but her parents pressured her to drop me. I still thought about her. Especially when I took a bath. A bath was rare for me—showers were more economical. But Annette liked getting in the tub to-gether and soaping up my circumcision. If she could encase it in one big bubble, that made her happy. She really was under a lot of pressure from home—to get good grades, get into medical school ultimately, and be somebody—and here I was, complicating the program, she'd say. "I need to be very, very cool, Scotty. Like ice. A surgeon has a life in her hands."

The situation with Annette was mainly why I quit college. I had the idea—at least at first—that if I ventured out into the world and made some real bread, her parents would like me. Look at my cousin Richie. Only four years older than me and worth millions—had his picture in *People* magazine with a starlet wrapped around his neck and barely graduated from high school. So I ventured forth, hope in my heart high as a flag on the Fourth of July. I did this, I did that, anything to get a toe in. I laid out good money for a quality clock with a loud alarm, and guess what? I was not only getting nowhere in a hurry, I was developing a tic in my cheek.

I went to see Richie, who at the time was in Chicago. I said to him, "How do you do it?"

"Scotty, I can smell it."

"You can really smell it?"

"Am I standing before you in hand-crafted shoes?"

"What does it smell like, Richie?"

"Like honey in a tree. Hit the boonies, Scotty, while there's still time."

So I raced back out, led by my nose. I smelled until my head felt full of bees: there lay two pastures, one for each nostril. I could see them blossom into a condos-and-golf course combo—the kind of development that Richie had done so well with. But though I had sugar in my nasal passages, I had no money in my pocket. Frying hamburgers days and hawking life insurance nights wasn't good enough, the bank said, and Richie said, "Scotty, Scotty, you have to do it on your own, man, or there's no rush, no *release*. Believe me. Besides, I don't smell honey at your particular locations." But he did give me three new Franklins for a decent suit. He said "dress for success" wasn't just an expression.

How does all this relate to the Turtles? Well, they had thirty-two big ones and change in their savings account and almost two in checking. Thirty-four thousand right there, practically laid out on their lumpy sofa, fuzzy with Cleveland's hair. Sure the poor dog was shedding! Living like he did indoors, no real weather, no challenges to keep his hide healthy. I mean, he only went out the doggie door to poop and pee, maybe give a quick roll in something foul, then he came right back in. I'd look at those statement figures, and think Thirty-four, thirty-four, thirty-four—which just happened to be my exact age—and then I'd think about a lot of things, like the Mountain of Opportunity, my advance on forty.

I said to Jake, because she also had a dog—the weirdly quiet miniature poodle Rocky, that sat at the round table with Boog—"Cleveland needs to chase birds. He's a bird dog. We all need to do what we're supposed to do. *I* need to do something. I'm having terrible thoughts."

"How terrible?" she said.

"Criminal," I said. "Nothing violent, but serious all the same."

"Finish your supper, Scotty. And come back at closing time."

I ate. Then I went home, fed Cleveland, put iceberg lettuce I got on sale in the turtles' dirt, let grumpy Warren sit on my shoulder and pick pumpkin seeds from my hand. I felt peculiar. Like two or three different people—or like parts of two or three people put into me, squabbling strangers, what was going on? I went back to the Big Sammich and waited for Jake to lock up. Boog finished his game. On his way out, he said to her, "Is a Lexus all that hot? Tell me."

"You better buy one, Boog," she said.

"I better."

"You better buy a new dumpster from Scotty too."

"Okay."

He waddled off. Even if he bought the deluxe model from me, I still couldn't respect him. He had let himself go to hell—what did that say about his feelings for Ursula? I blurted all this to Jake as we walked to her place—not too fast because we took turns carrying the silent Rocky, and because she had one leg maybe an inch or two shorter than the other. You would never notice the little bounce unless you spent a lot of time watching her.

"I'm a bad person, Jake. I lie all twisted up in Jane and Evers' flannel sheets and imagine forging their signatures. I should be more like Rocky here, the quiet philosopher."

Her apartment was in one of those new split-level triplexes that charge you a fortune for a box. She had a lot of nice plants, though, so hers didn't feel like a motel room. She gave me a Dr. Pepper. Then she changed clothes and rolled out a rubber mat for her sit-ups. If she didn't do these every night, she said, her back would be a mess. I told her about Richie currently living like a mogul in Seattle, his glass penthouse, his particular *view* of things. "I mean, we are sitting there on very supple leather chairs," I told Jake, "and into the room breezes this looker wearing white silk pj's and heels five inches high. Richie tries to introduce us, but all she can say is, 'My God, Richie, my God, I am so late!' And off she goes. I say, 'Nice looking lady, Richie,' and he says, 'French women have some imagination—what does she have to be so late about?' 'So she's French?' I say, and he says, 'Yeah, the employment people sent her up.' I say, 'What do you mean Richie.' He says, 'She's the maid.' 'Maid?' I say. 'Come on, Richie.' He looks me straight in the eye, sad as a bloodhound, and says, 'Scotty, if you were in my shoes, if you had what I had, you'd know what I mean.'

"To this very minute, Jake, I don't know what he meant. And I'm related. We played trains together."

"Uh-huh," Jake said. She was now lifting her legs up and back and touching the mat behind her head with her toes, the short leg perfectly in sync with the normal one. Holding that position a moment, then returning to a straight-out prone position to repeat the exercise. I was watching from one end of the sofa, Rocky from the other end. She looked good, lifting her legs back and forth in that slow arc, breathing slow and steady, the blue leotard sucked to her body like a second skin, saying "Uh-huh" once in a while or giving me a smile. It was very exciting to watch her, and I said so. I also said, "I talk too much sometimes."

"Don't talk then, honey."

"The fact is, I got my dumpsters job through Richie. Among other enterprises he's into garbage big-time. Do I need big-time garbage behind me for a good self-image?"

"Do you?"

"But I'd be letting Burke down if I quit."

"Uh-huh."

"He's supporting three sets of kids."

"Oh, my."

"Lord, Jake, you're like one long muscle."

She sat up. She rolled her head around, exercising her neck. Then she looked at me.

"How much of Jane and Evers' money are you thinking to steal?"

"Good question."

"Come rub my shoulders."

I went over and knelt behind her and rubbed them.

"Hmmm," she said, "where'd you learn to be so patient?"

"I knew somebody in pre-med once."

"Let my straps down."

I did.

"What do you think?" She turned so I could see.

"I can't think, Jake."

"But you can think about stealing money."

"That was over there."

"Now you're over here."

This might sound boastful, but I could be pretty good with women, thanks to Annette. After she got a bubble over my circumcision, she'd stroke me real slow. The object was for me to break the bubble. But if it broke on its own, before I did anything, she'd flat-out quit and go study. This routine made a deep impression on me. In other words, after Annette if my mind could get a strong enough bubble up there, I was in business for a long time. If my mind couldn't, I was useless. So before I ever got going with a woman, I always excused myself for a few minutes and went in the bathroom and soaped up, to jump-start my imagination. It was also good hygiene, and I think my partners, not that I'd had many, appreciated it. The problem with Jake that night was, she had me so excited so fast, I barely reached her bathroom and got a bubble up there when I popped it.

For a couple of weeks I avoided the Big Sammich. I was too embarrassed to face her. Of course she had been sweet about it, told me not to worry, but I know she was embarrassed too.

I kept busy. I drove the territory in my used but still okay Eldorado, sold two or three dumpsters, got three or four good prospects for Burke to seal, which he did; and nights when I came home, after feeding everybody, I tore into the Turtles' house. I scrubbed windows and floors, vacuumed, filled a jumbo trash bag with dust balls and dog hair and candy wrappers from under their king–size bed; I made neat piles of all that clutter in the cellar; I even tackled the cupboard job that Evers had abandoned. When Ursula called one Saturday to ask where I was keeping myself, I told her in the kitchen, building doors. She came right over with her electric saw, and we hung those babies in no time. All I had to do was stain them later.

"I have never seen this house so *tidy*," she said.

I said a guy had to straighten up once in a while.

"And fly right?"

"Something like that."

"Would Jane and Evers ever be surprised."

"How long have you known them?" I asked.

"Oh, ages. Three years maybe."

"Where are they from?"

"Back east. Cleveland, Ohio, sounds right."

The dog came over to her. Ursula sat down and scratched his ears. "Cleveland," she said, "*you* need a bath."

"You need a bath," said Warren.

"I've bathed him," I said. "It doesn't do much good. He needs to chase birds. You hear that, Warren?" I sat on the floor beside Ursula and looked in Cleveland's old eyes.

"Does he know how?" she said.

"I doubt it."

"You should teach him."

"I wouldn't want him to break anything."

Cleveland looked at us, back and forth. He kind of reminded me of Richie, how his eyes hung.

"You ever been in love, Ursula?"

She laughed. "What a question."

"What a question," said Warren.

"Let me think." She rubbed Cleveland's back a while. Finally she said, "Well, I reckon I haven't."

"I reckon, I reckon," said Warren.

"I remember guys that made me want to pee all night waiting for them to show up," she said. "But that was just boom-
boom stuff—which I take it we are not talking about, right?"

"Right."

"You tickle me, Scotty."

"You tickle me," said Warren. "Tickle, tickle."

I got up and covered the parrot. I offered Ursula a cup of
hot Ovaltine. "It might be dangerous," she laughed, "given the
way we're talking. I'll just go on back and take a long, hot
soak in the tub and roll around this idea I'm getting for a new
decoration." She gave me a kiss on the cheek. It was snowing
in the lights of her pickup as she drove away.

I'm only human—if I had never met Jake, I thought, Ursula
would be the one for me, tall as she was. But I had met Jake,
and now what?

One night when I knew she wasn't home yet, I set a yellow
rose in a box against her door. The next night I left another
one. The third night I waited until I knew she was home and
finished with her sit-ups, then I knocked. This time I held a
yellow rose in my hand. I also had a bottle of Andre Cold
Duck and a sampler of Whitman's chocolates. When she
opened the door as far as the chain, I said, "I don't even know
if you're free tonight."

"Are you the flowers man?"

"I'd like to do this right, Jake."

We sat on the sofa with Rocky between us and sipped the
wine. We had a chocolate or two. I asked where she was born
and how she ended up in Moscow—if ended up was the right
phrase—and when was her birthday and what was her favorite season. Questions you would ask somebody on a first
date. She asked me the same ones back, more or less. We
made no references to the night I took her straps down. She
put on some really moody jazz—Ben Webster's breathy tenor

sax, Sarah Vaughan's throaty blues—and fixed a platter of cheeses and pickles.

"This is very nice, Jake. You are very nice."

"Why, thank you, Mr. D'Antoni."

The weaker part of me wanted to bury my face in her remarkable front right then, and stay the night, cozy and warm. But the stronger part said Here is a woman shorter than you with first-class muscle tone, a Gemini originally from Las Vegas, Nevada, who is crazy about the green buds of spring— who came to Moscow because her father had played football here, and met her mother here, which is all very romantic to her, and therefore she thought she'd enroll as a radio-TV major, but one thing led to another, as they do, and now here she is, managing the Big Sammich, meeting all kinds of nice, sensitive people, for example yours truly. And this stronger part of me said Let it build, focus on the long return. When we kissed good night, I noted that she raised one of her feet off the floor high enough for me to see a shapely calf over her shoulder—something that, when I see it in a film or a magazine, always creates a tingling sensation around my bald spot.

Christmas was coming up fast. I was wondering what to do about this least favorite holiday of mine—make the long trip again to Whispering Pines Rest and watch the lounge TV with my snoring old man and have him wake up and say, "Who the hell are you?" or what? Boog was closing the deli for almost three weeks, and that meant Jake would take some vacation time. She planned to visit her parents in Las Vegas, where her father dealt blackjack and her mother worked as a secretary at the university. I kept waiting for her to say Why don't you come along? Ursula was going down to Amarillo and taking Boog (actually he was driving them in his new Lexus with the full leather, the phone, the mahogany dash), so naturally I identified with them, more or less. I could board Cleveland and Warren at the vet's, and the turtles could hibernate away on their own, surrounded by all their mail. Evers, incidentally, was still writing me the Italian nonsense, which I continued not to read, though Ursula was getting letters from them in English. "They send their thanks for the cupboard doors," she informed me, "and want you to keep December's rent as a Christmas present."

"What are those two, anyway," I said, "old hippies?"

"If I told you what they really went to Poland for, you would be very pleasantly surprised," she said.

"Tell me, I'm into pleasant—I want all I can get."

"I can't. It's a secret. But here's a hint: do you know 'My Blue Heaven'?"

"'My Blue Heaven'?"

"The song, Scotty. 'Just Molly and me . . .'" she sang.

"This isn't more religious stuff, like their postcards?"

"Not saying."

She and Boog had a little party at her place the night before they left for Texas. And what do you know? She had a new set built that was practically a carbon copy of the Turtles's first floor—with emphasis on the kitchen. It included a good likeness of a springer spaniel peeking out from under the table and a red and blue parrot in a cage. Both plaster of paris.

Everybody there except Boog and me had some official connection to the Theater Department, either as teachers or as students who worked part-time at the Big Sammich. Even Jake, I learned, had taken an acting course or two. They all thought Ursula's set was "wild," "so fifties." What was *wild* about it, I couldn't see. Boog, for once, joined the human race. He sat at the table in a tall chef's hat and white apron and sliced roast beef. Ursula had on a house dress printed with pieces of cherry pie, and curlers in her hair. "Don't tell me," someone said, "Alice Kramden!" Ursula pressed her cheek to Boog's for a picture. I had to admit they were cute. As for

Jake, she wore a glittery, white, elf costume and was playful and sexy. And as for me, I had semi-major riots going on under selected areas of my powder-blue, raw-silk Mr. Frisco that Richie had paid for—a suit more than a decade old, though it still shimmered because quality never goes out of style.

After a couple of cups of punch I was calming down. I had gotten some insights. Boog, for example, was kind of like Ursula's big dog. No matter how heavy or old he got, she would never abandon him. Which was more than I could say about the Turtles and their feelings concerning Cleveland! Especially if they went to Poland for *religious* reasons. Furthermore, who, in real life, is originally named Turtle? Nobody I knew. So they definitely had some problems. As for this Las Vegas problem, I suddenly had the answer.

When I took Jake home, I hesitated at the door. I said, "It's late. I probably shouldn't come in."

"Is it really that late?" she said.

I looked at my watch. "Almost two o'clock."

"Tomorrow's Sunday."

"Aren't you leaving town on Monday?"

"Tuesday," she said.

"Even so, you have packing to do, right?"

"Mr. D'Antoni, you *may* come in for a minute."

"If I came in for a minute, I'd probably want to stay an hour, maybe longer."

"Well, as I said, tomorrow *is* Sunday."

"Today is Sunday."

"Is this some kind of foreplay, honey? Because if it is," she said, grabbing hold of my necktie, "it's working."

I hadn't thought of it as foreplay. In my mind it was strategy, good psychology. It was also making a substantial part of me miserable. Why couldn't I simply have said Hey look, let me drive you down to Las Vegas. I've already checked out one of those gambling hotels that let you stay cheap, so you don't have to worry about me sleeping at your parents' house, if you are. I won't even take off my coat. I'll just be a friend who gave you a lift. A friend who's got business in Las Vegas. And who knows? Killing time, maybe I *can* sell a couple of dumpsters while I'm there, though probably not. Probably that market is already wrapped up solid. Anyway, I'll be there to bring you back, that's the whole point.

Because, in a way, part of me thought she might not come back, and this made me nervous.

So all the way home, still smelling her, I practiced my speech. And in the Turtles' cold bed too, trying to sleep. I could still say the speech to her on Sunday—or better yet, Monday. Give her Sunday to think about me just kissing her on the cheek and returning to my car. She *did* like me, I knew that, so why wouldn't it work? Why wouldn't she accept a free ride in a used but comfortable Caddy over driving all that way alone in her tiny Geo? Anybody would. Geos are nothing but coffins waiting to happen.

On Sunday, the rates low, I phoned Richie. Maybe he did have a finger in the Vegas garbage market.

"Who's asking?" he said.

"Me. I'm planning a little Christmas vacation down there. Possibly I can combine some business."

"My advice is stay away," he said.

"Actually, my girlfriend's parents live there."

"What a sorry place to spend Christmas."

"You've been there for Christmas?"

"Are you kidding? I've been everywhere for Christmas."

"Remember when we were kids? Your fabulous train?"

"Don't hurt me, Scotty."

"Those times are gone, aren't they, Richie?"

"What are you into, pain on purpose?"

"I think I'm in love—but how does a guy know for sure?"

"How old are you, Scotty?"

"Some days I feel sixteen, some days a hundred."

"Go hit a rock with your head," he said, and hung up.

Maybe I *was* into pain. Maybe that was my mission in life, to collect enough pain so it would get sick of hanging around and leave. Who knows? What I do know is, my great strategy regarding Jake Kelly didn't pan out. I drove over on Monday morning and she'd already left.

I got back in the car. What to do now? Man, I had the whole day on my hands, and it weighed eight tons. I wanted to hide and fly at the same time. I found myself heading west, and in my mind, driving along, I imagined her beside me. We were crossing Snoqualmie Pass in one great big glass-ball-beautiful snowstorm, quiet and happy. Then on to Seattle. Taking the elevator up to Richie's glass penthouse. "This is Jake, the one and only," I would say. "We're on our honeymoon." Of course he would be bowled over by her.

But I only drove west as far as Moses Lake, from which I could make it home that night. I paid a couple of calls, at a McDonald's, the hospital—my heart really not in it—though guess what? Two signatures. Before leaving town, I treated myself to a piece of pie at a little diner called Mama's. Here's more good luck. The woman waiting on me is actually Mama herself, who that morning baked the delicious pumpkin pie I am eating. Heavy on the ginger, which I like. She is six times a grandmother, she tells me. "And look there," she points to a photo hanging above the cash register, "who is that?" I say, "It's you—on a motor scooter." "That's right," she says. "An old Cushman Eagle. When my dear Charley died three years ago, I said to myself Tillie, you can pull the tarp over your head or you can ride point. I ride that machine every day the streets are clear. That's all I ask for, Mister. A clear road." She said to come back again. I promised I would. You always promise you will, what does it hurt? Then I drove home to Moscow.

I fed sad Cleveland. I told him he was looking sharp. He flopped his choppers on my foot when I sat down to give Warren some time on my shoulder. "Well," I said, "here we are." "Here we are," said Warren. I thought about the turtles burrowed in their cozy dirt, the brown iceberg leaves scattered above them. I thought they had a pretty good deal. But then I thought about clear roads and how right Mama was, and where was I? Fresh snow was falling, icy flakes making little ticks on the kitchen window. It's a sound that's life in a nutshell, if you ask me, both comforting and lonesome. Hello in there, hello in there, they seem to say.

Genealogy

S ammie was staring at the space marked Experience on
an application form. The form was for a job she had no
interest in. If she got it, she would spend eight hours a
day in a windowless room and couldn't wear jeans. She
would put folders in filing cabinets and take them out again.
She would twist paper clips into skinny little wire people and
in general go nuts. But what else could she do now that she
was back in Iowa? Teaching her refugees English would pay
about half the heat bill this winter. "Have a goat," Thuy had
said all smiles, when she explained her situation, "for the
milk." "Oh, sure," Sammie said. "I could keep it in my land-
lord's marigold patch."

Sammie had told her students about living in Iowa years
ago when she was a young girl. She told them about the
small farm her parents had owned, about the goats they
raised, the honey bees, the popcorn they planted above the
orchard that sold as far away as Chicago—with their names
on the jars! She told Thuy and Tuon and Mai and the others
that her parents had a barn with a good space for a mule, so
they traded for one and put him in it. Howard. She told her
students, with the aid of pictures she drew on the blackboard,
that her parents had carved ducks and wove rugs and played,
if they could believe it, the spoons! But she did not tell them
that one spring—the spring Sammie was fourteen—they

picked up and moved to California. To make Oceanburgers in a restaurant in Oceanside.

Sitting at her kitchen table and circling the word Experience on the application form, Sammie remembered that they bought the restaurant, Happy Joe's, without seeing it. They saw only a photograph mailed to them in Iowa by Happy Joe himself. The photograph showed the owner, roly-poly in a tall white chef's hat, standing at the entrance to the place. He had one arm around a pretty girl and the other arm around a soldier. The girl held a pinkish poodle and was helping it wave a paw. And in a letter Happy Joe wrote something like this: that Oceanside had beaucoup servicemen and beaucoup tourists and every one of them was crazy about his Oceanburgers. He said the place was King Solomon's Mine, but he'd made his bundle and now had his sights set on shoeless days in a hammock under the palm trees watching the sun do its thing. Sammie's parents had had a good laugh over Happy Joe.

But they did it. They went out there, with all seven kids in the school bus her dad converted into a camper before campers were popular, and made Oceanburgers. The only thing special about the burgers that Sammie can remember was the bright blue cardboard whale they were served in. For just about a year—and oh it got long—her parents, and she and her sister Ursula too on weekends, filled those cardboard whales with Oceanburgers.

Then they sold Happy Joe's to their best customer, a soldier who had chipmunks tattooed on his biceps. When he flexed his muscles the animals' cheeks puffed out. His name was Boo Rapp, and Sammie had a terrible crush on him. She wrote "Boo" on her kneecaps in red lipstick and wore jeans so no one would see it and refused to go swimming until his name burned through her skin to her soul. Oh yes. But they never even kissed because Boo was a man with a mission and a motto: no hot women and no hot cars. And no booze or

funny tobacco either. Just Oceanburgers. Retail success was
his aim in life. He'd joined Uncle Sam's Army to save up cap-
ital and to keep his nose clean, and if he'd slipped once—
those chipmunks—a man wasn't a zombie either. He told
Sammie all this one night in the parking lot over a Dr. Pepper
they were sharing, and to this day, though she can laugh at
her youth, she cannot drink anything sweet from a bottle. Her
parents of course were elated that Boo Rapp came along—no,
elated's not the right word. Lucky. Lucky that he came along,
his discharge imminent and his aim in life clear, for they were
ready to move on.

Sammie sighed. They were thirty-nine that year, the same
age she was now. Now they were sixty-four and doing what?
Oh, she could fill the space marked Experience with twenty-
five years of geography and good intentions and dreams, and,
like a piece of chopped meat on a bun in a cardboard whale,
what would it all mean?

Sixty-four. Divorced. But sharing the same house. Her
mother downstairs, her father upstairs—in Aunt Jelly's former
sewing room, paying rent—and out front on the lawn a sign
advertising Vitamins and Foot Care. And at the bottom of the
sign her mother's name in Old English lettering: Thelma
Goodrow Dunley. All right here in Des Moines, an hour's
drive from the goats and bees and Howard the mule they
picked up and drove away from a quarter of a century ago.
And now back—how many times had they been back? back
through?—all but the twins, the babies, Holly and Teak. Me
and Ursula and Brendan and William and Georgia, she
thought, listing their names, from the eldest down, in the
space that asked for Experience. "And Thelma and Jack," she
said aloud, adding their names too. Then she looked up and
gazed out the window at nothing.

No, not nothing. A freeway. And over it a bridge for school
kids to walk on, to get back and forth, swinging their lunch

pails, smoking their brave cigarettes, shrieking, spitting down on cars, yelling out, "I do *not* love Junior Potts!" "Tell us another one!" And straight up the freeway the capitol's golden dome—bright as a hat from the Renaissance—which her parents had marched to, arms linked with hundreds, to help stop the war. Hell no, we won't go! Boston, Columbus, San Francisco, Madison, Denver—you name the place, Jack and Thelma and their seven kids were there, holding up signs, smiling at the pigs. Pigs. She had to laugh. They'd raised pigs too for a while; even had one, Bridget, whose mother tried to eat it, housebroke. And Dan Rather said, "Get those kids with the pig!" And for three seconds—you couldn't blink, Aunt Jelly said—they were on TV, coast to coast, the whole family, American as all get out, while the country fell apart.

Which made her think, now, of sweet Holly and handsome Teak. In fact, if she had a TV set she could flip it on and probably see one or the other, at that very moment, suffering some awful hokey dilemma. Soap stars. Is that ironic or what?

"Do you watch them, Poppa?"

"Talk, talk, talk."

He'd walked over to have supper with her last night. When she answered the door there stood a goofy Richard Nixon in a long brown coat, holding a Target shopping bag. "Trick or treat," he said, sounding so small behind the rubber mask that she wanted to close the door, count to ten, and try it again.

"It smells like a damn hospital."

"My apartment?"

"This thing"—and he took off the mask. "Did I scare you? I scared the lady downstairs."

"Mother?"

"Not your mother, no. She has no time or inclination to have her blood excited. The lady below you, your friend the dancer. Let's see what she gave me." He reached in the shopping bag and pulled out a Tootsie Roll. He studied it a moment, then put it in his mouth like a cigar. "Say, girlie, which way to the egress?" The eyebrows hopped, but his voice—oh, such a little instrument it had become. She hugged him. Was she dreaming, or was he even smaller than just a few days ago? In the short time since she'd been back, her father, daily, seemed to be going away, inch by inch. Please, Poppa, no jokes. Stay. She helped him off with the heavy Army surplus coat, and gave him a glass of Bushmills. Food. I will feed this little man whose hair should not be half so white. Whose eyes seem elsewhere.

"Where are you, Poppa?"

"Good question."

"I mean—a penny for your thoughts."

"Your mother gets these Masons from the reservation." He laughed. "Now that's a song title for you—'Masons from the Reservation.'" He ruminated, pulling his chin. "I refer to these ladies, retired, who come on a bus. She snips off their corns and oils their bunions. What an occupation."

"Oh, dear."

"That's what I say."

"No—I meant we're having corn chowder tonight."

"Ah well, I should keep my trap shut." He sipped his whiskey. "But I'll tell you one thing: *I'm* not moving into one of those abominations."

"You won't have to, ever."

"Nor bounce from one unlucky child to the next."

"No, Poppa."

He gazed at his feet. "You're all back now. Except for those two. Holy Saint Francis! One's supposed to be a nurse, I guess—she wears a white cap—she's up to no good with a pair of doctors! And the other one's—what's *he* supposed to be?—he's up to no good with a pair of women lawyers! Talk, talk, talk. Don't they ever get tired of it?"

"So you have seen them."

"*Seen* them? I have witnessed a mockery of two-thousand years."

Then the witches and goblins and hard-to-guess-what started coming up and knocking and asking their riddles. On the sofa her father held the Nixon mask in front of his face, and said, "I'm the one." Or, "Me. I'm the answer." Sammie heard him and his pleased chuckle, but the children, eager to move on, paid no attention. When the last of the beggars had come and gone, she and her father sat down to the chowder. He said to her, "Your mother, Thelma Goodrow Dunley, is making her *own* genealogy now. Because she's discovered I'm making one. Can you beat that? She comes into the genealogy room at the Historical Building and pretends not to see me." He chewed, scowling. "It's a good laugh when all the chairs are taken except the wobbly one directly across the table from my spot. Hah!" He looked at his daughter. "Damn it all, Sammie, this is good grease, but I wish we hadn't discussed your mother's profession."

"Poppa, tell me about the genealogy you're working on."

"No one sits in my chair. They know I'm coming, the old farts." He wiped his mouth. "I'll tell you this: it's difficult."

"Finding information?"

"Your great-grandfather, John Peter Dunley, was fifty-five when my father was born. His wife was thirty years younger, the first foreigner, far as I can determine, to marry a Dunley. Tweet, her name was. Norwegian. All of that stuff's easy. It's the sitting there *thinking* about them that's difficult. Their lives. What was in their tickers. All these old people—my colleagues—scrabbling for names and dates and going home happy as larks—well, names and dates, Sammie, what good are they?"

He stood up and looked for his coat.

Leaves, yellow and slick, stuck to their shoes. She was walking her father home. A cry, now and again, issued from the darkness, a late ghost or goblin dashed across their moony path. The little man beside her was quiet. Then her heart quickened when she remembered how once he brought a wooden peacock that he'd carved and painted, without them knowing about it, into their kitchen and set it on the table. She was just tall enough to see it stand there all fanned out on perfect black feet. Hold still, he said, don't wiggle the table. That was to her, because she was so excited. He fixed a feather in her hair, and gave her mother one too, and then she and her mother closed their eyes—for he'd told them to do that, and wish, wish hard—and when they looked again the wooden peacock was real, and was stepping around the sugar bowl. How did he *do* that?

"Poppa—"

"I'm not deaf."

"I know what you mean though. Names and dates are *not* enough."

"We've discussed this."

"Okay. But tell me how you turned that wooden peacock into a real one. You remember when."

"Ahhh—"

"Tell me."

"Nothing to tell. I don't remember."

"You do remember."

"There's your mother's sign, lit up like Christmas. Foot care. Hah!"

"Wait, Poppa. Please. You can't forget the one you carved. We had it for years. We took it to California that first time. It was beautiful!"

"California? It's warm. That's all you can say for it. Look, your mother's in the window. Spying on us. Where's my mask?"

He found it in his Target bag and put it on.

They went in then, into the front room that years ago was Aunt Jelly's parlor but that now—Aunt Jelly gone to the grave—was her mother's office. One entire wall was lined with little jars of vitamins and teas and wooden rollers to exercise your arches on, and on another wall hung big posters of feet like tracks made by someone who could walk up any obstacle, feet with the bones showing through bright as icicles, and arrows with bold legends pointing out what exactly was what: PHALANGES OF GREAT TOE, CALCANEUS . . . Her mother turned from the window, from tendrils of ivy flowing over and down the sash, and said, "They tried to steal my sign, the rascals. So I put a sunlamp bulb in the drop cord and hung it out." She looked Sammie's father up and down. "I thought we ran this bum out of office."

He shot both hands in the air, his fingers making Vs.

She sniffed, and said to Sammie, "Did you and the President step in something? I smell a bad odor."

Her father brought his hands down and mumbled.

"I think it's the mask," Sammie said.

Pulling the lower part of the mask away from his mouth, but not taking it off, her father said, "That's what *I* said. Now I'm going up to my cell. Goodnight."

Sammie hugged him, whispering, "You *do* remember that peacock. Don't lie to me." Then she helped him remove his coat. He draped it over his arm. He stood there facing them, still in his mask, and suddenly Sammie felt as if they were all in a play, a school play, something silly, and this boy shows up on stage playing Richard Nixon home from the wars with an old Army coat over his arm and tufts of white hair sticking up every which way around the top of the mask, and she's ready to laugh because it's *supposed* to be funny, this boy always makes them laugh—but something isn't going right, the boy just stands there, in a smelly mask with grotesque cheeks.

And then her mother said, "Don't forget to take that ridiculous thing off your face, Jack Dunley."

His back stiffened. He left the room. Her mother called after him, "I'll make some tea if you like?" They heard him climb the stairs, mumbling. Her mother sighed. "He won't be back. It's just as well." She went to make tea for herself and for Sammie.

Sammie stood alone in her mother's office. She felt small, displaced. She looked at the big feet on the wall. She went over and touched one. The slick paper crackled and she thought of crickets, of straw and hay and how they smell on summer nights. She thought of Howard the mule and how good he smelled when you came running into the barn first thing on cold mornings. And how his skin shivered to shake off flies. The mule and maybe the barn and house too were gone now, but maybe not. And maybe what she ought to do was pack them all in her rickety Volvo and drive out there. Maybe that would snap them out of this!

Then she heard the tea kettle whistle in the kitchen. Followed by another whistle, behind her. She turned. It was her father. He had a finger to his lips, meaning she should be quiet. He tip-toed into the room hunched over like a thief. He was holding something behind his back. He tip-toed over to her mother's desk. What he had behind his back was a mouse in a trap, which he now placed on the desk. Then he pulled from his pocket the Nixon mask and placed it, face up, over the trap. He winked at Sammie. "Let's see how quick she is," he whispered, and left the room.

She looked out her window at the children on the bridge. The name Junior Potts hung in the gray air, and a girl in a coat bright as autumn, yellow and red, whirled around at two small boys and faced them. They pretended to be afraid of her, making noises like the wind, "Ah-woo! Ah-woo!" Their knees went all wobbly, their arms dangled. They looked like the marmosets that Sammie fed and fell in love with one summer at the San Diego Zoo, the summer her parents sold Happy Joe's to Boo Rapp because they'd made a mistake, they were bored to their bones making Oceanburgers, they hated Oceanside—no, the military, the government's policy in Vietnam, law and order, everyone in his little box, coffins, the cardboard whales they served the hamburgers in were daily signs of it—beaucoup, beaucoup, her father said bitterly. And now Sammie saw him trying to make Boo Rapp understand something, drawing maps, writing numbers on napkins, getting red in the face, turning over a catsup bottle and hitting the bottom, barking beau*coup!* beau*coup!* as if the word were rifle fire, sending spurts of catsup all over the counter, and Boo Rapp shaking his head, smiling, oh no, not him, no sir, and flexing his muscles showing how the chipmunks chewed and chewed.

At length she looked up, focusing on the bridge again, and saw the two monkeys run past the girl, each holding an end of her yellow scarf and raising it like a banner.

When did they stop *liking* each other? She asked Ursula, she asked Brendan and William and Georgia, all of them rosy-cheeked and smiling and shrugging their shoulders, busy, working at their jobs. Ask *them*, they said. How do you ask your parents a question like that? she said. And they said, Don't ask then, Sam.

She spoke to Ursula through the wire fence at the day care: "I know you and the others are only pretending indifference, because otherwise none of you would be here."

"Where would we go? Where would I go?" Her sister was swinging one end of a skip-rope; a little girl held the other end, and a second girl was jumping over it. The girls were counting in Spanish.

"You lived in Mexico. You loved it there."

"I like it here too, Sam. Especially now that you're back."

"But *why* are we back?"

Her sister laughed. "Oh, Sammie," she said "you're such a philosopher." Then to the rope–jumper: "Okay, Marvella, it's Jimmy's turn."

Sammie spoke to Georgia at the co–op, helping her unload bags of bran and wheat germ from a truck. She spoke to Brendan while he raked leaves for the city, to William while he chopped wood at Living History Farms. They all said she was such a philosopher. They all said they were glad to see her back among them.

But she wasn't a philosopher! She was just as simple and down to earth as they were. She taught people the basics—to say, "Hello. Goodbye. I live on Brattleboro Street. My name is Tuon and Mai and Minh. I wish to take the bus. Please make change for me." No, Thuy, not to cause different, you smart aleck. We are talking about money here, coin, filthy lucre. To take the bus. To use the telephone. To get from one place to another you sometimes need exact change. And to that, Thuy, her quick one, sang, *Precise* different, yes? Yes. Yes, indeed. Meantime, Thuy, holding up his legal tender and speaking clearly, is brushed away by the busy clerk. And her parents, meantime, not saying much at all, have made change.

Games!

What she wanted to know was why, after all the marching and handholding and passion they'd been through, her parents were like *this.* Never mind the divorce, her father paying rent—those things were silly and superficial. What she wanted to know was underneath. What she wanted to know had blood in it, surprise, purpose, memory. Yes, something besides names and dates!

She noticed she was making a small circle on the application form below the names of her brothers and sisters and parents, going round and round on the same track. She stopped that. She gave the circle a long beak. Now she gave it wings, an eye . . . and all over again she could see her parents, side by side in the orchard, *covered* with honeybees. It was as if they were wearing suits, bee-woolly, bee-buzzing long johns. No, not buzzing—humming. Like the end of a tune staying in your head at bedtime when you lay quietly on the pillow waiting for sleep. And it never occurred to her to be afraid for them under all that swarm. In fact she sat down in the tall grass and watched, astonished, as the swarm, moving ever so slightly, rippled and shone, causing her parents' shapes to seem like reflections in a warped mirror, or on water. And then two more interesting things happened: first her parents put their gauze-and-bee-covered faces close to each other— whispering? trying to kiss?—and then, suddenly, like a blanket, the bees were pulled off. Who pulled them off? At the kitchen table Sammie put her head down, resting it on her forearms, and closed her eyes. She wanted to savor that memory. Underneath her arms lay the application form, her brothers' and sisters' and parents' names, the crudely drawn bee. She had those things in her head too. The nose on the bee-drawing was her father's, long and fine. He was in the orchard with her mother, their bee-furry faces almost touching, and then the bees were gone. Her mother had leaves in her hair and was saying his name . . . Jack, oh Jack . . . as if he had just surprised her, made her laugh. He *did* make her laugh. And Sammie watched them, quietly laughing with them . . . and then when they did kiss she closed her eyes and kept them closed, and was quiet as a mouse . . .

Now another time came to her . . . Oregon . . . when they were living with some other families on a farm. They had goats and fruit trees and chickens. A morning's walk brought you to the ocean. Ursula was not with them now; she had gone to Canada with a boy from Berkeley. Then Brendan, who was nineteen, went somewhere. No one would say where. He had refused to register for the draft. Sammie can still see him collecting the round black goat droppings—the goat balls—he said he planned to mail to the Pentagon. Then William, almost eighteen, was gone, along with the rooster who stayed in his room and followed him everywhere. One morning Sammie found her mother wiping her eyes in the hen house but, as with Brendan, neither she nor anyone else said a word about William's absence. Georgia and the twins attended school in the little town; but when Georgia turned sixteen she quit and caught a ride with some people who were passing through to Oakland. She got a job in a vegetarian restaurant down there. That left Sammie and the twins. The twins were thirteen. They said they were happy just where they were, for a change. They were tired of demonstrations, running off here and there. Agnes, a college dropout who lived with them, made puppets, and Holly and Teak were making puppets now too, and putting on shows after dinner. They invented a couple named Joe and Mrs. Joe who had several children—Spiro, Dick, Pat, John, Martha—and a pet bulldog named Jolly Edgar. Despite repeated instruction, Jolly Edgar was always leaving his "secrets" in the house where people would step in them. The children were not very smart either, and Joe and Mrs. Joe were forever teaching them some simple lesson: how to fix a flat; how to brush their teeth; how to wash their socks, without being seen, in a gas station restroom. Holly and Teak's audience loved these skits. Night after night their audience wanted to see them again, roaring in laughter even before a skit had begun. Her eyes still closed, Sammie saw their flushed faces. Then she saw her parents again, in the orchard. Her mother's hair was long and red and sparkling with leaves. Her father was dancing up and down, holding his first fingers out from his head like horns, saying, "Baa–baa," and coming after her.

In the middle of this reverie, she heard a noise, not very loud. She looked up. Someone was knocking at the door. She did not want to answer it. She wanted to go back in her head to the orchard again and hear her parents laugh. But the little knock came once more. No, she thought, whoever you are, not now. She waited. Again it came. Quietly she went to the door and listened. It could not be her father, for his knock was a loud, no-nonsense pounding. Perhaps it was Donna, the dancer from the apartment below. She listened. Finally she heard footsteps going away, down the stairs. Then the sound of the outer door opening, closing. She returned to the kitchen and looked out the window. She saw little Thuy beside the house, wearing that blue baseball cap that was too big for him and the red satin jacket he found at Goodwill that said "Fred's Electric" on the back in blocky yellow letters and was also too big for him. Thuy was looking at the sky, his round face under the long bill of the baseball cap in a wide smile. It was snowing—very lightly—the first snowfall of the year. He held out his palm. Sammie watched him, a little man in a bright red jacket, a figure—from this distance—who might have been five or fifty, trying to catch snow. She looked at the gray sky and wished more snow would fall for him, big fat sparkling flakes, enough for a snowman! He was walking toward the bridge over the freeway now. She opened her window. "Thuy!" she called. "Thuy!" But he was near the bridge now, too near the noisy homeward-bound traffic to hear her. When he stepped on the bridge, he suddenly thrust out his arms as if he were a circus performer balancing himself on a wire. Sammie watched as he moved across the bridge—her bright clown carefully placing one foot in front of the other. In the middle, he paused, jerkily tilting his torso left, then right, back and forth several times like that, in a parody of almost losing his balance. Then he rushed to the other

side. He ran down the walkway, his red jacket billowing, filling with air, and disappeared.

Sammie stood by the open window. She gazed at the gray,
goat-colored sky. She listened to the traffic hum. Closing her
eyes, she could hear the ocean, a swarm of bees, a crowd of
people singing a hymn.

The Inheritance

A week before her forty-fourth birthday—one she'd celebrate with her face in real light—Lila rushed from the laundry room to answer the phone and heard a man's laugh—a whisky laugh—and then, "Can't you guess who this is?"

Unfortunately she could. "It's you, Lester."

"Aw, call me Lucky, honey. Ain't we still friends?"

She saw his one good eye winking at her.

"What can I do for you, Lester?"

"Hope I got the right Lila LaRue," he said. "Who'd fry up the best prairie oysters in Moose Falls, Idaho? You sound different. How the heck are you?"

Guarded, she said, "Okay."

"I'm glad to hear it. Now listen, this is all the way from Atlanta, so I won't keep you. You know, a course, about Russell."

She said she did.

"Figured so. Anyways, why I tracked you down, which took a while, is there's some inheritance for Bobby Lee. Oh, ain't nothing like the pile a gold we was always looking for"—Lester made his laugh—"but enough, Russell reckoned, to buy a gen-you-wine first class fishing pole. And you know, Lila, how much your husband enjoyed seeing that boy chase fish."

Lila saw a mountain of shadow. Husband? Nightmare, *leech* were more accurate. And even if he could no longer reach out and grab hold and hold her down, you could bet a whole paycheck that anything coming from him had to land you smack in a grimy tunnel. So her immediate thought was no thanks. She was trying to be happy, *was* happy. She had a nice house now in Lewiston for her and Bobby—no, a nice *home*—with a sweet yard and a plum tree. She had a decent car that didn't have a lien on it, or phony plates, or stall every time she tried to go somewhere important. Like the hospital when he broke her thumb to get at that fifty-dollar bill she'd been keeping back for Christmas. She had her own money now because she had a good, responsible job, a job that meant something, working with children who needed help out of *their* grimy tunnels. Where mice nibbling spilled Frosted Flakes under the table might be their steadiest friends—

No—no thank you. There had been too many nights suddenly waking up in a hot sweat knowing that Russell, at that exact sticky minute probably, was doing something lousy, somewhere. Not anymore. For nearly six months now, or ever since she learned he was gone, she was sleeping through to sunshine and a normal wholesome breakfast with her tender boy who had seen enough meanness to last him—and her—forever.

But she hesitated. The word "inheritance" had landed in a soft place near her heart and wouldn't go away. Bad as he was, Russell was still the boy's father; and she would never try to erase those good feelings that Bobby might be holding onto—was holding onto—for Russell *had* taken his son fishing a couple of times, and Bobby still remembered those trips—not often, maybe, but when he mentioned them and how much fun they were, it touched her, hard. The man had given the boy so little.

Okay, if this inheritance could buy him a fishing rod, she'd let Bobby have it.

"You can send us what there is, Lucky."

"Well, it's a inheritance you can't exactly put in a letter," he said. "What it is is pick up money. *Easy,*" he added quickly, "believe me."

Oh no, here we go again, she thought. Another scheme.

"Lester," she said, changing her mind right there, fast, before anything bad could get started, "I'm not sure we want to get involved in any easy money, thanks all the same"—and she was about to be rude, to hang up, when she heard him say, "It was Russell's dying wish, Lila. I had to bend close to his mouth to hear it. Ain't ashamed to tell you I bawled."

She had been standing; now she sat down—as it happened, in the one kitchen chair from her life with Russell that hadn't been broken. She looked at the rabbit decals Bobby had fixed on the arms—for his dad, because this had been Russell's chair. Theoretically. Honest-to-God, she couldn't remember one meal, not one, at which all three of them sat down together.

"It's up in Moose Falls," she heard Lester say.

"What is?"

"Bobby Lee's inheritance."

"I don't call him Bobby Lee, I never called him Bobby Lee."

"Okay, Lila, okay. Don't get sore. Are you getting sore? The guy's gone. And that's another thing. Virgil his daddy and Luther his brother who I don't think you ever met won't budge till I do something about them ashes. Man oh man, if it don't rain it snows. And here I am, stuck in the middle again, trying to make peace. Can you just tell me one thing—?"

The line went dead. She didn't know, or care, what happened. She returned the phone to its cradle, then sat tense, hoping it would stay quiet. Pieces of Lester's voice were still in her head, like the squeaky insistent noises in one of those mechanical animal toys someone was always donating to the Center that she did not like because they gave the kids dumb ideas about animals. Push the "4" on the turtle's shell and a haywire voice says: *"Four! Four!* I'm *four!* Can you say *four?* Say *four!* Say *four!"* Quietly she retired such toys to a special box when nobody was looking. She would retire Lester *Marble* and the bad memories of Moose Falls, where she had not stepped foot since that freezing night she zipped Bobby into his jacket and fled, with two quarters in her pocket. It took her nearly seven years to get warm.

She put her hands on the rabbit decals and pushed up from the chair. In the bathroom she splashed water on her face. She finished starting her wash. Then she went to the fridge and took out all the vegetables she could find and began to chop them for a soup. Yes, that was the end of Lester Marble and the inheritance and whatever else he was squawking about.

When Bobby came home at noon from playing next door at his friend Eddie's house, she fed him her good soup and two slices of oatmeal bread that was still warm enough to melt the butter. She was exactly where she wanted to be on an April Saturday, or on any day: feeding this eleven–year–old boy with green eyes like hers and carrot–colored hair she wouldn't deny came from Russell and buckteeth the dentist said would straighten out just fine, sitting in a bright kitchen you could see a wonderful drawing of on the wall beside them where she put up some of Bobby's other drawings and marked his height and kept her jars of basil and thyme and cinnamon on a shelf the two of them had built together. After lunch she would work in her garden and see Bobby and Eddie pass from one yard to the other doing what boys do, and that night her new friend Dan Sawchuck would come over for pizza, and then they'd go to a movie. He was, with–out doubt, the nicest man she'd ever dated, and they were getting closer. The thing she needed to do, though, hard as it might be, was tell him about her other husbands. Lester Marble surfacing and dragging a shadow into her light underscored *that*.

Bobby said, "I've been thinking about your birthday."

"You have? Thank you, honey."

"How we're getting up early to catch a steelhead for dinner? Eddie'd like to help, but I said it was your birthday and you had to decide."

Lila's heart expanded. How many boys his age were so considerate? She wet a finger and reached over to smooth down a wild sprig of his hair.

"Honey," she said, "it would please me very much to have Eddie join us. For the party too, don't you think? With Dan coming, and Cheryl and BonAnn from the Center, Eddie will give us three boys to go with us three girls. And just in case we don't catch our steelhead, I'll have a lasagna standing by, how's that? And of course the carrot cake, our favorite, with extra creamy cream cheese frosting—to heck with Lila's Plan A to Reduce Her Spare Tire!"

He laughed and asked to be excused.

"You may, Mr. Bobby."

As he was leaving, the phone rang. She counted ten rings, took a breath, and answered.

"Lila, it's me again. We got cut off because that card I bought ran out of time and being a little short, I had to go find—"

"Lucky," she interrupted, talking fast, "I am very sorry, I am not interested in any inheritance from Russell. I accepted the kitchen chair he brought to my apartment in Cottonwood when he was trying to win me back but never, not once, sat in to have a real family meal with us, and only because Bobby's decals are on the arms, so I am hanging up now because I have to."

"His last dying word was your name, Lila, his dead last."

She said nothing.

"Did you hear me?"

"I did."

"That's right, his dead last. Said he'd been so damn dumb, and if only life had dealt him a decent hand, just one, things coulda turned out a whole lot different, but there it was, a kick in the hinder, excuse my French."

"Sounds to me like his last word turned into the kind of self-pitying speech I heard too many times. Lester, I have to go now."

"A dying man's last wish is a secret thing, Lila. Secret."

"Lester, you are troubling yourself over nothing. Russell was a liar, a cheat, an awful man, and you know it. I cringe to my toes when I think of how many times I believed him."

"I know, I know, believe me, I know. Many's the time I said Russell, that wife you got's the sweetest gal ever made by Gawd, go home and get down on your knees and *tell* her, Russell, tell her how blest you are. She is a *saint!*"

"I am not a saint, Lester, don't get carried away. But I *am* tired of all this useless talk, so, for the last time—"

"No—wait! Lila, please don't hang up. I am in a kind of fix here. His ashes and his daddy and Luther are camped at my trailer waiting for me to do the right thing, which is what I am trying to ask: will you let us come up there to Idaho and put them remains to rest?"

"You are free to do whatever you like, Lester."

"But I need your help."

"You need my help?"

"Virgil belongs to some church, I guess, don't ask me to explain, it's nothing I unnerstand, but he looks at me and says he won't quit till we do are duty, and I tell you, Lila, I can't sleep. His eyes hang on me day and night. A man ninety years old, almost, but nobody to move off a idea once he puts his mind on it, and this is his one and only idea, day after day. Now, Lila, my card is about to run out again, and a woman wanting to use this phone here at the Mobil station is giving me nasty looks, and I can't go back to Virgil without a answer. Will you just please say you will let Bobby Lee— excuse me, I mean Bobby—help scatter Russell's ashes up at Moose Falls? This is the whole truth now, Lila. It was the main part of his dying wish to get saved, him and Virgil talked it over, and the upshot was that his daddy, his brother, and his son could do that, together, his blood kin, by putting their hands in his ashes, at the place where I am asking you to help us. Then I believe he said your name, and I swear to you, Lila, he had real tears in his eyes."

She was tempted to ask, sarcastically, if there were any *more* parts to Russell's teary-eyed deathbed speechmaking, but she only said—fast, so her voice wouldn't crack—that she would think about it and hung up. Then she gazed out the kitchen window at Bobby and Eddie, who had their fishing gear spread on the new grass, checking it over down on their haunches and fluttering like two angels about to take off.

The rest of that afternoon, no matter what she tried to focus on—her garden, the shelves she was putting up in the tool shed to hold the jars of tomatoes and plum jam she planned to can, the filing and polishing of her toenails—Lucky Marble's pinched, blind socket and his brown watery good eye kept popping into her head. She had to admit he was not a truly bad man, a little overly winky and slick with people he was trying to sell something to, but deep down a man you might reach if he was sober and you were really hurting. Like that time he came with a truck and helped her move out of Cottonwood and didn't tell Russell about it or where she and Bobby lived next, and he slipped a fifty in her coat pocket and said "Well, it wasn't me" when she mentioned it later. She accepted his help for all the work she'd done, all the meals cooked and other chores, back during the Moose Falls days that came crashing down after he and Russell had taken big payments from those California hunters to go packing for elk and then abandoned them at the mountain camp, no licenses, hardly enough food, just her there trying to explain. Explain what? That her husband and his partner, who were supposed to be hauling up the main supplies, decided that getting drunk with a couple of women in town would be more fun than showing their foolish customers where to bag the promised trophies? Of course she didn't know all this until later, and could only offer more beer and crackers and guesses. Bobby, just a baby then, had saved her—who could get mad at a woman nursing a child?—Bobby and the fact that she could saddle all their horses for them and lead the poor hung over saps down the trail to their cars. By and by Lucky had tried to apologize to her, in his way, but Russell never said a word about it. Not one. Okay, he bought her a horseshoe diamond ring—which he soon enough took back and sold when a finance company came after them for defaulting on another deal she knew nothing about either, until it crashed.

So she didn't much care where his ashes ended up. Though it did nag her that maybe she owed Lucky. More important, didn't she owe Bobby?

Showered, her nails looking not too bad in mauve (at least she resolved *that*), she came downstairs just in time to see Dan Sawchuck pull up. She needed to get everything square with him, too. She watched him step from his Jeep, a guy, finally, tall enough for her. How was it possible every man in her life, until now, had been so short?

Dan brought frozen yogurt and Alaska ale, and he whispered in her ear, when she was stirring sauce at the stove, how lucky he'd been exactly two months ago to visit a certain grocery store and get stopped.

"I was feeling these boulder–hard turkeys, and then I raised up and turned around," she said, turning from the stove to face him. "Almost a whole year we shopped at that store, and often on the same day, but why on *that* day was I bent over like a heron in frozen turkeys? I *hate* frozen turkeys!"

"Why?" he said.

"I believe everything happens for a reason," she said.

"Your cart was in my way," he said.

"I looked awful! I had on my worst glasses, that slide down my nose. And not one of my best colors, except my panties. Oh, oh, I've gone too far."

Dan Sawchuck laughed. He *did* like her—no man could laugh like that, easy and natural, and not like somebody. He also liked how she peeled mushrooms, he said. He'd never seen anybody do that. Or make pizza from scratch. Well, he hadn't seen anything yet. And then Lester Marble's toady eye popped into her head, her resolve to tell Dan everything.

"You okay?" he smiled.

"Getting closer to it." She kissed his bearded cheek. "Now, if you would go give that boy of mine a whistle and tell him eleven point two minutes exactly. I am fixing to pop my Pizza Lila DeLuxe in the oven."

Sitting at dinner with candles and a table cloth and a nice handsome man asking Bobby how things were going, really interested, and Bobby really interested in him, both of them like old friends, and the food the way it should be, and no knots in her stomach, no pain down her back, well, you could shoot her now and she'd die happy.

"I told Eddie's dad your uncle Terry was a goalie for the Detroit Red Wings," Bobby said, "because he's a big hockey fan, and you should have seen the look on his face."

The look on Bobby's face right then, she thought, was pretty darn beautiful, and if he could have a father like Dan Sawchuck she *would*, honest-to-God, die happy. What was he going to think when she told him about Omaha Fashions and

Broker Cowboy, never mind Baby Tattoos, who followed Russell. "Widow" had been easy to say, but technically it wasn't true. Technically she had four divorces on her record. Four! Lord God, why didn't she try them out first, see how they fit? Why did she have to marry them!

That night Dan took her to a movie at the college where he taught, an old Woody Allen picture about a man who wanted a divorce—oh boy, her favorite subject—from his crazy wife so he could marry a perky widow nothing like the other one. And he does marry her, at his beautiful seaside house, with his three grown daughters there, all of them in favor of their dad's new marriage except the hard-faced one who was stiff like her mother and really cold to the perky woman, refused even to dance with her at the wedding—boy, that must have hurt!—but in the end the woman *saves* the cold daughter from drowning. Afterwards Dan had a lot to say about real life getting smothered with *posturing*. Lila liked how he came up with, to her, the perfect word. And held her hand in front of his college friends outside the theater. That was very nice of him, and so was having a glass of wine with them; she only wished she could have contributed more to the conversation. But the truth was she didn't think the movie—the *film*—was that complicated. Here was a couple that found each other just in time and enjoyed being together, so what if the widow wasn't sophisticated like the other one, she had something you can't put a price on—*life*—and a down-to-earth view of things. Like she said, a man either cheated or he didn't. Anyway, that was Lila's opinion too, and Dan agreed with her.

In his Jeep later it occurred to her that maybe now was a good time to straight-out tell him about her past, and she was about to start when he suddenly laughed.

"Okay, what did I do," she said.

"I was just laughing at—how I carry on."

"Sure it wasn't something *I* said, with your friends?"

"No, no." He looked at her like he did when he was about to kiss her. "You, Lila, are a natural treat."

"Well, it is true that I have cut way back on my sugar and salt."

Then he *was* kissing her, and that's no time to resurrect four divorces.

On Sunday afternoon Lester Marble called again.

"Did you decide?"

"I just don't know."

"Lila, Lila, I am between ten rocks and a hard place on this, can you open your heart?"

"The truth is, Lester, my life is going so right I can't take a chance on anything connected to Russell—"

"He is a box of ashes, Lila! All we need to do is toss 'em out and it's done. Two hundret percent done. Oh Jesus, didn't I help you once or twice?"

She took a deep breath. The man sounded like he was drowning. She could see his toady eye blink a mile a minute. She couldn't stand this.

"If I help you, Lester—I am saying *if*—I don't want any inheritance involved."

"You got it."

"And I can't take much time."

"What's a scoot from Lewiston to Moose Falls—one hour?"

"Two."

"We get there, toss our load, it's done. How's next Sunday?"

"I can't. Saturday's my birthday and—"

"Birthday! Lordy, lord. Well, happy birthday!"

"Thank you."

"Lemme think."

"Friday. I have Friday afternoon off, and Bobby happens to get out of school early."

"Oh, boy, *this* Friday? I don't know. Muffler on my car's shot, I'd get stopped for sure, and Luther's pickup goes maybe—"

"It's this Friday or nothing, Lester."

"Okay, okay, if Virgil and Luther and me we leave Atlanta right away in Luther's rig and don't stop but to pee and eat a burger, we can be in Lewiston by Friday. Where you at exactly?"

She didn't want them coming to her house. She said, "There is a new café called Mama's—got that?—Mama's, on Main Street, near the Public Library. I will be in Mama's at one o'clock, Lester, with Bobby, and if you are there we will go scatter those ashes. If you are not there, we're all done. I don't wish to be hard, but my checkbook is almost balanced, if you know what I mean."

"Hard ain't in you, Lila."

"Don't be too sure."

She was sorry she hadn't talked all this over with Bobby first. But it was something he'd want to do, wasn't it? He knew about his dad—she'd showed him the card from the Georgia funeral parlor that was forwarded from their last address (he took it and put it in a drawer in his room)—and he'd understood about cremation. He hadn't asked what happened to the ashes, though he was smart enough to wonder; anyway, she hadn't started any discussion about them. Now, she could close that chapter, because sooner or later he *would* ask. So Lester Marble's reappearance in their life was probably a good thing after all. Everything happens for a reason.

Wednesday, after dinner, she said to Bobby, "On Friday afternoon your grandfather Virgil and your uncle Luther will be here from Georgia with Lester Marble—remember him? He helped us move one time?"

Bobby nodded.

"They are bringing your dad's ashes to scatter up in Moose Falls, where you were little. It was your dad's last wish that you help do this. I should have asked you first, honey, but you were outside and I had to make a quick decision when Lester called about it."

Bobby didn't say anything right away. He had been preparing to do his homework and he continued to arrange his papers and books on the kitchen table. Then he said:

"Will you be there?"

"Of course I will."

"Then we can do it together."

She went around behind his chair and hugged him.

"Did I ever meet my grandfather and uncle?"

"No, you never did, honey. They lived down South, and for one reason or another we never went to visit after you were born, and they never came to Idaho." She added that he would like his grandfather. "The one time we met he called me Sister, just a real nice old guy with nice manners. Luther I never met. So he will be a first for both of us. Now, how about you and that homework?"

They'd never met because Luther was in prison for shooting off a man's ear and maybe a bit more, facts she hoped Bobby would not learn for a long time—or ever. She also hoped she hadn't made a big mistake with this ashes promise.

That night she dreamt Russell was not dead after all—that he and Lucky had pulled off another slick deal—and she woke in a hot sweat. The air smelled foul, as if someone were burning tires under her window. Then she saw Max, her first husband, and Randy, her second, and that spoiled kid Booster she married after Russell—all of them stomping their boots on her porch, laughing and hooting at her and Dan Sawchuck, who were only trying to have a nice conversation. That might have been a dream too. Because the next thing she knew the alarm was going off, though at first she thought it was a fire truck and her house was in flames.

On Friday morning she finished her bimonthly paperwork at the Center by eleven, then looked in on Cheryl and BonAnn at Word Time. They had the kids in two half-circles on the floor and were alternating holding up cards. A Mozart CD was playing, not too loud but loud enough. This was Lila's idea, thanks to a discussion she'd had with Dan about giving children good music to hear. Cheryl said it still gave her a funny swirly feeling now and then, and BonAnn said it made her go home and play Johnny Cash real loud for a while, but both said to Lila, whatever works, don't mind us chickens.

She sat on the floor and watched the kids eagerly raise their hands to recognize an old friend or make a new one: *Shirt! Heart! Shoelace!* Clapping twice for two syllables. Maybe some of the girls would grow up and not have babies too soon like their mothers. Maybe some of the boys would grow up and—Suddenly one child, Heather, began to vomit. BonAnn quickly got her to the bathroom; Lila attended to the small spot with paper toweling while also holding up a new card for BonAnn's group. In a few minutes BonAnn brought Heather back. She was fine but needed some TLC. Lila took her aside and sat with her on a bench. Heather threw up almost every Friday; Lila was afraid it was because she did not look forward to a weekend of unhappiness at home.

Then it was lunch time. After every child, including Heather, was settled before a tray, Lila said she'd see BonAnn and Cheryl at her house tomorrow, and they should dress casual—remember?—because they were having a bonfire with the cake! She left to pick up Bobby at school. Her plan was for them to have lunch at Mama's before the others arrived.

But when she and Bobby stepped through the door, there was Lester Marble waiting by the cash register. He'd shrunk down since the last time she saw him; and though his hair still sat on his head like an explosion, it had turned white as a ripe dandelion, and the good eye was more watery than ever. She tried not to appear surprised: he resembled a queer kind of angel-troll one of the Center kids might have drawn.

"We got here, Lila—we made her. Luther's pickup did better'n I thought." He sounded like a man in a place he should behave in, like church, his voice just above a whisper. An odor came off him that reminded her of those sprays some people use in their bathrooms to make them smell like candy stores. "And will you *look* at this here boy," he said, a little louder, the watery eye all winky, acting more like Lester the salesman. "Lemme shake your hand, son, been a long time."

Bobby, shy at first, gave him a big toothy smile.

"Lila, you just gotta be proud."

She smiled at Bobby.

"Okay, you two, let's innerduce Bobby to his folks. Hey, they see us acomin'!"

The two men at the corner table bore stony expressions that suggested they were as good as anybody else in there, and by God nobody better try to push them out. When Lila and Bobby sat down, however, the lean old hawk-nosed man looked her straight in the eye and said, with a gentle intimacy, "Sister, it's a pleasure to see you again, praise the Lord," his leathery face skin softening around the pale blue eyes she remembered.

"Thank you, Virgil." Putting her arm on Bobby's shoulders, she said, "This is your grandson."

The old man studied him a moment. "I believe he is. Will you shake my hand, boy?"

"Yes, sir," Bobby said, taking his grandfather's hand across the table. It was, no denying, a tender moment Lila was happy to see.

As for Luther, he seemed, now that she got a closer look, like a goofy giant, especially beside little Lester. His pinkish eyes appeared to be going in six directions at once. This man shot another man's ear off? Maybe he was hoping to hit a tin can on a fence post, or a duck in the sky. There was nothing about him that suggested a steady aim—one sure connection to Russell, besides the red in the skimpy fringe of hair hanging off the sides of his otherwise bald head. His voice came out almost squeaky when he told Bobby he was real glad to meet him. Holding his jumpy, rabbity eyes more or less still, he said to Lila, "Hour yeh?"

"Well, well, well," said Lester, "we are all here. Just like a family reunion."

Lester's comment stopped her. Here *was* her family. Complete. There was not a soul on her side. Dad who never knew about her killed in Korea, mother dead from drinking before Lila got out of college. No siblings or cousins. None of this was fresh news. But to see the fact of what she and Bobby had for family at one table was—well, she didn't know what it was, only that it gave her a lonely feeling.

Virgil cleared his throat as if to speak, and everyone waited, but he said nothing, gazing at the plate before him. An awkward silence set in. Lila had noticed—couldn't help but notice—a box next to her silverware wrapped in gold paper. She was touched. They'd brought a present: either for her, for her birthday, or for Bobby. Now, in the silence, she ran a finger along its edge, hoping someone would speak up. It was bigger than a box of candy but smaller than a hat box. Finally, since obviously no one was going to introduce this subject, she said, "Hmmm, look here, Bobby. What could this be?"

Virgil, Luther, and Lester all looked at their plates. Being shy, she figured.

Then Virgil raised his shining eyes.

"It's my boy Russell," he said.

Maybe sixty seconds went by, maybe twice that, and finally the cheerful waitress came over. "You folks about ready?"

How Lila ate even half of her spinach salad with those ashes on the table she didn't know. It was something to do. Bobby, though, got through his cheeseburger—thinking what? Lester and Luther cleaned up their fries and eggs and apple pie. Virgil just let his toast sit there but finished his buttermilk. What did they talk about? The weather. How the trees in Lewiston were way behind the dogwoods in Atlanta. Bobby's school. He liked it fine. That was good, real good. No mention of the ashes again. Lester tried making a joke about Luther having eggs with his catsup. Then, serious, he said he remembered the way to Moose Falls and Lila and Bobby could follow them. It was the closest that he—or anyone—came to mentioning their mission; though when the waitress brought the bill and Virgil picked it up, he placed his hand over Lila's and said, "We're much obliged to you and the boy, Sister."

In the parking lot, Lester pointed out Luther's pickup. Just then she thought she saw Dan Sawchuck go past on Fifth Street in his Jeep. Taking Bobby's hand, she started toward her car a couple of vehicles away.

"How are you, honey? You okay?"

"Sure." Then, "I think that's Dan driving in."

Glancing back, Lila saw Lester, Luther, and Virgil still standing side by side behind their pickup, watching her and Bobby, the white-haired troll and the giant flanking the lean old man hugging his box of ashes.

Dan stopped and rolled down the window, smiling.

"Need a lift, guys?"

You don't know, she thought. Then hearing her voice sound pitched too high, too hurried—"We just had us a bite—next item on the agenda's a little chore. What's up?"

"You won't believe this," he laughed. "I've got to give an exam—on Friday afternoon. Finals time." She saw that he noticed Lester, Luther, and Virgil; he *had* to be thinking they were very suspicious looking ducks.

She said, "So I guess we better let you go. See you tomorrow night?"

"Counting on it. Hey, Bobby, good luck fishing."

"Thanks." Bobby glanced at Lila. "I was just thinking, Mom, since Eddie's coming with us—"

"Like to help catch that steelhead?" she asked Dan.

"Love to."

"Have breakfast with us—about six?"

"I will, thanks. Meantime"—he looked at their audience—"I must be blocking those guys. So—"

Dan was shifting gears, ready to go, when Bobby said: "That's my grandfather and Uncle Luther and Lester. They're waiting for us."

"Oh," Dan said, "I see," though Lila could tell he wasn't certain what he saw. He looked at her, and she gave him a smile she hoped was coming out better than the rubbery bunch of lip it felt like.

She said, "They're sort of passing through. Can I explain later?"

"Of course," he said.

Then he was gone, and the three men now seemed to her like the shadows of misery. She got in her car, with this innocent child beside her, to go to a place she'd never wanted to see again.

Lewiston behind them, she licked her lips. "Bobby"—he was looking at the clasped hands in his lap—"tell me what you're thinking?"

"Oh," he shrugged, "I don't know."

"Seems like all of a sudden a lot's going on."

"Uh-huh. Will my grandfather and Uncle Luther and Lester live around here now?"

"I don't see . . . no, I don't think so."

"My grandfather's pretty old."

"Isn't he nice? Just about the nicest man we know."

"Dan's nice too."

"Oh, well, yes."

"Will you and Dan get married?"

"Oh, honey, I don't—I mean—would you like that?"

"Sure. Wouldn't you?"

"He's very nice, isn't he?"

"You said one time he makes you feel lucky."

"I did say that, didn't I. Does he make you feel lucky?"

"Maybe—" and Bobby smiled at her.

She latched on to the green light in his eyes as the best possible sign—for Go, for A Clear Way. Though if she could wrap him in her arms right now, for insurance, she'd feel a lot better. Because luck—the rich, slippery idea of it—seemed to flirt in the flick of tree shadows across her windshield, now waving hello, now waving goodbye, back and forth, until, on the final long climb into Moose Falls, the oily exhaust shooting out of Luther's tailpipe got thicker and blacker and luck began to resemble a blob hobbling uphill on crutches beside them, a thing that wheezed and coughed and kept squeezing her sore, red, runny eyes tighter together. If that made any sense. Because look—this was the point—who in his right mind wants to take a chance on a woman who four times promised to love somebody in sickness and in health until death? I mean, after four times . . .

Moose Falls didn't help much. It was still a potholed muddy street with a bar, a general store, a meat locker, a taxidermy, a café—a street with old yellow snow pushed up to the sides, melting and keeping the potholes full. If the man-sized carved-pine hunter leaning on his flintlock rifle in front of Shoot's Café suddenly came to life, he'd most likely send a thin stream of brown juice toward one of those potholes and give you a hard squint, because he didn't know you and you'd made the mistake of looking at him too long. "We got business?" But if he did know you, he'd say your name and you'd say his, and you'd stop a while and spit with him, if you were a spitter, and not have to say another word. You were in town, as he was, because neither of you was in the woods, or in the bar yet or the café or one of the other establishments—and since all of that was obvious, you both knew pretty much everything that was necessary to know. For now and maybe forever.

Most likely you lived in one of the trailers or unpainted shacks or half-finished log houses spread around like uncompleted thoughts or mistakes no one was going to finish or correct right away, so no point wasting time in discussing *that*, though some, not many, tried to better themselves with a rose trellis, or a porch, or a couple of fruit trees. In the midst of those trailers and shacks was where she and Bobby had lived once—in a partially finished log house with a rose trellis beside a porch and two apple trees out back. You could say Russell lived there with them—*when* he came home.

They parked beside Luther's pickup in front of Babe's, the bar where Russell and Lester and the other outfitters had hung out. Lester came over to her window and said he had to check on something in Babe's. "Then we'll do them ashes. I mean the funeral," he added, glancing past Lila at Bobby. "How you doin', son?"

"I'm fine," Bobby said.

Lester left then, and Lila said, "It will be more like a"—she searched for a good word— "memorial, honey, than a funeral. A remembrance"—this was hard—"of when you and I and your dad lived up here and enjoyed these woods." Her heart gaining weight, she said, "A memorial can take lots of different shapes—you don't even have to see it, the feeling's the important thing." She wanted to explain what she meant so clearly it would be like a brand-new morning, cloudless and trouble free—but all she could think of was a poster on the wall at the Center that asked HOW DO YOU FEEL TODAY? And listed several choices: happy, sad, silly, angry, surprised, proud, excited, scared, bored, anxious. Pick a word, sure; but was it all that simple?

Seeing Lester come out of Babe's wearing a smile he hadn't gone in with got in the way of her thinking. She followed the pickup into the hills above Moose Falls, the list of words still in her head waiting for her to do something with it. Them. She tried putting a couple together—*proud-happy*—but felt no closer to a brand-new morning or anything.

They stopped beside a meadow patched with snow, old stumps, and piles of slash poking up, and Virgil, holding the box, gazing slowly around, said, "No." She mentioned the creek where Russell and Bobby had fished, and they got back in their vehicles and drove to where they could go on foot. When they arrived beside the creek, Bobby said he thought he remembered it.

"Well, I reckon you do," Lester said. "I know you and yer daddy had you some *big* times snagging those old fish." He coughed in Lila's direction, and she caught the sweet odor of whiskey.

Virgil said, "Is that right, son?"

Bobby looked at Lila, then at his grandfather and said, "Yes sir."

The man laid his hand on the boy's shoulder, a hand of freckled, papery skin and bone that shook some, and Bobby reached up and covered it. Lila wanted to hug them both— would have—but Lester, clapping, coughed out, "Well, okey-doke, reckon we got are spot."

Virgil brushed snow from a fallen cedar so he could sit; he sat there collecting himself. Then he turned to the box. He peeled off the gold paper. He pulled apart the two cardboard flaps held together by tape and looked at the gray contents. Lila took Bobby's hand, waiting. Lester winked his watery eye at her. Luther's rabbity eyes ran loose. Virgil's eyes were closed. He was feeling something for Russell. She tried—really did try—to remember something good about him but could not.

"Lord a journey . . . keep fast our ties . . ." Poor Virgil was exhausted. If it wasn't for him—and Bobby—she'd be out of there. They were the only real point to all of this. Virgil muttered something to Luther, who said, "Yes sir." He dipped both hands in the box and filled them. Virgil set the box between his feet and, with effort, filled his hands. After Bobby took his turn, Virgil said to Lila and Lester, "Please, help yourselves. We are all but one." She went first, telling herself, as she touched them, that they were just like ashes from the stove. But standing close to the rushing, noisy creek, her eyes watered. It was such a beautiful idea, being one, though how could just saying it, like saying words on a list, ever get you there?

When the ashes were all gone down the creek, Virgil seemed revived. His eyes looked bluer, and in his hand lay a soggy leaf he'd picked up. He caught Lila watching him muse upon it, and smiled. "Sister, I reckon I'll have to keep this Idaho leaf." Then he said he wanted to buy them all something hot to drink.

Back in Moose Falls they parked in front of Shoot's. Lester came over from the pickup and said Virgil was fast asleep—

"like a old contented angel"—and he and Luther decided not to wake him.

"Well then," Lila said, "we'll be heading back."

"Aw, lemme buy the boy a pop. You drink pop, dontcha, Bobby?"

"Once in a while," Bobby said.

"When yer sociable, right? Okay, a deal. And lemme buy you a beer, Lila. Come on—we're all free and clear now, praise the Lord—and besides, life is short."

She let Lester and Luther lead them to Babe's. Stepping inside, she saw the elk and moose and deer heads above the long bar staring straight out like always, and at the bar half a dozen patrons, mainly women, simultaneously turned their bright surly eyes toward her, as if jerked by a string threaded through their noses. She led Bobby across the wide-plank dance floor to a booth.

Tonight the place would be hopping. Hopping and hoping. She'd been there too, though it was painful to remember the woman she was in those days, sliding around, heating up under her flannel shirt, being kissed and kissing back. And meaning it! From one to another, and all of them keeping their hats on. So they could seem tall enough. Did she ever dance with a man she could look *up* to? Right. That football hunk in Missouri, Lamar, when they were King and Queen at Homecoming. But he wasn't even her date, just the top vote-getter for men. So they only danced once, at the crowning.

Then she was off, teaching first grade in Omaha. Hang on, Lila, here you go: take Max, in his nice little shop—dresses, shoes, everything a girl needs—to have and to hold, till— whoops, Max has something on the side, a girl who doesn't need a stitch on, which our not so little wife, leaving school one afternoon a bit too early, not feeling well, gets to see in her own home. But hang on: here's Denver, here's Randy, who buys and sells, lots and lots, fast, in and out, a glow, yes, of health, to cherish—whoops, he's gone, he was just here, is still here, but gone, the drugs, the drinking, plus minus, minus, minus. She needs air. Fresh air. Gets on a horse, likes it, likes how they smell and move those big muscles and—hang on: here's Russell saying they could ride all the way to Idaho, where it is high and quiet and you can breathe. You like to breathe, right? Right, right. But no: wrong, wrong, and again wrong. That's three strikes. She should be out. No. One more whoops, a rebounder she's with such a short time it's like having a cold, a boy named Booster who carries his name stitched on both biceps inside hearts with eyeballs for Os. One morning, waking up alone, she is not able to move for a long time, feeling nothing.

"Lila?"

Lester's grinning.

"I said what kind of beer you want?"

"I don't care. Cold."

"Come on, Bobby, come choose a pop."

Now Luther, at the bar, is grinning. At her? She looks down, at the table, and the initials and names, carved deep, come up H.A. and B.A.W. and BULL and BIG HIT and R.A.H. Shouts in the wood. Like *happy* and *sad* and *silly* on the poster? Are they *all* that you can say? No. Picking at the ash—the dirt—under her nails. No. And suddenly she remembers Valor—before she left Omaha, helping out with those delayed kids. Sees him in all that furious silence, those charges he made. At *her.* Here come Lester and Bobby, both smiling, and setting down on the table—what's this?—cartridge boxes full of quarters?

"Look, Mom." Bobby lines up four boxes of quarters in front of him and whistles.

"Now, Lila," Lester says, "it ain't but a few dollars for the boy. From the machine."

"What machine?"

"For that new fishing pole."

"I asked you a question, Lester," trying to hold his toady eye.

"You know, in there"—sheepish—"in the Gents, Lila."

She can hardly breathe. Her son is stacking quarters, Lester has scooted back to the bar, and she's stuck in the middle. Everyone is smiling—Bobby, Lester, and even Luther, his shoulder holding up the winky troll's arm. Valor comes back. They didn't say *delayed* then; they said *mentally retarded*. And Valor, with his odd beautiful name, was the worst. A biter, hair all over his back, three years old, he sought her out, came after her, his teeth like a fish's, sharp. At home his parents kept him in a big roofed playpen, a cage, because they were lost, didn't know what else to do, but she was going to help this child, and by God she did. Not right away, not soon, but little by little she got him to sit in her lap, got him to sit at a table with the other kids, by God, they all said, by God. And now . . .

Lester is bringing her beer and Bobby's pop. A troll having grown several grand, generous inches.

"I promise you something, Lila, and then I almost don't do it." He sets down the bottles. "Hey, Bobby, how much you git?"

"Thirty dollars . . . wow."

"Buy you a nice little pole."

Her son takes a gold matchbook-sized packet, shrink-wrapped, from a cartridge box and holds it out to Lester. "This got in here by mistake."

Lester reads the legend, "'Rugged'N'Ready,'" and grunts. "I'll give her to Luther. These ain't much use to me no more." Bending down, his white hair and watery eye both coming at her: "Now, Lila, don't be mad. I sold the old boy here the machine, but Bobby gets to keep what me and him flushed out."

She can't help it. She's laughing. Maybe it was the word *flushed.*

Lester's eye glows. "That's right, money's money, ain't it honey!"

"Goodbye, Lucky."

Outside, she and Bobby stop at the pickup. Virgil's profile is still as stone. She reaches through the window and touches his cold hand. Pats it.

"So long, Virgil."

"Is my grandfather okay?"

"Now he is."

The last of the sun slants across the street, filling potholes with a dark golden sheen. Walking toward her car, she bends over one.

"That's right, money is money, and this is a hole full of mud and spit."

"What, Mom?"

"Oh, I guess I'm just practicing, Bobby. Getting things straight."

The Great
Depression

The year she turned fifty (her age had *nothing* to do with it) Rita Soluk walked out, took a stroll, a simple one-two, buckle my shoe. Was she angry? Giving up? Off her nut? "You decide," she said to the pressing sky. "I need air."

She wore what she'd worn for three days, jeans and a T-shirt that said HOT PEPPERS. She had her cowhide shoulder bag, toothbrush, comb, extra underwear. Nothing complicated. She closed the front door, pointed her stuffed-up nose toward the parking lot of that joke called Seven Oaks—not an oak anywhere, just a bunch of puny bonsai the developer stuck in the gravel after shaving the land and planting his condos—and climbed into her Honda, through the passenger side because the driver's door didn't work. Okay, so she *drove* off, if you want to be accurate. And her allergies had nothing to do with it either.

Rita aimed the car west, the odor of Detroit going, going, blowing her nose and tossing the tissues over her shoulder. *Of course* she'd thought about Bernie—saw him reading her note, shrugging. "Sure, sure, go ahead. See how far you get." Something like that, no fireworks, no throwing things; the lawyers, the Feds, but especially the doctors who rewired his pump (as he would say) had changed all that, calmed him down—scared him, if you want the truth. So he probably shrugged—

no, did shrug—then got on the phone to deal and rave with someone, anyone, as usual. Had she been there, a fly on the wall, she might have said, "I see you're handling this okay, Bern."

"I'm making calls, doing business. You do the same."

In fact she laughed—somewhere between Lansing and Grand Rapids—because she could imitate Bernie Soluk like a hiccup, write his dialogue, his gestures, his *dreams*. Twenty-four years of practice, that's why. "I'm climbing into myself, Reech, coming back. Hey, all that pounding I took from the law, all that pork I lost—I can take on anybody, anything. So go. Go scratch your itch. Come home when nobody wants you."

Bernie her bear. Her former bear. Down from two hundred forty when they were flying high to a man who ate fruit cocktail and kept touching his chicken chest to make sure something in there was ticking. He'd dropped a hundred pounds. But refused to have any of his suits altered. He said he'd get it back—all of it. He wasn't talking about the lost weight. He meant his money, his power, what they had before everything changed.

"Including Nick?"

"Maybe," he said.

"Tell me how."

He stared into space. She joined him. Because on this subject, their son—the health of their son—there was not far they could stretch anymore. Nick was twenty-three, and for almost eight years, a third of his life, he'd been hooked on poison, chaos, junk—in and out of so many jails and hospitals and reeking flop joints he had become a kind of fiction to them, a rattling voice they heard from, when they heard at all, in the middle of the night, across hundreds of miles; and when they actually did see him he looked made up—as an actor can be made up—to play someone older, someone experienced in the ways and deeds you can grip your chair to follow in a movie, but not into real rooms smelling of burnt hair or dis- infectant, crawling with roaches.

In her Honda, following the sun west, Rita thought about that not-real, winking, sly older man her boy was pretending to be, and of course she thought of the last time he called.

"Here's what you should do, baby."

"I am not your baby."

"You should take a break, Ma, relax."

"Where are you, Nick?"

"On the phone, sweets."

"You're hurting me again."

"Now *listen*. Ma. Please."

She listened to his breathing, to cars honking in the back- ground. He could be anywhere—New York, Cleveland, L.A. Then, almost whispering, almost crooning, he said he was *in a program*, had a *nice* girl, was getting *cleaned up*, so not to worry, *okay?* And please, please, please think about *leaving it alone.*

He hung up. That was in December. Seven months had gone by. Seven months of silence like death. You could go crazy waiting for the phone to ring, or you could go to your dumb job, or see the shrink, or pick up the dead flowers on your parents' graves and leave fresh ones, or ride the exercise bike that Bernie only glanced at, with Chopin mazurkas plugged into your ears, or kick the Honda's frozen door, or stand in the bright light of the fridge at three A.M. spooning spumoni into your face.

Or, Mother of God, hear your sister-in-law explain for the zillionth time how her brother was framed, watch her sit at the kitchen table watching Bernie eat fruit cocktail out of the can and hear her tell him, as if he hadn't attended his own trial, how *everybody*—including so-called relations—all stood on the sidelines looking the other way. Hear her describe the fourteen months he'd spent in prison as if she'd been by his side every single day suffering the injustice of it, the pain and humiliation—until finally Rita could bear it no longer, and said, "Lillian, enough"—not angry, not loud, certainly not loud enough to stop Lillian once she got started, but loud enough for Rita to hear in her own voice a new tone—no, an instruction—that said *No more*, that said *Not one more complaint, excuse, or accusing finger.*

She left the kitchen then, her head like a fish, swimming, and went to Nick's room—the room they kept for him in case he came home, his things laid out, hung, ready: the ski jacket, hockey skates, posters, books, maps; the baseball glove from junior high when he ran and ran, always on the go, laughing; the bedspread with John Lennon's face woven into it like a god's; and in the closet, in the drawers, fresh clean everything a boy wanting to grow up normal and dress smart could want.

And then she staggered, almost fell down, because a light came on, the light bulb over the dumbo's head in the comics—over *her* head. That wasn't Nick's cozy, thoughtful room, never had been. Not like this. It wasn't even a room, for Christ's sake, it was a parody, a cruel joke, a mausoleum—and she got rid of it. While Lillian in the kitchen, fresh from church, raged on and on in her Sunday best, Rita wiped her eyes and quietly made two neat piles of all Nick's things; she wrapped one pile in a sheet, the other in Lennon's face, and tied them like hobos' bundles. Next morning she called St. Vincent de Paul's to come get them. As the truck pulled away, she sat down and wrote Bernie the so-long note. That's how fast it happened.

Then she was gone. Moving west. But where, exactly? Just past Grand Rapids she saw signs for Holland and Lake Michigan, and naturally she thought of Harry. She'd had no intention of seeing him, did she? Laying on her sweet, crazy brother a dismal story he didn't need and would only worry

himself sick trying to grasp? No—their father's death earlier
that year had contained enough sadness and confusion to last
Harry for a long while. Adding her own troubles, however
softened, was simply not necessary. Maybe she would breeze
in and say to him, "Harry, I need your help. I'm looking for a
nice used street cleaner to buy, to drive out west on old two-
lanes, maybe get in on some small-town parades along the
way." Wouldn't he be ecstatic? Hell, he might even have one!
All gassed up and ready to roll. A big, round, white, elephant-
looking thing. This was her brother's true territory—the goofy,
the eccentric—not what she had to offer. No, she wouldn't tell
Harry anything. She'd simply stop for a spell at the one place
she'd known all her life and breathe that familiar, comforting
air until she could at least see the road better.

She followed the signs to Holland, got turned around a little because the short cut their father had always used now led
to a permanent barricade—shocking her momentarily—but
then, twenty nervous minutes later, just as the sun like some
fiery halo knocked off a saint's head seemed to touch water
over where Chicago was, or ought to be, she arrived and
climbed out of the car. Harry stood on his front porch—a
porch packed like a flea market annex with stuff the world
had thrown away—stood in the midst of scythes and warped
kayak paddles and bowls of buttons and old brown bottles
shaped like swans, and he smiled his gap-toothed, jack-in-
the-box, angelic smile as if he'd been waiting for her, as if her
troubles were all over, because he had just what she needed.

"Hey, what *took* you so long?" he said.

They hugged and whooped and finally, breathless, they fell
back in the sand dune in front of the house. Harry's house
now—his inheritance, and rightly so—but in many ways her
house too. For the memories, the stories. For all the summers
she spent there. My God, she was born in that house! And

Harry, three years later, almost was too. Their father said they tried, had a big welcoming party standing by, a tremendous bonfire on the beach, lots of good food and drink, the *best*, but Harry wouldn't come out, wouldn't come out, so they packed up—hell it was damn near October, people had to go home, go back to work, enough was enough, and they left too, joking, "Well, maybe *next* summer he'll show"—and after ten minutes back in Detroit Harry decides okay, he'll come out now and be baptized.

Sitting in the dune in front of the house as the fiery halo took water, they remembered their father, Big Jake Lupinski, while letting thin streams of sand pour from their hands.

"I can hear him singing 'Danny Boy,'" Harry said.

Ah yes, the "Danny Boy" story. Really a couple of stories tied together, though where one of them ended—ended loud—the other simply stopped after barely getting started.

"He was such a showman," Rita said.

"I think," Harry said, "that Pop was like a poet."

"The Great Depression of the Thirties," Rita intoned.

"I remember," Harry nodded.

"Did you ever hear him just say 'the Depression'?"

"I don't remember."

Always—always—that whole line, as if he were narrating a documentary, for Christ's sake. She could hear him now, see him take possession of the room and declare that during The Great Depression of the Thirties, a couple of years before Rita was born, he acquired this house on this gorgeous lake "for a damn song—can you imagine that?—a song. I'm not kidding." And then in his surprisingly fine, pretending-to-be-Irish tenor he would sing that song. *Oh Danny boy* . . . He'd be having a drink, of course, and holding a cigar—not a cheap cigar, either—and more than likely be tanned dark as beef jerky, wearing white flannel trousers and a blue blazer with crossed oars on the pocket, and a *tie*. And when the song was tenderly over Big Jake Lupinski would gaze at his wife Dolly—who *was* Irish, full-blown—and then at Rita and Harry and whoever else happened to be there—a long, slow, sweeping-around-the-room bulldog gaze that was supposed to show the epitome of deep feeling, which every damn time he did it he pulled you in for a few seconds, caught you as if by the throat, had you ready to spill the soppiest tear ever, even though you *knew* better. Knew it was all a setup again, wasn't it? How could a man sing so sweetly and gaze into your eyes like that and then at the exact moment you were ready to melt—how could he almost blow you away with a great bellow of laughter? A tremendous bellow—and his big meaty palm slapping down on something hard. And then, as if not one thing had happened—no song, no near melt—"Ladies and gentlemen, who needs a fresh bump?"

Bang, it's over. Okay, so that was one story. But exactly *how* he got the house for singing that song he never explained. Just, "Charm, kid. Pure charm."

Big Jake in his blue blazer with a cigar in one hand and the world in the other. A self-made man, he liked to say. He *was* charming. Her girlfriends when she was twelve, thirteen, called him Jake the Prince. And successful. Oh yes, a huge house in Grosse Pointe, always long, sleek cars, and "You, your mother, and Harry," he'd say, "who dresses better?"

That's how it was growing up. New this, new that, *nice*. At St. Hedwig's, where she and Harry went to school, because it was *his* old school—driven there across town by Dolly usually—the nuns almost daily would whisper to her, "Please thank your father for his generous gift of . . ."

Oh hell, she couldn't remember half of it. Flowers, books, furniture, *statues*. The point was Big Jake Lupinski had done very well in Detroit and put his family in a good neighborhood, the *best*, and was generous to nuns—and to many others—and could have afforded to take his wife and kids anywhere in the summer, or buy a vacation spot (his phrase) ten times better than the little house on Lake Michigan, but that's the place he most wanted to be and—above all—it was the possession, the gaining of it, that he was the most secretive about. Why?

Not even her mother could, or would, help her. Watching another handful of sand stream out, she remembered asking—again!—was it *really* true that he got the beach house for singing "Danny Boy"?

"Sure it was true, didn't Jake say so?" Dolly, also a singer, would sing.

"But *how?*"

"Ah, you'll have to ask him that."

"I did."

"And?" Her mother's green eyes flashing.

"He said charm."

"Then that's the answer, isn't it?"

The secret was frustrating and puzzling *and* romantic, and one day she got a good answer—all by herself: he'd won it on the radio, in a singing contest! Or so she romantically thought—for two or three more summers—until a Dutch kid whose snooty parents had a place up the beach said to her, "Don't make me laugh."

But Jake laughed. "A singing contest? Not on your life, kid."

Then—a jolt—she saw him that last year when he sat in his Grosse Point house like a toad. Went nowhere. Pulled all the curtains. Did nothing that she could see except watch—stare at, moronically—television. She tried getting him to talk— about anything. The weather, baseball, his garden, his formerly prize tomatoes. "Tell me how you got the lake house, Pop?" Surely *that* would pick him up. But here's what he finally said: "Go ask your big-shot Bernie Soluk."

He was bitter, God he was bitter, and so damn full of self-pity she wanted to throw an ashtray at him, a lamp, all that

Polish crap on the mantel, his oh–so–precious awards. She also wanted to *reason* with him. Sitting beside Harry—Harry the innocent, who all during the mess had been told nothing, since what was the point?—she remembered trying. Remembered looking the bitter unhappy toad in the eye and saying, "Let's set the record straight. Just you and me. Private."

"I'm watching something. You're in my way."

She whirled, turned off the TV.

"You're watching *me*, Pop."

He raised his eyes. *What?* the suddenly fierce expression said. *You?*

He was getting mad. Good. Here it comes, the old fury. Any second now he'd be yelling that nobody lectured Jake Lupinski! Nobody! He'd throw his arms around, he'd thunder.

He stood up. He seemed confused. He walked over to the fireplace and took down a plaque and a sword—both bearing his name—and in a small voice that sounded like his vocal cords had been twisted into rusty wires—not looking at her— he asked did she think these were garbage? No thunder, no rage. Just this one question. Then he glanced at her, slipping away.

She was desperate. "Pop! Pop! You know what your business was? Scraps. Stuff smashed, tossed in a heap. Is that *all* you can handle?" Did he understand what she was saying? She said, "Listen—I go to this woman, Dr. Shi, who is not any older than I am, who sits in her nice office, in her nice clothes, and waits for me to talk. Anything, she says. Anything at all. I don't know how to start so I say I miss Dolly. I tell her Dolly was like a beautiful bright bird, always singing something—or she was like the first star at night. Harry said that, remember? Said we could wish on her picture. And when she fell, was falling, she said to us, Don't fight, you hooligans, I mean it. Which confused us, because we *didn't* fight. Not ever. Not then, because everything was nice. She made us hold hands and promise, remember? Because if you *do*, she said, if you do—but she didn't finish, and poor Harry kept saying, No, no, we won't, we won't, over and over like he was saying his beads. And now, I tell Dr. Shi, Bernie Soluk, my husband, and Jake Lupinski, my father, don't speak. Bernie's sister, Lillian, *will* speak—to Bernie, who doesn't hear her, but not to me, who does. As for Nick, ah, once in a blue moon he speaks long distance—always long distance, even when he's right in front of us. Why did everything turn out like this? Because Bernie went to prison for a while, and his son seems to be trying his best to go him one better and go there forever? Because Jake did not go to prison but maybe should have, same as Bernie, his partner and son-in-law, except that Bernie Soluk testified that Jake Lupinski hadn't set foot in the office in ten years, that all he did now, this retired widower, was grow his prize tomatoes, collecting more honors because he was clean, spotless, like his lily-white shirts? Is that, all of it, what's eating you, Pop?"

His eyes, shiny-wet, seemed loose.

"I tried to tell Dr. Shi what a phony showboater you'd been, but I broke down. Not that any of that was relevant—the 'Danny Boy' stuff and so on—so I focused on the trial. The main event. A full ten-rounder with nobody on our side throwing much of a punch. It is fascinating how Bernie let all the blame fall his way—without really admitting anything. You live with a guy almost twenty-five years and you think you know this and that, and what do you end up knowing? *Did* he slip money to those guys at the shops to let his drivers pick up brand new steel along with the scrap and make that nice crooked profit? And *if* he did, he paid for it, yes? Can we now, please, move on to a new event?"

That was it. That was her speech. Her last words with Big Jake Lupinski. Who then, when no one was looking, did move on to a new event by taking himself and his precious-nothing secrets out to Holy Rosary cemetery and lying down with them on his paid-for plot all night in the rain. Next to Dolly. And got himself pneumonia and a gleaming walnut casket and a church full of flowers and a bunch of priests saying what a wonderful devoted friend he was. Which shut even Lillian up for a couple of Sundays.

Rita looked at the house he'd left Harry and shook her head. She wanted to cry. Look at it. A pile of gray boards surrounded by what? You need a brace of pink flamingos? A Wurlitzer? Tarnished candlesticks? A *sword*? She found a tissue and blew her nose. You know what she wanted? She wanted to hear Big Jake Lupinski sing 'Danny Boy' like he did. Who—out there—could give this ragged pump she hauled around a bump like that?

"I knew you'd be here today," Harry said.

"Yeah, how?"

He smiled. "Hey, smell this nice clean air."

How could she smell anything with her equipment? Blow, blow, and more blow.

"The little waves are nice too, huh?"

Yeah, sure, nice.

She said, "Harry, a person gives you a sword, what is that?"

"You talking about Pop?"

"No—the Pope."

"The Pope? I can never remember—"

"I'm sorry, Harry. Ignore me."

"Hey, Rita."

"Hey."

"Don't you like to see the very tip of the sun?"

"I like to see everything, that's my problem."

They gazed out at the melt of yellows, purples, and reds. They'd seen this show a thousand times. More. It always got you, always, and always left you.

"I'll tell you the truth. Ready?"

"I hope so."

"I knew you'd be here because you're my sister." He found her hand and held it—softly, carefully, as if it might break like an egg.

The paw of a high-strung cat, one that might suddenly lash out, was more like it. In her view.

"Didn't Pop say blood is thicker than water?"

And if your nose itches you'll kiss a fool. And—

She took her hand back; she had to blow again. Maybe in her next life she'd be a whale.

"You got a cold? I can make some tea? Just like Mom did."

"Let's sit a little longer, okay?"

"What if Jesus came by, Rita?"

Oh, Harry, Harry.

"I mean for a swim, because *look* out there. Is that something?"

She looked at the lake in its just-after-sunset slate-rosy sheen and thought to say that as she understood it Jesus preferred to be *on* the water—walking—he was that kind of guy—maybe a showoff, maybe even allergic. Nobody ever talked about Jesus' health. His bouts with germs, headaches, teeth. Did the guy, *if* he was human, never suffer anything common like acne? He makes headlines for those Big Plays, but what about between the acts? Did he, he just for starters, fill his pants as a baby? Harry did, Nick did, everybody does. It's natural, normal. So is becoming friends with people. You talk, you share, you don't bullshit. Or if you do, then you laugh about it, right? Clear the air. If you're human. But it's hard. We're into either/or too much. Good or bad, win or lose. Even though we know, deep down, it's an impossible way to live, really. We're such hypocrites, most of us. Such graspers. Why? Because *nice* after a while is too dull? Is it? Oh no. Nice was more difficult, more elusive, more *something* than anything. On that she would wager all she had.

She could hear the soft waves rub and rub the shore. It was soothing, touching, almost human out there; and then she thought—surprising herself—well, maybe he just might come by, for Harry. And no big deal. No gawkers, no mob, nobody else would even know about it, because why should they? Only the two of them, dog-paddling around, between the pink flamingos, wagon wheels, and jars of buttons on one side and the ruler-sharp horizon line on the other. It made a kind of sense because—

He had her hand again in his big gentle palm and was standing up. She stood with him. She took a breath, a deep one, a lung-scrubber, and let him lead her, shoes and all, into the lake, up past her thighs, her belt. In a moment, reckless, she bent her knees, dropping, soaking her HOT PEPPERS. How funny. How simple! How—

"Nice," he said. Then he let her go so he could turn over in a somersault. He came up all smiles.

"What are we *doing?*" she squealed.

"Don't you remember?" He made another somersault. And another. A forty-seven-year-old kid. A nut. A lovely nut.

She pinched her nose and tried a somersault too. My God, she did it! Without holding her nose she did it again—and again—keeping up with him.

Finally they stopped to catch their breath.

"Really, Rita, you know it's nice."

"I do," she said. "I do," because—oh hell—it really was, and it was all—right then—she needed or wanted to know.

Tornadoes

When I was a kid, walking home from school, it seemed kindly women in town were always calling out:

Halvard, come help me finish this pot of cabbage soup!

Halvard, I'll bet you could eat some fresh hermits!

For the longest time I thought they just understood my late afternoon hunger. I had no idea how much my old man figured in. Not that he wasn't often on my mind too.

I can remember more than one winter day like this—lying flat on the pond, hearing the ice crack, and watching my breath bloom and slide away in the spiraling snow . . . trying to imagine nothing, nothing but sky, under my back. I'd pick out a snowflake and follow it—him—down, waiting to see if he would land on me, and where. I wanted to catch him, save him in the red and black squares of his old hunting coat I always wore.

I can also remember looking at his picture in the trophy case at school. There he was, vaulting, my old man, sailing past a fleecy cloud, his bare legs leading him to glory. He was halfway there, still gripping the pole, his shorts just ticking the bar. Sometimes I'd look too long and forget where I was and my heart would beat hard for him to *get over*. But another part of me knew I didn't have to worry because there he was again, in another picture, all freckles and bright teeth and tight curly hair, an all–American boy, smiling out at anyone who stopped to admire him and the gleaming statuette he held high in the air.

Your father had such promise! a teacher said to me once. Mrs. Swift. She was a well-meaning woman who taught me geography, who helped me appreciate the great difficulty most people have in simply getting from here to there, and I heard no disappointment in her voice, only wistfulness, praise.

I heard somebody else say once—not to me and not in these exact words, but this was the idea—that we lived in a house that might have been patched together from several other houses knocked apart in a tornado. I knew about tornadoes. I had seen blades of grass sticking out of a telephone pole as if they had grown there. Like a high-wire artist I had walked, one foot carefully in front of the other, from the top of a giant oak down to its bushy exploding roots and leaped into the soft hole, finding a long red worm to catch bluegills on, finding a ring of good wet clay to dig at and shape into a wide, smiling face. But I never thought of our house as anything unusual. Even if we did use a lot of scrap lumber, and had every color you could think of in the roof, and used that gift oak as well. We cut it up and smoothed it out and polished the grain so it looked like the rolling hills at daybreak. Over which—the real hills—I pulled my wagon, hunting for beautiful stones to cover our floor with.

How are you and your father getting along these days? the women in town would ask as I ate their soup and cookies. We're busy, I'd say. We're busy on the house. I would say the same at school to Mrs. Swift and his other teachers I inherited. I would say it again at Bender's Store when I picked up a box of Quaker Oats or a sack of Red Man tobacco or some nails. We're busy on the house!

I was not around yet when Bender's had the parade for him. But there was a picture of that too, in the store in the meats section. It hung on the wall over the big butcher's block, along with pictures of other local citizens who had done something noteworthy—won a blue ribbon for their bull or a seat in the state legislature, or lived to one hundred as Mrs. Ida Muldowny did, still milking her cow. There she was next to my old man, resting her head in the cow's ribs, squeezing out a good stream.

What my old man did to get his picture up in Bender's—above and beyond winning the high school pole vault event for 1938—was jump out of an airplane in France on D–Day wearing a parachute that refused to open. There was no picture of that, of course, nor any showing the lucky thing that happened that saved him—unless you count the one I drew with crayons and that looked more like a giant vanilla ice cream cone with a spider on top than a man riding to earth on another man's parachute. The picture above the butcher's block in Bender's showed him sitting in the back of a truck with my mother, his four limbs wrapped in plaster, pointing a crutch in the sky. And smiling out at the crowd as he did from the trophy case at school, all freckles and bright teeth and tight curly hair. An all–American boy still. And my mother pretty enough to be in the movies.

In many ways it was a perfect picture of a man used to falling and landing, if not exactly on his feet, certainly among the living. And always to applause, reward. Was he lucky? I heard people say when they talked about the war. Was he *ever* lucky. Well, that was only part of the story. Imagine a man falling from the stars. It's a long way down.

His bones mended, in any case, and he and my mother went to the State University. She got a job as a secretary there. He planned to become a teacher, a coach, and go back to West Branch High where they were waiting for him. Meantime I was born. We lived in the Quonset huts with the other GIs and their families. We had a cocker spaniel named Chance.

There is a picture showing the four of us in the front yard of our Quonset, my old man holding out for Chance a bone with a ribbon around it (it was Chance's birthday), my mother in a babushka holding me. I know they were happy, you could see it in their beaming faces.

The scowling, threatening expression on my face made my old man think of Edward G. Robinson, the actor, and from the day he saw that picture he called me Robinson. Or, if he was feeling good about something, Not-So-Impossible Robinson. One time, when I was old enough to think about it, I asked him what Not-So-Impossible Robinson meant. Suddenly pretending he was on a horse, he said, Whoa, Robinson! And then I got that name too. My mother, I'm sure, always called me Halvard. All adults did. But Robinson was the name I preferred, although I never would have told my mother that, or anyone else. Kids called me by my last name, Link. Lanky Link.

After my mother and Aunt Frony died in the accident, we just had Uncle Albert for family. He lived up the road from our place, in the house where my old man lived as a kid. Uncle Albert and Aunt Frony raised him. They had a beautiful place. Two apple orchards, a big red barn, and the Curly Creek curled through their walnut woods saying its name all the way to what became our place. At one time Uncle Albert farmed 360 acres, beans and corn and hay mainly, but after the accident he rented out his land and sold his hogs and cattle and didn't do anything until he took up raising canaries as a hobby. I can remember Uncle Albert putting me on his knee and asking, What would you like, a brother or a sister? He was sipping his afternoon glass of buttermilk, and I was having one with him, that's how I remember the question. I was four. My old man had just graduated, and we were all back in West Branch, Chance too, staying at Uncle Albert's and kicking up grasshoppers in the sun as we walked off the measurements of the different rooms of the house we planned to build, on the hill next to the pond down the road.

Then before summer was over Old Joe Bender who had the grain elevator ran into Uncle Albert's Hudson. His brakes failed coming down the big dip out of town. He was driving out to visit Uncle Albert. My mother and Aunt Frony were going in for their Saturday shopping. Old Joe, who was not very old—he was called that because his son was named Joe too—retired when I was in the first or second grade and moved to California. Young Joe took over the grain elevator. Young Joe's grandfather, Pete, was the one who started Bender's Store, and he was still there, in his white apron, the pencil behind his ear, when I stopped by for my Quaker Oats or my Red Man. He never let me pay for anything.

If you drove Uncle Albert's pickup from the WEST BRANCH sign at the edge of town, down the big dip and straight out Curly Creek Road to the bridge we built that crossed the creek where it ran past our house, the speedometer would tick off exactly two miles. Across the bridge was seven giant steps (my size), and eleven more brought you to our chopping block, which sat, in a sea of sawdust and chips, where a front porch would be. We got around, my old man and I, on foot mainly. But if we had to haul something heavy from town, like a bag of cement or bundles of roofing shingles, we used Uncle Albert's pickup. Climbing in the cab, my old man would make an engine-starting noise with his mouth, and then sing songs like "Sleepy Time Gal" and "Who's Sorry Now?" all the way to town and back, one right after the other. He never blinked when we passed the corner at the bottom of the dip where Old Joe's brakes failed and two small white crosses stood to the side in a wild black raspberry patch. You had to know they were there.

The first time I remember my old man telling me how he met my mother he had a white blanket draped around him like a ghost and was shaking all over. I suppose he had the flu. We were sitting in the main room on a bench we made from part of that tornado oak; we had a nice fire going, and staring at it he said he wished Jill were there to make us some mushroom soup. Like she did in New York City when he got off the boat all wrapped up in plaster. He said that's how they met, over bowls of soup and one spoon. And she kept coming back, he said. It was that easy.

Often in the fall we would sit outside against the chopping block, sit there for hours and watch the ducks make circles on the pond, and look for the geese to come down from Canada on their way south. Across the pond and the field where Uncle Albert's renter planted corn or beans you could see the red barn turn darker on our side, dark as a plum, and through the orchard closest to the house you could see a bright flash, like fire, where the sun going down reflected off a window. Aunt Frony's baking a pie, my old man might say. And then he might laugh and finally dip his fingers in the sack of Red Man he suddenly remembered he'd been holding; or he might just continue to sit quietly, and forget all about the tobacco.

Once when the geese came honking and honking overhead, surprising us, my old man, all excited, said, By God! We'll have to go up to Canada one of these days. Soon! I'll show you where I met your mother. I said, I thought you met her in New York City eating mushroom soup. I said that? he said. Oh no. No sir. We met up in Canada. Way up there where the map almost quits. Where those honkers come from. Listen!

Over the next few years, he told me that they had met each other, found each other, in England, in an ice cream shop at the University, in Uncle Albert's walnut woods, in his orchards, in so many places tears would come to my eyes at the mention of her name, tears I did not understand. I had to turn away, and then, near the end, I had to walk away.

The spring I was fourteen a tornado funnel dropped out of the sky, black and swirling, and lifted the roof off Uncle Albert's barn while we watched, sitting against the chopping block. The roof rose up in one piece like a pair of white wings—rose up high enough so you could see daylight between it and the barn—and beside me my old man grabbed his ankles and rocked forward and back, shouting, Whoa, Robinson! Whoa! Whoa! Then the roof fell back to where it belonged, more or less, and the funnel tore a path up Curly Creek Road toward town. Not much damage was done there, though, because after the funnel climbed the dip it continued up and, in effect, bounced completely over West Branch. Four years earlier, however, a tornado came through and wiped out the grain elevator and half a dozen houses and the Mobil station and, down where we lived, it knocked over the giant oak plus a lot of other trees. It also either blew Chance in the pond or he ran there, confused, and drowned. Our house wasn't touched; neither was Uncle Albert's, but all of his canaries died. After the sky cleared, we ran over to see how he was and found him digging a hole in the orchard where the sun-lit window blazed through to us. Then he dumped the milk pail full of yellow birds in the hole. It was between the two tornadoes when my old man kept telling me where he met my mother.

That's all there is to this story, because the summer after the second tornado my old man's heart stopped. He was thirty-six. I found him one morning on the bridge we built over the creek, a coffee can of crawlers and the cane pole we used for bluegills beside him. The creek was low, but there was still enough water falling over the stones to sound like hands clapping in the distance. Looking at him there and then in the trophy case at school or above the butcher's block in Bender's, you could not tell that he changed much.

I Have Work
To Do

Mrs. Woo brought out the box of ashes and asked why was I saving such dirty trash in the coat closet. I said it wasn't trash, it was my mother's remains. She blinked at the box. Then she carried it to the dining room table, carefully as if it might do something, and set it down. She crossed herself. "Oh, baby," she said, "I am so sorry."

"It was a while ago, Mrs. Woo. It's all right."

"All right?" Her eyes got wide.

"The mourning period's over."

"No, no, no, no. You must not talk like that."

"Well . . ."

"Candles!"

"Mrs. Woo, please. Just take—"

She ran to the kitchen and began opening cupboards, mumbling Spanish. Mrs. Woo was Puerto Rican; the name came from a Chinese wine-seller—"passed on"—who had left her some lucrative rental properties and the nice house she lived in—"in the Marina!"—so how could she stop using his fine name? She gave me this information the first day she came to my apartment, for the interview. She didn't *have* to sweep up after other people, she told me. No, no. But a few *select* customers, clean ones, she would take on for *diversity*. Besides, she was not afraid of a little work—look at her arms, still firm, yes? And look at me, a tidy man, she could see this in one glance, so okay, she would add me to her list, because she had an opening. She had an opening because Larry, she said, had foolishly left San Francisco for Vermont! "Very cold. Very big mistake. Wait and see." Her other clients, besides myself now, were George the dentist on Wednesday—"very sharp specialist for caps, see my two up front?"—and Mr. Spiros the movie producer on Monday. I was the youngest, she informed me, Mr. Spiros the oldest. She tapped under her lavender-lined eyes. "His sad dark little bags here—more vitamin E I told him!" Anyway, my day was Friday. On her second visit, to begin cleaning, she discovered my mother's ashes.

She found some large fruit-shaped candles that Allison had brought over for a reunion I wasn't quite ready to—what?—assess? She placed them around the box of ashes and lit them—a pineapple, an avocado, a honeydew melon, a pear. I couldn't help seeing Allison's smile, that slow–curl–into–a–burst–of–generosity she was incapable of holding back.

"Hey, these smell nice!" said Mrs. Woo. She pulled out two chairs. "Now—please sit with me. And tell me about your dear mother."

"Mrs. Woo, I have work to do."

"No, no. It would be bad luck. Very bad luck."

"I have a deadline."

"Don't say such a word. Come." She took my hand.

I sat down beside her.

"Now," said Mrs. Woo, crossing her legs. She wore—because, as she'd told me, she *could* wear them—tight white toreador pants. "Begin. Sweet memories, Hymn. The nice times. We need that, yes?"

My mother once hit me in the clavicle with a feed bucket. I was approaching fifteen when it landed, on the verge of becoming an intellectual dandy, full as I'd ever be of myself and my own opinions. My opinions, after I'd polished them, came from my mouth, I felt, like inscriptions off a stone. I was in high thrall at the moment, flush, my hands whirling under certain essential words, trying to explain to Oscar Duclercque my destiny—specifically my need to mark the world *soon*—when daylight wobbled and the hard-packed ground flew up. She glanced down at me and said I had fresh horse shit in my pompadour.

As everyone knows, mothers can be powerful. Mine could pitch hay, pitch a battle, and pitch my dad's heart around the barn without breaking much of a sweat. She stood maybe three fingers over five feet. She had hair the color of hot coals, back-lit green-gray eyes—like a wolf's—and tiny ears that cupped out some and that she rarely hid. Outdoors her hair was always tied back so her hat would ride snug. Her stride could seem suddenly petulant, as if she had to stomp out superfluous thoughts in a hard rhythm. From a shouting distance, she looked like one of those small tough gristly cowboys you avoided crossing in a hot debate. It astonishes me to realize that until I was almost fifteen, I did not ask where she came from or even how old she was, never mind what, deep down, she really wanted out of life.

I approached my dad with a standard question about meeting. He said she showed up one day right where my boots were planted and asked for work.

"From where?"

"From off a migrant truck passing by," he said. "She'd been picking Delicious apples and got tired of it."

"Then what?"

"Some time expired." He looked like he might smile. He was cinching up the saddle on Buster. This conversation took place the morning after she'd whacked me with the bucket—a monumental surprise. She was now a subject I felt I ought to look into deeper. Before, she was just my mother, like anybody's, I figured, although what did I really know about mothers? The only ones I had observed up close were at school, and since they were also my teachers the picture wasn't clear. Where they would say Let me show you, she would say Figure it out, it'll mean more.

My dad was leading Buster out of the barn.

"*Then* what?" I said.

"You were born. Right over there. In Ginny's stall."

I looked at my horse's stall. I was born there?

"She put down clean straw first," my dad said. Then, up on Buster, he did smile, and rode off.

I remember when I got to my feet, following the bucket-whack, Oscar Duclercque smirked. I asked what seemed to be funny. His smirk sprung into a shape that widened his face. He pushed in a fresh pinch of Copenhagen.

"Your mom is one sure-fire lady—always," he said, clearly in admiration.

The thing is, I admired her too. I had come to appreciate and like figuring out things on my own. Dreaming. Reading. And it was no secret that my view of the world went way beyond our ranch, beyond Idaho. I mean, I did my chores—I didn't whine (my parents both let me know what they thought of whiners)—but I never saw the scene around me as anything much more than a phase I had to get through. It's a condition, if that's the best word, I've had all my life.

I wanted to tell Mrs. Woo something short and sweet and truthful to get this over with: that my mother basically let me go my own way because she had gone her own way. Instead, I said, "Her name was Louise. But she preferred Lou. Almost at the last minute I learned that she was the only child of a lawyer who had done very well in the lumber business, up in Spokane, and then something happened and they were poor."

"Oh," said Mrs. Woo. "Oh, baby. Poor is no good. I *know*."

"After an interval, however, she married my father, Hymn, Senior, and helped turn his so-so ranch into a respectable operation."

"Ah," Mrs. Woo brightened. "She had comfort then."

"Lou would have hated comfort."

"No."

"Yes, indeed."

"How can you say such a thing?"

"Here's sort of an illustration: she rescued a one-eyed woman named Jewelle Gomez from some dismal job and brought her home to be our cook. Jewelle fried everything—I mean fried it. To all three of us it was immediately clear that mealtimes would be a hard row. Maybe a week went by. Finally my dad said, at the table, "Where in glory did she learn to punish good steak so thoroughly?" Then we heard sobbing from the kitchen. Next day my mother took Jewelle into town and bought her several presents—blouses, scarves, shoes—and when they returned she had Jewelle join us at the table. She ate with us from that night on, and my dad always found something on his plate to praise."

"Your mother had a heart, I think."

"My dad was crazy about her."

"Oh, baby. This touches me. I love romantic men."

"He was also old enough to be her father."

"Hey, older men are *okay*." She gave me a consoling pat on the arm. "But he has passed on too, yes?"

"No."

"He is alive, your father?"

"Alive is not the first word he would choose."

"Oh my god, baby. Will this be sad?"

Will this be sad? I was ridiculously quick, at one point, to quote the philosopher Hobbes, who said that our lives were solitary, poor, nasty, brutish, and short. "Do you *believe* that?"

Allison asked on what amounted to our first date. "Sure," I laughed. We had both showed up to interview for a job at an ad agency, were kept waiting longer than we liked, and went for a walk. Possessing high opinions of our abilities and almost no money seemed the only things we had in common. But about six months later, part-timing here and there, no richer, we said: why *not* share expenses? And then, as if overnight, we got real jobs, good ones, and were glowing. How could it be otherwise? we said. Look at us! Were we stars or what? We moved to a considerably better apartment. We were like two kids at the beach, with our toy tools, shaping, smoothing, trying to make everything bigger so it would stay, overwhelm. At the height of all this, I got a call from my dad. Lou was dying.

I had never expected that to happen, not so soon; worse yet, neither did my dad. She looked at us as if, damn it, we were going to disappoint her at exactly the wrong moment. We straightened up. She nodded. Not right away, but when things seemed steady enough, she held our hands. She told us that when she was a girl, men came to the door and took away the piano and pictures off the walls and rolled up the rugs intricate with tendrils and birds and took those too. One night her father crawled inside the dog's house under a big Douglas fir in the yard, and her mother sang a lullaby to bring him back out and up to their bed. Days later he boarded the train; he was gone for a long time. When he returned his hair was white, and soon, it seemed, her mother's hair, always so golden, was white too. He said he had a plan to save them. He said that for years, getting smaller and smaller until he was gone. Her mother sat and worked large puzzles. Lou would help her. They were all really the same puzzle, she said: a scene of the country, great sweeps of grass with a stream curving through, a rustic cottage on a hill in the distance, or a castle ruin. Over and over in their little

Spokane apartment, Lou said, her mother put such placid, sentimental pictures together piece by piece, and she helped her because the woman's vision was failing.

It was the longest story I had ever heard my mother tell. I thought I got the point of it, and was back if not hard by Hobbes at least in his shadow. What my dad took from the story, he never said. He held her hand until the undertaker came, and then he went out to the barn and slept there. In warm weather once in a while he still spends a night out there—when she stomps into his head and sifts down around his ribs and grabs hold, he says. But mostly he falls asleep in his rocker on the porch. In the cold months he stays pretty much indoors and reads, or is read to by Cheyanne Duclercque, Oscar and Jewelle's youngest daughter who calls him Grandpa-daddy and bakes his favorite cookies. I drive up to see him when I can. We walk around the place. "Two Hymns—and neither one can sing a lick," he once laughed. When I leave, he always reminds me, "Don't forget."

"So," I said to Mrs. Woo, after telling her all this, "there it is, a love story. I've given love stories some thought. They're not easy. Endings are especially hard. Usually the man dies first, and the woman, if she lives on long enough, runs the risk of becoming silly and losing everything—that's how it seems, anyway. Men run the same risk if they live on. So far my dad's been extraordinarily lucky. As for those ashes, he asked me to keep track of them, I think, so that I'll remember how little they mean."

After a minute I said, "Well, Mrs. Woo, that's basically where we are."

She stared at me. She had *been* staring at me. When I smiled and shrugged—there just wasn't any more to say—she stood up, very slowly, as if the chair or she herself might break, then she bent over and one by one blew out Allison's candles. For a moment I saw Allison holding them in her arms, saw that smile at the peak of its generosity begin to fade.

"Here," she'd finally said, "keep them anyway. You never know when you'll need some light . . ."

Mrs. Woo walked to the door. There she half-turned. I could have stopped her maybe, told her what she wanted to hear. I could have lied to Allison, too. Said I loved how we were climbing higher and higher . . .

Sometimes I wish I could paint. The way a woman can hesitate at a door, gazing down, deep down, as if beyond floors and rock and fire, with no view to report . . . only that silent, helpless, mysterious and lovely profile.

Leaving

Hymn lay under the comforter and saw the convent door... a kind of trapezoid... and then he saw Sylvia step through it, a bag in each hand and her head bare, leaving the order. He had not been there, of course; she told him about it—how her bags contained nothing but a toothbrush, some underwear, and a book of short stories. How bright the sun shone, and how she felt both gracefully light and awkwardly off balance at the same time. She wore a heavy tweed skirt and a blue middy blouse. Her hair was cut short as a boy's. She was twenty-eight, and she had an immediate craving for a tart apple and the salty-sweet cream rendering of peanuts. He embraced these details, savoring them. As he had before. Not often. But often enough, out of nowhere, a goofy door would open in his floating thoughts, and there she'd be, a slender willow, her white cheeks and reddish cropped hair caught by the sun, her mouth wanting a green cooking apple, a Jonathan, anything with snap and pucker to it, and a spoonful of peanut butter. He couldn't imagine not having that memory. Not having any memories. He had tried and the emptiness, the nothing, the idea of nothing made him oddly mad, as if rope bound his arms, a straitjacket. How could he never again think about when they first touched hands? It was exactly a year after she had stepped through that door—July 14. Simply a coincidence, she said later, just as her leaving the convent on that date was only a coincidence. Bastille Day and its symbolism—prison, revolt—was not on her mind at all. Snap and pucker. "Your name—it startled and charmed me," she said. He was stretching his lunch hour at the advertising agency to take a summer school course—Shakespeare's Major Plays—and there she was, in the first row, alive to every word. The day they formally shook hands, they had carried their coffees outside for the break and shared a shady bench. He said, "I think my favorite line is Lear's 'I will keep still with my philosopher.'" She smiled, nodding approval. They sipped in silence. But the next day they returned to that bench—"You don't *appear* crazy," she said—and slowly, shyly, they began to say the kinds of things that men and women say when they can't help it. By the time fall arrived they were, as they confessed, in sweet ache for each other, and he was—mercifully—no longer employed to find clever ways of saying almost nothing. They said their vows under a plum tree, the leaves turning from green to yellow. The old pastor was against it, he wanted them *inside*, but that young assistant went along. What ever happened to him? How lucky they felt! They loved their leafy town . . . Sylvia able to walk to her school, he to his . . . they said to their students *look . . . listen . . .* They planted a garden behind their house. And a tree that produced small green tangy apples perfect for pies. Every Halloween they carved pumpkins—Catherine the Great, Boz, Humphrey Bogart they named them. On a questionnaire once—he couldn't remember what for—they said they liked the rhythms of the witches in Macbeth, popcorn, the roly-poly peasant Pope—John—who stirred things up before he died, Louis Armstrong. They liked many other things, but there was no more space. At the first serious packable snowfall they always built a mule and rider they called Quixote. Always, didn't they? Yes, they liked to see these two travelers brave every blow and then slip slowly into the sweet smell of spring. They hoped for

children, often reciting favorite songs and riddles before
falling asleep. They framed a copy of Rackham's drawing of
Rumpelstiltskin, that "indescribably ridiculous little old man
. . . leaping, hopping on one leg, and singing." Wasn't it still
up? They faithfully attended Mass in the handsome stone and
cut-glass church that German and Italian immigrants, long
before, had joined talents to erect. Was it that unlikely, happy
marriage of the stolid and playful they were mainly drawn
to? One Sunday, in the middle of the old pastor's sermon,
Sylvia raised her hand from the first pew—and kept it raised
until the flustered priest said, "Yes, yes, what is it?" She wanted
to know how he felt about the possibility that Jesus' *imagination* was his gift, the real point of it all, that the rest of us re-
sist. The priest said he would talk with her later, privately, if
she didn't mind. When the meeting came about, he advised
her to go to confession, seek forgiveness, pray harder. On
Sundays after that, she elected to look for something outside
she hadn't noticed before rather than attend church, and he
joined her. "Why are you smiling?" she asked. "Methinks
sometimes I have no more wit than a Christian," he replied.
"*Twelfth Night*," she laughed. "Sir Andrew Aguecheek. That fool."
They were retired then. Did they feel retired? They pretty
much said to each other what they'd said at school. And—
always a refreshment—they got rid of things. Out went the
little car they rarely used, the TV (when had they last turned it
on?), his two neckties, her dress-up shoes, a flowerpot full of
pencils too short to really grip. In nice weather they worked
in the garden—they came to smell like their garden, which
was lovely—or rode their bicycles to a pond beyond town
and watched a green heron step thoughtfully. Or after dinner
walked to a hill above the railroad tracks and waited for the
night train, delighted, yet again, to hear it approach and
whistle and continue on without them. They liked the quiet
philosophy it brought, how the stars afterwards seemed

brighter, more receptive, smarter. When the harsh weather kept them in, they read, baked bread, canned the garden's last produce. Their tomato juice was especially spicy and had *body*. Responding to letters from old friends who had moved to condos in warmer climates, they sent feathers, leaves, their homemade fudge. Were they dotty? Getting senile? Most things that occupied people's thoughts seemed to them like . . . like the pieces loose in the box that you were supposed to be able to put together "in minutes" by following the Easy Instructions. Planting a flag on the moon? On Mars? Well, okay. But what about the notions the honeybees faithfully hatched? The lyrical fish? Among their closest friends they counted the worms keeping the ground supple, and flickers on the job above, and Rabelais, Emily Dickinson, Huck Finn. "I wouldn't mind," he said, "a raft and a river. I know something about them." Yes, that raft he once built—out of driftwood so bleached and smooth—well, it held not only him but Honey too. "Did I tell you about Honey? My collie?" "No, you never did." He didn't? Never told her about Honey? She was singing—slowly, softly, as if from a dreamy distance—"I'll be down to get you in a taxi, honey. . ." Such a comedienne, his angel, listen to her! Of course he told her. She was having fun with him. He could see that raft. See the two of them on it. And see that red-tailed hawk again too, circling the sunny field, signaling *come, come*. They stopped there for lunch . . . for an avocado, a fresh peach with cream. . . and afterwards, drowsy, they rose to the guest room upstairs, feeling invited, and lay in sheets still smelling of clover from drying outside. He must plant more clover, another apple tree. Yes, by God, another apple tree . . . and see her under it, sun-lit, filling her basket. "A songwriter says the most popular vowel sound in the English language is oo. As in boo-hoo," she said. And she began singing.

Pavol Hudák,
The Poet,
Is Talking

"Pavol is drinking hard cider for breakfast. You would not guess this, but he is a very good pick-pocket. He travels to pretty Levoča, a prosperous town. I could make a fine living here, he thinks. Rich merchants, doctors, foreign tourists. I can slip money from their coats and trousers like a magician. So this is what I do, I move here. You yourself, Gary, can see how successful I am, as I drink cider for breakfast while others slave away.

"One morning in the Main Square I observe a beautiful woman walking toward me. She is such a wonderful sight, my eyes go weak as she approaches. I can only look at her face a few moments, then I must look down, at her basket of flowers. I am suddenly bashful, like a boy. I even stumble as we pass each other. I am in the clouds, a confused and lucky leaf. I touch my chest to calm my heart. Wait. Breathe slowly, Pavol. What is this? My purse is not in my shirt here, where I always keep it. I am certain I brought it with me when I left my room only moments ago. I stopped nowhere, saw no one—no one except the beauty. Is it possible *she* took it? I am ashamed and astounded at this thought, and curious too. Very curious.

"I turn, I run after her. My heart is beating. I say to her, 'Excuse me, please. I must ask you a stupid question.' Her eyes are a glory to look at. 'I am only Pavol, a poet and, to tell the truth, a pickpocket. I ran after you because I am curious. Did you by any chance take my purse? Please, you can relax. I won't tell the police if you did.'

"She looks at me a long moment. Up and down. I tell you her eyes are the color of grass and sky. Impossible, I know, but that's the truth. Finally she says, 'Yes, in fact I did.'

"We talk. I want to say a poem to her, but this other news, of her great gift, as good as my own, is what we discuss. In short, I suggest we work together. We can be fantastic! So this is what we do, Gary. We become a team. We make so much money we buy a house. We become lovers, of course, it is inevitable. And one day we decide to marry. Why not? We can have children. We can teach them what we know. We can retire into a nice old age and let our kids do the work.

"So Slavka becomes pregnant, blooms into a garden, a moon. Forgive me, but I lose myself remembering. And it's amazing how this new condition makes her an even better pickpocket. Because she doesn't seem the type, does she? She can get closer to people. They trust her, offer their arms, and so forth.

"Then the baby is ready. I run for the midwife. The best one. She brings out from Slavka a boy, Pavol, named after me. He is fine looking, has those miracle eyes of his mother, and is healthy except for one thing. He holds his left arm close to his chest. I try very gently to pull it away, but he resists. He will reach up to me with his right hand, but his left he keeps to himself, clutched in a fist beside his heart.

"Time, I think, will fix things. Perhaps his coming into the world during winter was too shocking, too cold, although the midwife took care to bundle him quickly and hold him close. I watched, so I know.

"Thus we wait, doing all we can to encourage little Pavol to relax his arm, open his hand. We bathe him, caress him, sing to him. Not even my best poems, whispered in his ear, will help. The doctors (some whose pockets I once picked) all tell us the same thing: do not worry, nothing physically is wrong, after all, he is only an infant. But I am impatient—Slavka too—and we take Pavol to a woman in the country who is said by many to have old wisdom. A few even call her a witch. In truth, she looked like one, her hair all stuck out, no teeth.

"She gazed at Pavol a long time. She started to touch him but pulled her hand back. This made me nervous. I was ready to leave. She said, 'No—wait.' Shivering, she gathered her rag of a shawl tighter. She tossed more sticks on her fire. Then she threw a handful of grain into the flames. 'Give me money,' she said, 'and I will tell you what to do. Give me money now.' I paid her. She counted it, the witch. Then she said to go home and tie a small piece of gold on a string and dangle it over the baby.

"We followed her instructions. We tied one of Slavka's gold earrings on a string, and I held it like this. I could see him look at it—his fabulous eyes had birds in them, a whole forest. He raised his right hand. I moved the earring closer to his left hand. Slowly, very slowly, the little hand came away from his chest. The little fingers began to open. They opened so slowly I thought a week went by—and this is why, Gary: he was already holding something! Something very shiny! Do you know what it was? In his little palm he was holding the midwife's wedding ring!"

Pavol the poet looked into his own left palm, then he looked at me and winked.

I raised my glass. "Very good," I said.

"Do you think so?"

"Absolutely."

"Will it make me rich?"

"Don't you mean richer?"

"Of course!"

He clinked his glass against mine, gave me another wink, and said, "To happiness!" He finished his cider in one gulp. Then, lifting his face toward the sky, eyes closed, he recited the following poem:

> Really. You saw a hawk there
> swooping without mercy
> on yellow hens . . .
>
> That's life
> diving
> head down
> onto childhood.

Sleepy Time
Gal

In the small town in northern Michigan where my father lived as a young man, he had an Italian friend who worked in a restaurant. I will call his friend Phil. Phil's job in the restaurant was as ordinary as you can imagine—from making coffee in the morning to sweeping up at night. But what was not ordinary about Phil was his piano playing. On Saturday nights my father and Phil and their girlfriends would drive ten or fifteen miles to a roadhouse by a lake where they would drink beer from schoopers and dance and Phil would play an old beat-up piano. He could play any song you named, my father said, but the song everyone waited for was the one he wrote, which he would always play at the end before they left to go back to the town. And everyone knew of course that he had written the song for his girl, who was as pretty as she was rich. Her father was the banker in their town and he was a tough old German and he didn't like Phil going around with his daughter.

My father, when he told this story, which was not often, would tell it in an offhand way and emphasize the Depression and not having much, instead of the important parts. I will try to tell it the way he did, if I can.

So they would go to the roadhouse by the lake and finally Phil would play his song and everyone would say, Phil, that's a great song, you could make a lot of money from it. But Phil would only shake his head and smile and look at his girl. I have to break in here and say that my father, a gentle but practical man, was not inclined to emphasize the part about Phil looking at his girl. It was my mother who said the girl would rest her head on Phil's shoulder while he played, and that he got the idea for the song from the pretty way she looked when she got sleepy. My mother was not part of the story, but she had heard it when she and my father were younger and therefore had that information. I would like to intrude further and add something about Phil writing the song, maybe show him whistling the tune and going over the words slowly and carefully to get the best ones, while peeling onions or potatoes in the restaurant; but my father is already driving them home from the roadhouse and saying how patched up his tires were and how his car's engine was a gingerbread of parts from different makes, and some parts were his own invention as well. And my mother is saying that the old German had made his daughter promise not to get involved with any man until after college, and they couldn't be late. Also my mother likes the sad parts and is eager to get to their last night before the girl goes away to college.

So they all went out to the roadhouse and it was sad. The women got tears in their eyes when Phil played her song, my mother said. My father said that Phil spent his week's pay on a new shirt and tie, the first tie he ever owned, and people kidded him. Somebody piped up and said, Phil, you ought to take that song down to Bay City—which was like saying New York City to them, only more realistic—and sell it and take the money and go to college too. Which was not meant to be cruel, but that was the result because Phil had never even got to high school. But you can see people were trying to cheer him up, my mother said.

Well, she'd come home for Thanksgiving and Christmas and Easter and they'd all sneak out to the roadhouse and drink beer from schoopers and dance and everything would be like always. And of course there were the summers. And everyone knew Phil and the girl would get married after she made good her promise to her father, because you could see it in their eyes when he sat at the old beat-up piano and played her song.

That last part about their eyes was not of course in my father's telling, but I couldn't help putting it in there even though I know it is making some of you impatient. Remember that this happened many years ago in the woods by a lake in northern Michigan, before television. I wish I could put more in, especially about the song and how it felt to Phil to sing it and how the girl felt when hearing it and knowing it was hers, but I've already intruded too much in a simple story that isn't even mine.

Well, here's the kicker part. Probably by now many of you have guessed that one vacation near the end she doesn't come home to see Phil, because she meets some guy at college who is good-looking and as rich as she is and, because her father knew about Phil all along and was pressuring her into forgetting about him, she gives in to this new guy and goes to his hometown during the vacation and falls in love with him. That's how the people in town figured it, because after she graduates they turn up, already married, and right away he takes over the old German's bank—and buys a new Pontiac at the place where my father is the mechanic and pays cash for it. The paying cash always made my father pause and shake his head and mention again that times were tough, but here comes this guy in a spiffy white shirt (with French cuffs, my mother said) and pays the full price in cash.

And this made my father shake his head too: Phil took the song down to Bay City and sold it for twenty-five dollars, the only money he ever got for it. It was the same song we'd just heard on the radio and which reminded my father of the story I just told you. What happened to Phil? Well, he stayed in Bay City and got a job managing a movie theatre. My father saw him there after the Depression when he was on his way to Detroit to work for Ford. He stopped and Phil gave him a box of popcorn. The song he wrote for the girl has sold many millions of records and if I told you the name of it you could probably sing it, or at least whistle the tune. I wonder what the girl thinks when she hears it. Oh yes, my father met Phil's wife too. She worked in the movie theatre with him, selling tickets and cleaning the carpet after the show with one of those sweepers you push. She was also big and loud and nothing like the other one, my mother said.

Burial

Leah Robinson, who lived across the street, offered to call our relatives. I said I would. But I didn't call anyone.

Up in the hotel room someone got for us, I found a long piece of string. To pass the time I tied it, slowly, into many small knots. To pass more time I went out and walked a lot. Jay usually came with me.

Then on the Thursday after Christmas we walked to the funeral home, a minister read a few words, and they cremated Jenny. That afternoon at the Greyhound terminal on Keosauqua I bought a ticket for Mexico.

I got as far as the edge of the desert. I drank whiskey at a picnic table between my motel and the highway until I passed out. When someone slapped me awake I stuck out my thumb. A guy in a van took me all the way to Denver. His name was Poppy.

"It used to be something else," he said, "but all the used-to-be's are back there, you follow me? From D. D. Eisenhower to Tricky, including all the wooden fish with numbers on them you paid a quarter at the carnival to scoop out with a net in-between, you follow me? I mean, I caught the winning TD on the last play of the last game of my senior year in high school, and Ike was still in office. And married the prettiest, richest, most spoiled lady in town the next year, under handsome Jack. We were nineteen and had all of our dream furniture, baby. You follow me? During the week I traveled my territory, the entire state, selling high school yearbooks. On weekends I came home to my stuffed prize from the top shelf. Some guys understand, some don't (I myself chuckle over it now if I'm in the right mood), but what drove me out was her Goddamn belching. I mean she brought up these great froggy blasts from her toe-jam, man, and turned them in to words, like a cancer croaker. In bed, you follow me?

"I split. My father-in-law tried to get me drafted, but I hotwired cars and ran red lights until they caught me and gave me a little time. He was satisfied, I was satisfied. Then after handsome Jack went down, I fell in with a chick who was socially conscious. Did the whole number with her. I mean I liked it, made me feel good marching and running the mimeograph machine, staying up all night smoking a lot of cigarettes planning our next move. We shall overcome, right? I'll tell you how much I liked it. The chick was creamy, an ice cream cone, vanilla, man, and *all* that time, about two years, I never balled her once. Not that I didn't try, you understand. But two years, man, is a long time to be more or less faithful to the same chick without balling her. She was a real believer, you follow me?"

There was more to his story—a commune, a bar he started, some dealing, one or two other business ventures, but I kept nodding off (his dope, my lack of sleep) and finally I slept a while. When I heard him again he talked about running a novelty shop with "a fine lady" who made most of the jewelry.

"I'll tell you how I got my name Poppy, man, it's a nice thing. My lady's kid called me that the first time he saw me. I mean I'd just met her, and pretty soon we see we want to jimmy a little, you know, so she invites me over. She's got a kid, wow. Like I thought she was maybe sixteen, and here's this two-year-old boy sacked on the couch. It turns out she *is* only sixteen, but that's another story. The point is, she shows me this fantastic jewelry she's made out of nothing—pennies, washers—and before we ball or anything I say, 'We gotta go into business!' Next morning the kid sees me and says, 'Poppy!' I say, 'Right, man, that's me,' just playing along. But—and here's the good part—when Fizzy and me start the business and it takes off, man, I remembered when it all started, you follow me? I mean I believe in signs. So I changed my name legally. And guess what we're gonna call our new store? Poppy's Place!"

It was about ten o'clock in the morning when he dropped me off at the bus station in Denver.

"What day is it?"

"Monday, man. Wash day." Pulling away he flashed me the peace sign, smiling, and I saw he had a gold eyetooth.

I felt weak. Inside the station I sat down. For a long time I waited for my body to stop trembling, feeling old. I wanted a bowl of hot soup. Steaming, nourishing bowls of chicken noodle, tomato, onion, mushroom came to me but I couldn't reach them. I sat up straight, like a good boy, but I couldn't get out of the chair. The bowls of hot soup came to me one by one, each with a big silver spoon, and disappeared, untouched.

Finally I was up, outside. The sky was high and skull white. I found a restaurant, got down chili and coffee, then I found a hotel and slept until the next morning, when I boarded a bus back to Des Moines.

I knew what I'd done to Jay and felt weak all over again. I knew it before I climbed in Poppy's van—knew it probably even as I was leaving the funeral home—and now in that droning bus I kept seeing a vision of myself as a child's stick-figure drawing with a balloon-shaped head trying to leap off the writing tablet in a jerky silent-movie motion, but whenever I reached the edge of the paper there was another sheet

I had to run across and try to escape, followed by yet another, until I put my head in my bag somewhere in the middle of those gray flat fields of snow in the middle of Nebraska and vomited.

When we stopped for a few minutes in Ogallala I got some change and called her office. A woman answered.

"Is Mrs. Rau there?"

"I'm sorry, I don't know," she said. "Everyone's up in the coffee room. It's somebody's birthday or something."

"Who are you?"

"I don't work here. I'm just looking for an earring."

In Omaha—an hour's layover—I washed my face, threw out the vomit-covered shirt in my bag, and changed some bills. Her boss, if anyone, would know where she was. I got his home number.

"Jay resigned," he told me. "I tried to talk her into taking a leave but . . . well, I understood." He offered his deepest sympathies, etc., and I was trying to understand how I could have thought she would go back to work.

"Where can I reach her? I . . ."

"She gave us her dad's address in Michigan."

I called Schooltz's number in Houghton Lake. No answer. It was after midnight. Where could they be on a Tuesday night? Playing cards? They played a lot of cards. Jay too? But she didn't have to be in Houghton Lake—she just gave that address. Where was she, then? I tried the number again. Nothing. My bus was called. Still nothing. I was unable to move. I watched the janitors mop, the drunks slide in and out, red- and yellow-eyed, and I dialed Schooltz's number. At five o'- clock I walked around outside, stepping on cracks, breaking backs, and took a cab to the airport.

In Des Moines I called friends. No, no one had heard from her. Then I called our neighbor, Leah. She'd seen her in the hotel the day after the funeral.

"Did she say anything? I mean about her plans?"

"She was waiting for you, Billy."

"Was she okay? Was she all right?"

Leah started to cry, and I hung up.

I couldn't believe she'd still be there, but I called the Fort Des Moines anyway and learned she'd checked out on January 3, leaving no messages. She'd waited there five days for me. I tried Schooltz; still nothing. I went to the bank, then to the post office and picked up magazines, Christmas cards, bills, but nothing from her. Did I expect a letter? Dear Billy, here I sit . . . Five days in that box of a room.

She was waiting for you, Billy.

On the flight to Chicago I saw myself in front of a door, the door to her apartment, almost sixteen years ago . . . it looked just like a door in a hotel . . . she wore a white dress, her cheeks were flushed, we were going to her roommate's wedding . . . Then I opened the door again, the hotel's door, that room, after the funeral, and said I had to go out for a while. She sat on the bed and looked at me and said nothing. Not Where are you going, nothing. And if she had asked, I could not have told her, though I did know I'd need money. I went to the bank. I remember doing that. Then the bus station . . . arriving in Kansas City and buying a shirt and a duffel bag, because my turtleneck was wet and because I knew I'd be checking into a hotel sooner or later and ought to have a bag. And I remembered before that, before the funeral, walking past what was left of our house, knowing while I was doing it that I had never wanted to see that house again, and yet there I was, looking at the boarded-up windows, the caved-in roof.

At O'Hare, after we landed, it was a while before we could get to the terminal: they'd had a record snowfall, the captain said, and everything was behind schedule. The stewardess came by taking drink orders. I didn't want a drink. I wanted to move! Inside, finally, I kept trying Schooltz's number and heard only the same cricket-like signal, which was now staying in my head between calls. Where could they be? In the corridor people were walking past me in a hurry, back and forth, up the corridor and down, carrying sacks and bags, suits and fruit and babies, in wing tips, loafers, high heels, wooden clogs, mukluks, cowboy boots, sandals, sneakers, galoshes, on slim ankles, on thick, on flat feet, dragging a foot, dragging a child, all going up the corridor or down, which was what they were supposed to do, it was their job, their pastime, their passion, their burden, their nervous tic. And mine, too, once I left the phone and joined them.

Crickkk-ettt . . . Crickkk-ettt . . .

I asked the operator to try for me, to check the line, maybe something was wrong with the connection. No, she said, everything seemed to be all right. Then I thought, Carl and Eunice in the brown house stayed up there year-round. He even kept Schooltz's driveway plowed. What was their last name? Carl and Eunice, Carl and Eunice . . . but no last name came to me. Their other neighbors, their card-playing friends . . . Frank and Melba, Connie and Leonard . . . or Frank and Connie, Leonard and Melba. They were all just pairs of first names. The only people whose last names I could think of were our old neighbors, Ellen Shipley and the Hanks, but they were not there in the winter.

Pinky! He'd know if Schooltz was around. It was a Mobil station on North Shore Road, I told the operator, Pinky's Mobil or North Shore Mobil, something like that, or Pinky's Baits.

"I show a Martin's Mobil on North Shore," she said and I got the number. A man answered.

"Pinky?"

"That's me."

"Pinky, this is Schooltz's son-in-law, Bill Rau. I'm trying to reach him at home, but nobody answers. Have you seen him or Mabel around?"

"Say, is this long-distance? I can hear it buzz to Christmas."

"Yes. Have you seen them?"

"Not today or yesterday either, but he's around, they both are. Least they haven't asked me to check on their furnace like they do when they go away. Unless they asked Carl up the road, but I don't think so since his heart attack, you know."

"So you saw Schooltz when, a couple of days ago?"

"Couple days ago, Monday. Filled up the Olds. Where you calling from—that's some buzz, ain't it?"

"Chicago. I'm on my way over."

"Well, they'll be glad to hear that. Say, I see you sold your place to some fella from Saginaw, Mabel says. Hear he's gonna cut down all them nice trees and build."

"If you see Schooltz, Pinky, tell him I'm coming, will you?"

"Sure will."

"Wait. You haven't seen— I mean my wife went on ahead of me a few days ago . . . I wonder if she got there yet."

"Haven't seen her."

It was one o'clock. My plane left at two. I'd land in Midland a little after three, rent a car, and be at Schooltz's right around sunset. Okay, I thought, okay, okay, and I started to walk. I was excited. I hadn't reached Schooltz or Mabel, but I'd talked to Pinky Martin, bait man and furnace watcher, and considered that the next best thing, plus something of a good sign. At the concession I bought a sandwich and milk, but I ate too fast and my stomach bunched like a fist. I smoked a cigarette, trying to relax, trying not to think where she might be—because if she wasn't in Des Moines or Houghton Lake, where was she?

Schooltz and Mabel would know. Really the problem was not that difficult. She'd left Schooltz's address at her office.

Now it was simply a matter of reaching Schooltz. She was probably with them at that moment.

But if she was, why hadn't Pinky Martin seen her? She'd left the Fort Des Moines a week ago. Surely he would've seen or heard something of her around the lake in a week's time? If she flew straight to Michigan—if she even *went* to Michigan. Was she still in Des Moines? If so, where? I called all of our friends. Did she check into another hotel, not able to stand the Fort Des Moines any longer? If she did that, why no messages for me at the desk?

Suddenly my face felt hot. Maybe she didn't want me to know where she was? Maybe she went back to him, the lover she said she'd given up?

I heard my flight being called. I'd try Schooltz's number once more. All the phones near my boarding area were in use, eight men in dark suits with vests. Finally I found one free. A busy signal! They were home! Or I'd poked a wrong number. I tried again, slowly, and again the empty ringing. It had almost been like reaching someone.

We sat on the runway for nearly an hour, waiting our turn. I lay back and traced "No Smoking" on the roof of my mouth with my tongue, over and over, until I saw Jay in Michigan, at the cottage, racing me out to the dock for our morning swim. We bought the cottage—Realtor Mabel's "find" for us—the summer Jay was promoted to editor of *Midwest Politics*. The same summer my first book came out and Jenny graduated from nursery school. We'd been in Iowa three years then, and having a place in Michigan, if only for vacations, was like coming home. Jenny turned the fishing shanty into her playhouse, and at night, at the end of the dock, we could see *stars*. Most nights when just the three of us were there we skinny-dipped, Jay and I, and afterwards sat on the dock in our robes and drank a brandy, facing north, recalling the Upper Peninsula, and searching the sky for the star that lay brightest above the silo our last year up there, Jenny's first, when we lived an easy walk from Lake Superior. "It's that star," she'd finally decide, bringing our past forward, locating one more time a part that stood for many, all of them as romantic and private and fragile as the things we can do only once, and that we preserve in a single gesture or sign that others would consider ordinary or corny unless it was their gesture or sign too. I thought of Poppy then, his faith in signs and his verb "to jimmy."

Shortly before we landed I fell into a squeezed, deep sleep and dreamt an old dream in which I was wearing a red tuxedo and trying to scrape putty off my chin with a shoehorn.

It was after four when I entered the Midland terminal. First I called Schooltz—no answer—then I rented a car and discovered, as the Hertz woman warned, that the interstate was icy. The car would suddenly slide two or three feet to the side. I cut my speed from seventy to fifty, concentrating hard on the road. It was getting dark fast, and my eyes started to burn. Also, after a violent lurch moved me completely into the next lane, my hands and arms began to tremble. I needed coffee. I'd been up and traveling since Denver, forty hours ago. How many miles was that? And all the miles before Denver? I couldn't think about that now. I opened the window, turned off the heat, and repeated the alphabet until I shivered.

At a rest stop north of Clare I put my face in a sink of cold water, tried Schooltz again, drank a cup of machine coffee, and took another cup back to the car. It was pitch dark now. Every ten minutes or so a van or pickup hauling a pair of snowmobiles passed me, and across the divide traffic was slim too. People were home eating, that's where they were. Eating and watching TV in their socks or over at the Elks for the Wednesday night fish fry and bingo game. It started to sleet. I kept the speedometer steady at fifty, which would get me to

Schooltz's around eight. If I didn't hit a deer. I remembered the summer night after I graduated from college, driving up north in the '46 Chevy I'd paid a hundred dollars for. East of Mancelona, in the dusk, a doe bounded out. She was just a little thing, carrying probably her first fawn. I broke her neck, and my front end was smashed in, steaming. I had a bloody nose. Someone finally came along and gave me a lift into Mancelona, where I called the Conservation Office, sold the car for junk, and stuck out my thumb.

I pulled into Schooltz's at ten past eight. No one was home, though his driveway was cleared and the back door unlocked. I looked for signs that Jay had been there and found nothing—the beds were all made, the fireplace swept, the *National Geographics* and *Reader's Digests* neatly stacked on the coffee table. What did I expect to find? Everything we owned had burned. Then I remembered Leah giving Jay a purple comb, and I went back through all the rooms. No purple comb, no extra toothbrush, no dirty underwear that wouldn't fit Mabel. My mouth felt like flannel. I went to the kitchen again, for a drink of water, and saw in the sink a small glass with a ring of milk at the bottom. I got some milk on my finger and tasted it. It was fresh.

The phone rang, almost knocking the glass out of my hand.

"Hello?" It was a woman's voice.

"This is Bill Rau."

"Well, this is Eunice next door and I just called to see if Mabel left a note about where they are."

"No, where are they?"

"Well, they stayed in Cadillac last night. She was seeing about some property, and because of the storm that hit west of here, and pretty bad too I hear, they decided not to take a chance. When she called me she thought they'd try to be back tonight, but if not to check on the furnace. You folks find it working okay? Carl looked in this morning after clearing the drive, because we got some of that storm ourselves, and more now by the looks of it, and said it was on."

"I just got here. The house is warm, it must be on."

"You just got there?"

"About fifteen minutes ago."

"Well your wife must've come ahead then."

"What do you mean?"

"She was there this afternoon."

"Are you *sure*?"

"Well . . . yes." She sounded insulted. "We even waved."

"When was that? What time?"

"Well . . . it had to be around two because the mail'd just come and Carl and me was leaving for town. Just a minute, I'll ask him to make sure."

"No, no, that's all right."

"Carl," I heard her say, "it's Schooltz's son-in-law, he wants to know what time it was when we saw his wife in the yard, remember? Around two when Alfred come by, wasn't it?" To me: "Carl says right after the mail truck came by, around two. We thought you was all together."

"You saw somebody with her?"

"Well, no. We just thought you'd all come in the same car like always. It had Iowa plates and, well, we figured you and your daughter was in the house."

"What was she doing when you saw her?"

"Oh . . . just in the yard, standing there. Unpacking the car, I think. Is something wrong?"

"I don't know. She did come on ahead of me, but now I don't know where she is."

"Well, the car was gone and nobody answered the phone when we come back from town, about five, because I said to Carl, 'I should've told her about Schooltz and Mabel being in Cadillac, in case they didn't leave a note.' The house was dark but I called anyway thinking maybe one of you had gone to town and the others stayed home to watch TV, but like I say, nobody answered, which now naturally I understand why. Then when I see the lights I called again and you answered. Well, my goodness, where could she be, d'you suppose? On a night like this?"

I thanked her and hung up. She thought Jay was unpacking the car. Like a robot I checked all the rooms and closets again. But what was I looking for?

It was almost nine, and sleet was clicking the front windows. Beyond them, the lake was a plain of darkness; the darker shapes here and there were fishing shanties. I couldn't even make out the beginning of a tree line. Lake, timber, and sky were all the same—an emptiness spitting sleet toward me. I turned on the yard light, and the sleet bloomed into the shaggy end of a monstrous gray beard being whipped by the wind.

Where *would* she go in this weather? We had no friends up there that time of year. She wouldn't call on Schooltz and Mabel's friends (Eunice didn't even suggest that possibility). There was food in the house—

The cottage. And likely it was empty: Mabel had said the Saginaw man bought it strictly as an investment. And unless he changed the locks, which I doubted, she'd find the extra key Jenny always kept in the shanty.

The ice on the road was worse, but county trucks were out flashing their yellow lights and throwing sand. My armpits were wet. The cottage was just two miles away. I marked off the first bridge; the Wolcjacks' jigsawed black bear cubs with their names, Steve and Bea, written out in reflectors on the bears' bellies; the second bridge; the fussy pharmacist's spread protected by his Cyclone fence and dogs; the long curve skirting the cedar marsh; then straight ahead on the right our tallest Norway. But what I wanted to see was a car with Iowa plates parked beside the road, and I didn't. And nothing sat in the long driveway but weeks of snow. And the house was dark.

I got out of my car anyway—I didn't know what else to do—and looked at the snowmobile tracks and boot tracks that my lights picked up along the ridge of snow on the shoulder. It looked like several snowmobilers had rendezvoused there and gotten off their machines. Then I saw fresher tracks, leading to or from the house, I couldn't be sure. Angling the car so that my lights showed more of the yard, I followed the tracks in.

The snow was deep—up past my knees in the drifts. I followed the tracks to the back door, then around to the front where a chest-high drift lay the length of the house close in; but whoever it was didn't attempt that drift to get to the door, instead headed straight for the shanty at the edge of the yard. I could feel my heartbeat. They had to be her tracks—and she remembered the key. I reached the back door again. Locked. With a piece of oak off the woodpile I busted the glass in both the storm and inner doors.

Everything inside was shut off for the winter. But someone had had a fire in there recently. I could smell it. I lit a match and went over to the fireplace and found a candle. When the flame filled out, it wasn't even necessary to look in the grate. On the hearth I saw a cluster of orange peels and Jenny's key beside them.

When I got back to Schooltz's they were there, at the door, both talking at once. I walked past them into the kitchen and picked up the phone. They stopped talking. "Dial Eunice's number for me," I said to Mabel. When Eunice answered I asked for a description of Jay's car. "Oh dear . . . light-colored, white, I think, or maybe cream. Let me ask Carl." I waited. "He says a white Ford Fairlane, a '78." Then I called the state police and reported her missing—something I should have done two hours ago. Then I sat down.

"Can I have a drink, Schooltz?"

He got a bottle and glass, and Mabel twisted a Kleenex. After a couple of swallows I repeated some of the information I'd given the police: "She's been gone from here since at least five o'clock—probably two or three hours before that. Where, Schooltz? Where?"

"And where is that *child*?" Mabel said.

The phone rang and I leaped for it. It was Eunice wondering if she and Carl could do anything. Yes, I told her, don't call us anymore, we wanted the line free. I lit a cigarette. "In the last two weeks," I said, "has she written or called?"

Mabel shook her head in small jerks, ready to cry. "We haven't heard anything," Schooltz said, "since her card."

"What card?"

"Christmas card," Mabel said. "With the magazine subscriptions. We called to thank you for them and wish you . . ." She stopped, unable to continue, and Schooltz said, "We called Christmas morning and talked to Jenny. She said you was out on the golf course, skiing . . . and she was making a surprise breakfast."

"Is she missing, too?" Mabel waited for the worst.

"No."

"Well where *is* she?"

"In Iowa," I said and swallowed more whiskey. Then I went over to the sink and splashed water on my face. None of us said anything for a while. I watched the sleet come down. Schooltz poured himself a drink and rubbed the stubs on his three-fingered hand. Mabel twisted her Kleenex.

I'd taken a trip after Christmas, I told them, and this morning, when I got back to Des Moines, Jay wasn't there. "I don't know when she left, but she came here . . . apparently drove all the way."

Mabel went over to the TV set and returned with one of the Christmas cards that had been displayed on it.

"See, here's her card."

"And we already got one of the magazines," Schooltz added. "Didn't we, Mabel?"

"Yes, we did. It's beautiful. All that lovely . . ."

"Where'd we put it?"

"I'll find it." She hurried back toward the TV. "See, it was right up here," she called to us, "on this shelf with my paper-work, because I was reading an article . . ." She brought the magazine to the table and laid it next to the card, then turned away, facing the lake. She was crying. "If only you hadn't let the cottage go . . ."

Schooltz covered his eyes.

My fist hit the table. But the rest of my body seemed calm, and my head clear, as I watched the hand open and the fin-gers tremble. How could we keep the cottage? We were in love at the cottage.

"It's ten-thirty," I finally said. "She's been gone at least five and a half hours, more likely seven or eight. Schooltz, I want to take your pickup and drive around the lake."

"I'll go with you."

"What if they call and . . ."

"He's right," Mabel said.

The sleet had turned to light flurries, and visibility was im-proved. Also the pickup, sitting high, gave me a better view. My thinking was: after leaving the cottage she could have de-cided to take a drive on the road that followed the shoreline into town, which was the route we always took; it was slower than the paved two-lane, but prettier, and since she went to the cottage for that memory, maybe she wanted the shore drive too. And if she went around mid-afternoon, the weather was clear. If she got stuck or ran out of gas or had any other car trouble, there were two bars along the way she could have walked to for help. Or she could have simply stopped in one and be there now, waiting out the storm over a brandy.

I passed the Wolcjacks' cubs, our place again. I wondered if I should stop and leave a note in case she went back there, but decided she would have taken Jenny's key if she planned to return.

There were two cars parked in front of the Rustic, neither one a white or cream Fairlane. I described Jay to the bartender. He hadn't seen her but would give her my message if he did. Then I called Schooltz.

"Nothing," he said.

I took a black coffee back to the pickup and burned my tongue drinking too fast. It was eleven o'clock. The farther I drove along that twisting road looking for Iowa plates on the few cars parked beside it, suddenly being passed by whining snowmobiles—their insane engines leaving a ring in my ears—the less confidence I had in my direction. I lit a cigarette and fell into a chest-squeezing coughing fit.

In high school, my last year, I was jogging around the track, getting my legs in shape for baseball. I was jogging with wiry Bartholomew, who ran the dashes. I felt good, the air was cool and sweet, the grass starting to turn green, and after a few laps, without saying anything, we began to push each other, slowly at first, then in earnest, until we were racing—one lap, two, staying even, and just when I felt neither one of us could go on, that we'd tied, Bartholomew sprinted away as if from a man standing still. When I stopped I dropped to my knees, dry-heaving and belching rancid air, my chest feeling as it did now, stomped on and kicked in a fight I couldn't remember.

Bob's Big Perch Inn was up ahead, and I could see a white car parked in front. Yes, yes, yes, I said, hitting the steering wheel, please, baby, please. But it wasn't. And the bartender couldn't be sure he had seen a woman fitting Jay's description.

"Hey, Chuck," he called to a toothpick–chewer playing shuffleboard. "Them two women came in about nine, one of 'em have brown hair, or was they both blondes?"

Chuck scattered cornmeal and laughed, feigning innocence. "Shoot, Russell, how comes you always ask *me*? I don't look at other women, the old lady'd run me over." And he laughed again, wagging his toothpick. I wanted to hit him in the face.

"They was blondes, wasn't they?"

"If you say so, Russell."

"Wearing black snowmobile suits with gold trim, if that'll help you," the bartender told me.

I used his phone to call Schooltz.

"Bill, they found the car," he said. "It's up in the Hartwick Pines."

"But not Jay."

"They're looking."

It was midnight when I got back to Schooltz's. He was in the Olds, the engine running. Mabel handed me two Thermoses—soup and coffee—and a wool blanket. "A ranger found the car," he said. All I could think of right then, sinking into the seat, was how you keep walking in circles.

The Hartwick Pines were thirty miles straight north of us, just above Grayling off Interstate 75. Ten thousand acres of timber, some of it virgin white pine the loggers had somehow missed, and a branch of the Au Sable River winding through. You went to the Pines to hike or snowshoe or cross–country ski, or to take pictures of the replica logger's camp, or, if you were lucky, of a Kirtland's warbler. Or to have your picture taken in front of the giant Monarch pine, and to read the plaque beside it that tells you there's enough lumber in that one tree to build a five–room house. But why would you go there, in this weather, if you were Jay? Especially after having driven God-knows-how-many miles already? For the same reason she went to our old cottage, probably; it was another memory. All right. But why was she still there?

"Schooltz, why is she still there?"

"What?" When I didn't answer, he said, angry, "Take a damn snowmobile anywhere. You can't show me the ground I can't drive mine over. They'll find her—God damn it, it's their job."

"I know they will."

"Damn right they will."

I watched the flurries fly at the windshield or looked at the woods on either side of us. I remembered reading somewhere once, maybe on a plaque in the Pines, that there are eighty-five species of trees in Michigan. Or there were at one time. I tried to name as many as I could. I got to twenty. I repeated the list and lost two or three, tried again and lost a couple more. At the sign for Grayling—named for a trout long gone from the area—my head filled with a light buzz. Here Jay was wandering somewhere in the middle of ten thousand acres on a night most people would think twice about even taking out the garbage, and I was naming trees in my head like a kid counting cows or barns to pass the time.

"Schooltz," I said, giddy, "I've been counting trees."

"We're almost there."

He turned off the interstate onto a two-lane, M-93. We had only three or four miles to go to the ranger's house. The trees grew closer to the road now, and it was slicker going. Suddenly I thought of something that froze me.

"What if she's not in the park? Schooltz, that car doesn't have to mean *she's* there! What the hell are we doing? It's one o'clock in the morning! You think somebody's going to be walking around in the woods at one o'clock in the morning? Somebody took that car away from her—

"Calm down."

I shut up, but I was shaking all over. At the ranger's house we parked behind the state police cruiser, its blood-red light revolving, hitting our hood. They were waiting for us.

The next two hours were a play of facts and surmises and questions and answers and explanations and attempts at explanations and bullhorns and whining snowmobiles—mainly whining snowmobiles—all given or asked or offered or called into or driven over trails and roads in scenes that my mind kept sliding away from and coming back to because I had forgotten, it occurred to me, to tie my mind down.

The ranger, his wife, a state trooper, Schooltz, and I stood in a circle, and some of us held mugs of coffee. The ranger's wife held a small calico cat whose front leg was wrapped in a splint, and the ranger held a pipe that he seemed to want to light but never did. He looked remarkably like my cousin Robert—big shoulders, bull neck, a thick black toothbrush mustache. The state trooper summarized his findings and said there was good reason to believe that the subject was in the park. He never used her name until the very end. Once or twice it occurred to me to request that he say 'Jay,' but I didn't want to interrupt his recitation. Listening to him calmed me down a few times even to the point of feeling pleasantly drowsy. Also I was grateful that he gave only passing reference to the possibilities of an abduction or a rendezvous with a second party, both of which he seemed to dismiss with his hand. Like the ranger he was big in the shoulders and neck, but he was twenty years older, perhaps fifty-five, with the slightly gravelly voice of an uncle you liked a great deal.

The car, he said, had been found in the parking lot behind the contact station. Normally a ranger would have been posted there during the daylight hours to check vehicles for parking permits, offer assistance, etc., but bad weather the past two days had kept the skiers away—there was very little traffic in the park during the week anyway—and therefore no one had been manning the station.

"The car was spotted by a road crew about nine o'clock and reported to the ranger, who called it in to us," the trooper said. He himself had been there since eleven. He found only one set of tracks—excluding the ranger's—near the car. Despite new snowfall, the trooper said he got a pretty good fix on the direction she at least started out in, which was due east to the two-lane, M–93. He managed to pick up the tracks on the other side of it, where they continued east a few yards to the campground, but he lost them there because of some road crew activity in that area and increased snowfall. That direction, he said, if she stayed with it, would eliminate the biggest part of the park—almost three-quarters of it.

"Of course," he added, "she could have turned back anywhere along the line."

The ranger said, "We checked out the chapel and all the toilets west of 93 anyway—none of those buildings are locked— in case she did turn back. Also all the short trails right around the logging camp."

So they were concentrating the search east of M–93: the Mertz Grade trail, Hartwick Lake, the plowed gravel roads, the lesser roads, the virgin jack pine stand, and the Au Sable trail. They had three snowmobiles out now, and the ranger and the trooper were going back out in a few minutes.

"What can you tell us?" the trooper asked me.

I told him what I'd told Schooltz and Mabel—that when I'd arrived in Des Moines that morning she was gone.

"Wednesday morning," he said.

"That's right. But I tried several times to call her on Tuesday."

He looked at some papers on his clipboard. "She spent Tuesday night in a motel in Holland," he said, "Monday night in Gary, Indiana, and Sunday night in Moline, Illinois. These receipts were in the glove compartment." He paused, sipping coffee. "Not much else in the car—used Kleenex, some apples and cheese, orange peels. The keys were under the front seat."

"That's where we always keep them," I said.

"She's thirty-five years of age."

"Yes. And in good condition. We've skied out here, hiked, I don't know how many times."

"Last seen at two P.M. yesterday in Houghton Lake."

"That's right."

"Any idea why she'd come to the Pines alone?"

I shook my head. "Memories," I said.

There was a long silence. The trooper's eyes were fixed on his clipboard, the ranger's on his unlit pipe, his wife's on her cat, and Schooltz was looking at a snapshot of Jay he'd slipped from his wallet. My legs and head felt loose. Did I tell them Jenny was dead?

Finally the ranger said something about the Mertz Grade.

"I can't believe she'd be on the Mertz," I said, adding, stupidly, "not at night." I tried again, "I mean we never used that trail anymore. In recent years—in the winter—we skied either west, out the Aspen trail, ending up back around the Monarch pine, or out the Au Sable."

The ranger nodded solemnly. "Be difficult knowing where you were now. Even for an expert."

Schooltz gave the trooper the photograph. In a white gown, white gloves, shoulders bare, orchid corsage on her breast, Jay at seventeen, her eyes filled with a sweet quizzical shine from somebody's flash, is off to the prom. We all stared at her.

Finally the ranger, clearing his throat, said he hoped she stumbled across one of the roads and stayed on it.

His wife said, "You'll find her. I know you will."

After looking at a map, we went outside. The ranger and I would take the Au Sable trail on a snowmobile, while the trooper and Schooltz, in a Jeep, would follow the plowed gravel road that ran almost three-quarters around our trail and ended up back on M-93 about two miles directly north of us.

Our plan was simple. The Au Sable trail forms a large circle slowly collapsing: flat on the bottom, humped twice on top, with fairly parallel sides running north and south. On the map it also resembles a torso with high shoulders (one of the images I forced myself to focus on whenever I felt drowsy). The west side of it, for about a third of its distance, runs within yards of M-93; the other two-thirds, which buckle away from M-93 as much as three or four hundred yards, are still within shouting distance of a dirt road that runs between M-93 and the trail. Almost the entire east side of the trail runs within a hundred yards of the gravel road. In the north, the gravel road was not much good to us, except for a short distance where it cuts back in near the torso's eastern shoulder. That same shoulder is where the Au Sable River enters the torso and continues on down as if around the heart and over the ribs toward where the left leg would begin. Twice the river passes under footbridges. If she left the trail and wandered due west toward M-93, we were in the best shape. If she wandered due east toward the gravel road, we had a pretty good chance there. South, the gravel road lies perhaps half a mile away at the closest point and a mile at the farthest. We hoped she did not wander south or north. We hoped she was not wandering at all, but waiting somewhere on a trail or walking on a road. Our simple plan was to drive around slowly and stop periodically and call out into the darkness.

The Au Sable trail is over five miles long. We figured to cover it in ninety minutes or less. The ranger, in his snowmobile suit, asked if I was cold. No, I wasn't. It was about five above zero and falling, he said.

The first time we stopped and he cut the motor I couldn't say her name right away. Then when I tried, using my own voice, it sounded as if someone else, a distance away, had called out. My ears were full of that insane engine whine. Also my throat was very dry; I scooped up some snow and ate it. Then I said her name into the bullhorn. "JAAAY." The sound might have been the deep scraping cry of a large bony creature who did not belong in those woods, who did not belong anywhere. "ARE YOU THERE, JAAAY?"

We waited half a minute, then started up again. We were following the post markers put down for hikers. Without a light you would not have been able to spot them, and come up close, as we did, and knock fresh snow cones off and see the deer hooves burned into their tops at an angle. We also saw real deer tracks in our light on the trail, and snow falling through the light, but no human tracks. The farther along we went the thicker the pines grew. When I called out her name against them, the scraping cry seemed to get smothered in the snow collected on their branches. And up in their tops I could hear the wind make a hushed whispering. Be quiet or go away, it seemed to say.

Just before we got to the river we came to a place where the pines grew so close to the trail that their lower branches made a roof over us. The ranger cut the motor and pointed ahead. I saw them—tracks that the new snow hadn't been able to cover completely; soft, regular depressions that rendered us both silent for a moment. Finally I said, "They've got to be hers." He got off the snowmobile for a closer look. "East," he said.

At the river we stopped on the footbridge and I used the bullhorn. It got a good carry here, upstream and down; but after its harsh echoes died away all we heard was the wind above us and the water brushing past boulders under our feet. Less snow was falling in the snowmobile's beam now, and we could see where the moon lay through a skim of clouds.

"We took off our shoes here last summer, and walked up-stream to the other bridge," I said. "It was a wonderful walk. We saw a doe leap across the river." I could see her again. I could almost smell her.

He used his radio to report our position, and to ask for news from the other units. One ranger had sighted tracks leaving M-93 north of Hartwick Lake; he pursued these on foot and followed them back to the road, where he lost them. The other units had only snowshoe tracks or signs of snow-mobile violations to report. The state trooper said he saw a nice buck, about eight points. I scooped a handful of snow from the bridge's guardrail and rubbed it over my face.

We left the bridge and started up Jay's and my favorite part of the trail, which runs parallel to the river. In the summer walking over the brown pine needles with their slightly spongy give and the sun speckled on them, and seeing the airy white rips of the stream only yards away, you felt as though you could walk forever, and why not if it was this good. Then at the second bridge you took off your shoes and lay back with your feet in the water, eating a piece of cheese or an apple and watching the tips of the pines sway easily, or listening to the birds discuss simple matters agreeably, and all of that felt pretty fine too, just being lazy there, getting drowsy in the sun. After a while you pulled your feet up out of the steam and worked your shoulders into a good position on the warm pine planks and fell asleep; and if someone was with you she was doing the same thing.

"JAAAY!" I called. And the scraping cry of the bony creature echoed and died, echoed and died.

When we came to the second bridge and found nothing to indicate she'd been there, I started to shiver and could not stop. The ranger took the bullhorn and said, "MRS. RAU, DO

YOU HEAR ME? ONE, TWO, THREE, FOUR. DO YOU HEAR ME, MRS. RAU?"

I looked upstream and tried to see where the doe had leaped across last summer, but the river beyond the bridge was just a black ribbon laid down between dark cloud-like masses. I began to mumble. If I said words, I don't remember them, but I know I made sounds with my mouth because the ranger kept saying, "What? What's that?" And I remember him turning around and taking off his helmet. Finally I stopped. His radio crackled and buzzed and he talked into it, soothing it. Or maybe he was talking to me. The next thing I remember is crossing the bridge, leaving the place where ever since the first bridge I had expected to find her.

Now we were riding down into the valley of the torso's neck. It was part cedar swamp and then scrub pine and the trail was very narrow. Twice we passed under low branches that formed roofs over our heads, but in neither place did we see any signs of tracks. That made no sense to me. I said so the first time, but the ranger said she could have left the trail at any point after passing under those pines where we'd spotted the tracks. Still I didn't think so, and the farther we went, the more nervous I got, while he seemed to become more matter-of-fact, or perhaps just tired. It was almost three o'clock. Each time we stopped I had to wash my face with snow.

We stopped again, and just before I used the bullhorn I saw fresh deer tracks at the edge of our beam; the back of my neck felt suddenly warm, and in a place in my head it was summer and the doe was leaping across the river. When she was midstream I called, "I WANT TO GO BACK TO THE SECOND BRIDGE! I WANT TO GO BACK TO THE SECOND BRIDGE!" The ranger turned and asked if we shouldn't finish the trail first, and with the bullhorn still at my mouth I said, "NO. THERE'S A PLACE I HAVE TO LOOK!"

Whether he thought I was on the edge of losing control and the only way to calm me down was to return, or whether he thought I had a solid hunch we ought to check out, he drove us back. At the bridge I got off the snowmobile and directed him to position it so that I could have some light along the river's east bank. He followed me as far as he could into the thick brush, maybe fifteen yards. That's all the help I needed, because twenty or thirty yards beyond that, under the roots of a cedar tree that had been pushed half over, I found her. Lying curled on her side with an urn of ashes in her arms. Breathing.

Below the
Gospels

Five years ago, when my daughter was three, she followed me out to the garden one morning. She wanted to help scatter the bird food, she said. "But this," I said, "is rye seed, my dear, and it's not for the birds. It's to produce rich nitrogen." "I know," she said. "What's nitrogen?" "Nitrogen," I said, "is the magical stuff that makes things grow—like carrots and spinach and sweet peas, your favorite." "I know," she said, "but the beaky blue jays will eat it anyway, just watch." "Anyway," I said, "let's hope not." "Anyway," she said, "tell me a story about growing, long or short, you decide, Poppa, because this fresh air is making *me* grow. Listen. Can't you hear it?" "I can," I said. "You're growing so fast you're whistling. You must be the wind. You better take a handful of rye seeds and toss them where I've raked." "I can't!" she squealed, "I can't! I'm blowing too fast—you better catch me if you can!" And then she took off running. Round and round the corral, then up toward the stand of tall fir—her favorite place—where she knew I would follow and hoot like an owl, searching for her. My God, she could run.

The truth is, we'd never expected to have a child; the doctors told Chloe her chances were almost nil. Two months after we moved out West, she got pregnant. We knew it would be a girl, and we knew what to name her—Melanie—after Chloe's great-aunt Mel. And she had been turning out a lot like Aunt Mel, too, vivacious, puckish . . .

The first year after Melanie was gone we kept finding things. Her crayon scribbles in a book. A glass bead. The second year was easier, thanks to all the trees we planted. Fruit trees mainly. We said the deer could get as fat as moose. The third year we went to Czechoslovakia, to teach English, and almost adopted a child there. Then in the midst of the Czechs' and the Slovaks' famous divorce, the mother, we were told, changed her mind. Now we're back home. Charlie Dreadfulwater, who brings our firewood, gave us a pretty little Australian shepherd-Rottweiler mix that Chloe named LaVerne B. We also have a green-eyed barn cat, Yah teh, who just showed up one day. Yah teh means hello in Navajo.

Chloe and I are freelance illustrators. We also garden and can a lot, and sometimes we go fishing down on the Clearwater that you can see a stretch of below our place, if you stand in the right spot. The river winds down from a group of mountains, the Gospels, and on nights when the moon is full the part we see glitters like a diamond bracelet. But lately we never keep anything, just catch and release. If we get a taste for fish, we drive twelve miles into town and buy some. If nothing fresh is available, we might go to the Blue Fox and watch whatever's showing and eat popcorn, or just come home the long way through Kooskia and make an omelet. It's in Kooskia where a huge cougar—eight or nine feet from nose to tail tip—is stuffed and encased in a glass box at a gas station. You can look at it while you pump your tank full. We don't buy gas there anymore or even glance over as we drive by. But we know the trophy is still up and we don't feel any different about it now than we did before we lost Melanie. It's still a sad display.

Some mornings on our mountain are so clear, so sharply etched, so open, that we can barely sit still. On such mornings we often hear, out of all the fresh silence, what we've named the Backing Up Bird, because its call reminds us of the regular beep a truck will make when moving in reverse. We love hearing this bird. We have no idea what it is, and have not tried to find out: what we know is enough—a song of one regular coo-like note appearing suddenly in the clear, fresh morning of green and blue. We stop working for as long as the bird sings, then when it quits we pick up our pens again.

The last time we heard the bird was late in the day, and when it quit singing we got a terrible craving for salmon. We hadn't had any in a long time. We liked it covered with garlic. So we drove to town. The store had three fillets left, about a pound each. Excited, we bought two. We'd eat salmon two nights in a row! We also bought a half-gallon of chocolate ice cream for dessert. Driving home the short way we played a tape of Cajun dance music that Chloe found in the back of the glove box. We howled along to "Two-Step De Eunice" and "Two-Step De Prairie Soileau" and "Two-Step De Mama." Chloe beat time on the pickup's dash, and I beat time on the steering wheel.

Home, I built a fire in the wood stove. Chloe put on the rice and sliced an onion and peppers, and I mashed garlic in lemon juice and olive oil. She ran back outside and got the Cajun tape from the truck and put it in her boom box. By God, we were cooking! Cooking and hopping around and chirping like we used to. I laid one of the fillets in a casserole dish, poured the garlic sauce over it, and noted the time when I should put it in the oven so it would be ready when the rice was. I made plenty of sauce so we could have some on the rice. She had a bottle of wine open and was pouring two glasses when the phone rang.

We looked at it on the counter. We pretty much knew who was calling. It was either Chloe's parents wanting to let us know they were halfway to somewhere now, or they'd arrived and it was raining, or they'd been invited to the Goldsmiths for cocktails and Jack had lost his mind and wanted to wear his winter plaids—or it was Chloe's sister Muffin with her itinerary, or wanting to describe the wallpaper in her new boutique, or to relate what Bradley said to her on his car phone that day and what she said back to him on her car phone. Bradley was a broker, like Jack, and the right age, the right height, right everything, and she *thought* they were getting closer as they drove around St. Louis keeping their many appointments. Chloe got steady updates on Muffin's latest business and romance ventures, as well as on where her parents were, or would be, at almost any moment in their retirement travels.

When Melanie was here we tried to remember to unplug the phone at dinnertime: settling her down and bathing her and making the meal and then eating in our usual circus was enough. For several months after we lost her, Chloe's parents and her sister refrained from calling when they thought we might be eating, though before that period of civility started there was an unhappy night when they all got together on Jack's speaker phone and took turns wanting to know, first from Chloe, then from me, how we could *stay* out here after what had happened. Neither of us could respond to a question like that—it didn't make any sense. Time passed, and they resumed their familiar routine.

I said, "Should I unplug it?"

Chloe nodded. But as I reached for the cord, she touched my arm. "It might be, you know, important."

"Right."

She answered the phone. It was her parents. I turned down the boom box.

That night, in bed, Chloe called my name. I said, "What is it?" She said, "You were yelling."

"Yelling?"

"Almost."

Then I remembered my dream. I had been invited to give a guest sermon at some church. I told the congregation I could not believe in their all-star God who had supposedly created man for his glory. I said, "It's too silly. On the one hand, he already has everything. On the other, look at us. How puny we are. And getting smaller by the minute. Hiding." Then I said to them, pontifically, "What I do believe is truth." They didn't seem to understand my sermon, and I felt wretched. But they were very polite.

A few nights later I was brought back to the church to try again. I said, "All right. It's all very basic." I still had that pontifical tone I didn't like. I *wanted* to say, "Listen, I'm puzzled by things too. But is that so terrible? Isn't there a richness in—in—" I gave up. Although it was all very clear to *me*, I couldn't seem to explain it. I woke. My face was wet. Chloe had her arm around me.

Chloe is almost fifty, I'm almost sixty. We married late. We have said to each other—and later deeply regretted it—that maybe we should not have married at all. Even now we find it hard to believe all the things we have shouted out, hissed, or even spoken calmly to each other.

Family stories have helped. There is one in particular that makes us laugh. It's about when we had been married almost a year and were having dinner at her parents' house. After Jack said grace, asking us to remember the less fortunate (his standard blessing), Cliffy, her mother, said she had a surprise for us. She'd managed, she said, to book a cozy suite at the Inn of the Grinning Walrus for our anniversary. It was her and Jack's gift to us. The Grinning Walrus, she said, was very unusual, very out of the way, and very romantic.

Jack raised his wine glass. "Here, here," he said.

I looked at Chloe. Her eyes didn't know quite where to go. Finally she said, "That's wonderful, Mother. That's very sweet. But—"

"That's your mother," Jack said, still holding his glass up.

"They are booked solid until Labor Day," Cliffy said, "But I managed."

"I say cheers to management," Jack said.

"Where is it?" I said. "This inn."

"Do you know where New Norway is?" Cliffy said.

I confessed I didn't.

"Why, it's practically on the way to St. Louis. They have an original pressed tin ceiling," she said.

For our anniversary, Chloe and I had been quietly planning a trip to northern Wisconsin, where we'd been married. We planned to rent a cabin and fish from a rowboat and roast our catch under the stars. We wanted to duplicate, if we could, our happy elopement. But instead we drove to New Norway.

Minutes after we checked in, still looking around the lobby—at the pictures of various walruses covering the walls, at the pressed tin ceiling—who should come waltzing through the front door but Cliffy and Jack. And bringing with them two old friends of theirs, Soozie and Deets Waterhouse—"to help keep the conversation flowing," Cliffy said.

"Anniversaries are so special," Soozie said.

"What I want to know is, where's the golf course in this burg," Deets said, giving me a horse wink.

"All the way from Kansas City," said Cliffy, "I had to remind your father, Don't get too close to them, Jack, you'll spoil everything."

"I know how to tail people," Jack said. "I could have been a private dick."

"Well," said Cliffy, "isn't this fun!"

Cliffy and Jack and the Waterhouses had rooms across the hall from ours, and after a late dinner, after we'd all said goodnight, Chloe and I, getting ready for bed, heard a knock on the door. It was Cliffy.

"We're just not sleepy over there," she said. "Come join us for a little cribbage?"

The place Chloe and I found to make our home is in the Idaho mountains. In the winter, unless you have a four-wheel-drive vehicle, you cannot negotiate our steep, twisting road. For all of the year we are almost three hours from the nearest airport. Yes, we tell our friends back East, we do have electricity. And a radio—and of course this old dial telephone. But no computer, no TV, no answering machine. You are like the rodents and birds and hairy dwarfs in your drawings, they say. Pretty much, we say.

We came out here soon after our second anniversary (I won't go into Cliffy's "Over the Rainbow" costume party organized in our honor) to see what we might find, and lucked into a house full of light. The man who built it had been an art major in college, and he made the house as a painter makes a picture, discovering what to do as he went along. The only reason he and his wife were selling it was because they kept adopting children and ran out of room. The reason that Chloe and I gave for leaving the Midwest was her allergies, all the shots she had to endure and was sick of. Out here she can breathe. And of course as freelancers we can do our work anywhere. Nor did it hurt getting that inheritance from Aunt Mel.

She had helped us even more in other ways. When Chloe and I were still living in Kansas City and absolutely needed to be left alone, we said we were spending time with Aunt Mel over the weekend. We often did anyway. She lived with her birds in a big house in Shawnee Mission and went out,

principally, for what she called "my socials." These were baseball games and funerals. The baseball games she attended
with her friends Mr. Spivey, Mr. Duckworth, and Mrs.
Popolewski. Mr. Spivey was a retired janitor who manned a
school crossing near the inner city. Mr. Duckworth wore a
wooden leg (he'd lost the real one working for the railroad)
and whittled richly detailed engines and cabooses out of pine
and balsa that Aunt Mel and Chloe flipped a coin to buy
from him. Mrs. P., as everyone called her, was a childless
widow like Aunt Mel who rang a bell for the Salvation Army
every Christmas; the rest of the year she ladled out soup at
the Rescue Mission downtown. They would all put on their
Royals caps and ride to the stadium in a special bus for senior citizens and have a great time. When we could, Chloe and
I rode with them or met them at the game.

The funerals, which Aunt Mel found in the newspaper, she
attended solo. It didn't matter whose funeral—or at which
church—the important thing was the covered dish she'd con-
tribute, the new friends she might make. This was how she
had met Mr. Spivey, Mr. Duckworth, and Mrs. Popolewski.
There were others over the years, but these were her friends
when we lived in Kansas City.

Both the baseball games and the funerals—not to mention
the canaries and finches and sparrows and parrots flying
loose in her house—caused Cliffy and Jack to keep their distance. (Muffin, away in St. Louis, didn't have to worry.) Of
course they invited Aunt Mel over for the major holidays and
her birthday—"or anytime you're in the neighborhood, Aunt
Mel," Cliffy would tell her, "*any*time, really"—but whenever
she accepted, which was not often, they seemed to walk on
eggs and half hold their breath, as if any second she might lift
her hat and release a squawking blue jay.

A hat was Aunt Mel's signature. She wore one from morning to night, outdoors or in. For visits to my in-laws I think

she always selected one of the most eccentric styles from her collection, usually a tall number in the stovepipe class that made you think of Lincoln. That might topple off her head into the soup tureen. "People like you and Jack who are so thin on top," I heard her say to Cliffy, "ought to cover up more than you do. Look at the ringmasters, the bishops, the wimpled of yesteryear!" Cliffy, who takes the lead in most conversations, took a far back seat to Aunt Mel, who didn't even have to say much.

Anyway, she left her money to a variety of charities and scholarship programs and to a bird refuge, and sums to her baseball group and to Chloe and me "from the Dinger Fund." Chloe's parents and sister said they had never heard of the Dinger Fund. "Who handles it?" Jack wanted to know. Chloe said no one handled it because it was a sports term; it meant a home run.

Cliffy said, "Why, that's utter nonsense. That's a perfect example of why Aunt Mel behaved so—" She didn't complete her thought. She was looking at Chloe, and Chloe's expression, I think, confused her. Perhaps even startled her, as Aunt Mel's could startle her. It was an expression that held almost no values, that carried nothing forward except an indifference of such clarity that Chloe, normally so responsive with her eyes and mouth and color, might have been frozen.

A large copper birdcage, with a replica of the Statue of Liberty on top, is what Aunt Mel bequeathed to Cliffy and Jack. Muffin received a birdcage too. When by and by Cliffy got over "the shock" of this "queer legacy" and discovered it was a clever place to keep Christmas cards, Muffin did the same with hers.

"One of these days," Chloe has said, "I would like to be able to explain a few things to my family. Or maybe just one thing." She says this wistfully, as if it's a dream, an important idea she'd give a lot to make real. In the meantime, she generously listens, saying "yes" or "I see" or "isn't that nice" when they give her a chance.

Once a year, in the fall, Chloe and I get in our pickup and say we are going to Kansas City. We wear our Royals caps. We say we will visit Mr. Duckworth and buy a carving. We say we will visit the Rescue Mission and greet Mrs. P., and then, we say, we can't forget Mr. Spivey at the school crossing. We know when he will be there with his STOP sign, working his long arms, clucking at the children to take care now, *take care*. He is an Ichabod Crane–like figure, nut brown, always smiling. We have slipped him and the others into any number of our drawings, along with Aunt Mel and her hats and birds.

But we don't go to Kansas City. We only take a drive along the river and come home. If it's not too late, we walk up the mountain above our corral with LaVerne B. and watch the sunset, the Gospels in the distance turning, for several rich moments, an apricot color. "Hello," we say, and chances are pretty good Yah teh will join us. It's the most peaceful place we know. Chloe and I have cleared away all the hogwire up there where the children of the previous owner kept small livestock. We have no interest in raising anything on that part of our land except what wants to grow there on its own. We've also taken down a blind that the eldest son had built. This area above the corral is where the eye naturally turns if you are sitting on our back porch, for it is heavily wooded, lush with promise—a place to view the early dogtooth violets, seek out the rare fairy slipper, a place where wild turkeys will send up their gargled hoots, where deer antlers may be found wound up in moss. It is also where, one bright winter morning, we first saw the cougar. I was cooking oatmeal, and Chloe, upstairs nursing Melanie, called down for me to look outback—hurry! I went to the door and saw a snowshoe hare racing towards the house, upright, like some Disney dervish, its ears and all of its limbs in a whirl. After it disappeared from view, I heard Chloe say, "Oh, look—above the corral!" There, stretched out in regal profile, was this magnificent tan cat, its long ropy tail lazily rising and falling . . . How can you *blame* an animal like that for being what it is?

My favorite image of Chloe comes from a winter morning not long ago when I looked out the studio window and saw her in a red hunting cap with the earflaps down. She also wore her fishing vest hung with flies and, around her neck, a scarf showing bright, leaping rainbows. She was sweeping fresh snow off the pickup. At first she didn't seem to be my wife. I mean, she had the same hazel eyes, same firm chin, same lips that, when I knocked on the window and waved, made the smile I love. And yet the red hunting cap threw everything off a little. But why? Because I couldn't remember at the moment where it came from? Because I wore one like it when I was young? Because her usual cap was a sailor's black watch cap that she wore as much indoors as out? Or was I only fantasizing someone not quite my wife? Someone I had dreams about when I had no one—who now, here, noticing my wave, waved back? Who soon would finish up her chore, come inside, cheeks all flushed, alive as fire, and pull her cap off, showing me her hair? And say she didn't really know why she did all that, out there, because—weren't we staying in today?

When she did come in, she stood by the studio door for a long time, looking at the floor; she seemed puzzled about something. She still wore the hunting cap, vest, and scarf. Finally she looked up at me and said, "Lenny, what if we were stuck in a huge building like a warehouse surrounded by boxes and sheets and rolls of hot information? And more pouring in every second. We can't move, there's so much. And no windows we can open, no fresh air. We can hardly breathe. Now what? I mean, *now* what do we do?"

"But we're not in such a place," I said.

"We're not, are we."

"We're here."

"In the mountains."

"We can go outside anytime we want," I said.

"And build a snowman."

"Build anything."

"I know," she said. She adjusted the red cap to fit more snug, gave me a big smile, and said, "Okay."

The Rock

The produce manager was fumbling with apples in a display case, returning to the top of the slope the ones that kept tumbling down to the edge at his waist. He was telling me about his son, a medic, who had been shot recently. "His first tour, first action." The manager used an apple in his right hand to touch the area below his left kidney. "Here," he said. "In the back. A .45." He shook his head. "We've had a helluva spring. First my son Rich got killed, we just had the funeral, then we get word that Jack's been hit."

I didn't know what to say except that I was sorry. I knew nothing about the produce manager's personal life. Our conversations in the past had been brief, about fruits and vegetables.

Now he was looking at an apple on the floor beside his foot as if it were a mystery. I picked it up and handed it to him. "Thanks," he said. "But he was wearing a vest, so it just knocked him down. Left a bruise the size of a watermelon." The manager started to smile, then turned almost grim. "He got the guy, though. Got him good."

"Your son got the guy who shot him?" I said.

"You bet."

"How?"

"How?" Now the manager smiled. "With his .45."

"With the guy's .45?"

"No, no. Jack was packing."

"I thought medics didn't—"

"It's a war, man, and the guy was a sniper."

"Was this in Iraq?"

"Spain."

"Spain? Who was the sniper?"

"A terrorist," the manager spat out the word.

"A terrorist?"

"One of those Basques. And I'll tell you, I was crazy myself when I first got the word. Lousy situation. Night, almost no light. Jack's a little turned around, trying to get back where he belongs, not expecting anything. Total surprise. Shot knocked him down hard, confused him—and when he could think he reached for his gun and it was gone. Found out later it was laying about ten feet away in some weeds. Anyway, there he is on his gut, feeling around for it, because he can *see* the sniper. Sniper's trying to hide behind a tree, because *he* can't get away, because two shore patrol guys are coming up. It was some kind of alley, I guess, with only one exit, and here come the shore patrol not knowing the sniper's behind this tree. But Jack's got the whole picture."

The manager paused; his face was flushed. He placed the two apples he was holding at the top of the display slope. They stayed put. He took off his baseball cap and ran a hand through his blond hair. He inhaled deeply, pulled the cap back on, then reached in the box beside him for more apples.

"Anyway, it all turned out okay," he said. "We can breathe again."

I said, "So Jack found his gun in the darkness."

"Well," the manager looked over his display, "not exactly." He glanced around the produce section, then lowered his voice and said, "Listen, I'm still a little . . . a little whacked about all this, you know?"

"Sure," I said. "Of course."

"Jack's got a tough situation on his hands, right? He can't play dead or the shore patrol guys might get it. But he can't find his .45. So, he finds a rock. When Jack was little, just starting to play ball, I'd catch for him. I always told him, 'Keep your eye on the target. Concentrate.' And that's what jumped in his head when he gripped that rock. He was one helluva pitcher. Made the All–Idaho team his senior year, the small schools division. Anyway—"

The manager glanced around the produce section again, his voice still low. "Jack had one good shot at the guy. One. He's about as far away as those onions over there, about fifteen, twenty feet. 'Keep your eye on the target,' he kept thinking, just like I taught him. Then when the guy sticks his head out just far enough, Jack stands up, takes aim, and fires. Bingo—right here"—the manager touched the back of his head with an apple—"and down he goes."

I nodded, smiling, but the manager look sheepish, embarrassed. "Hey," I said, "that's a good ending. A terrific ending."

"Well," the manager said, "that's how he got the guy. I told you the other way because, well, around here, you know, people wouldn't understand about the rock."

"They wouldn't?"

He shrugged his shoulders. "I don't know."

"Come on, anybody would."

"You're in a war, you shoot, you don't throw rocks like a kid."

"But Jack's a ballplayer, a medic—it's perfect," I said.

"I'm glad you think so."

"I do—and you can tell Jack."

The manager added the apples he was holding to the display. He seemed to be thinking this over.

"And you had a hand in it," I said.

"Some hand."

"I'd say a big hand."

"Well," he turned to his box of apples, looking at them.

"Listen," I said, "I'm sorry about your other son."

"Rich, dammit, was just in the wrong place at the wrong time."

"Was he overseas too?"

"No, no, he was driving his car too fast down by the river and lost control. Shouldn't have been behind the wheel at all. He'd driven all the way to Missoula to surprise his girlfriend—three hours—and found her in a bar with another guy. It's that kind of story."

He reached in the box, grabbed a couple of apples in each hand, and placed them—not gently—at the top of the slope.

"I'm sorry," I said.

"Kids. What can you tell them."

"You do your best."

"Some end up okay, some just—"

He turned from the display case and faced me. He seemed very tired.

"We never could tell Rich anything. He knew it all. From this high," the manager stuck out a flat hand level with his waist.

"I'm sorry," I said again, not knowing what else to say.

"Why didn't he call me? If he had called me . . ." The manager trailed off.

A woman appeared beside us and said, "Excuse me." She reached for an apple in the display. "These aren't mushy, are they?"

The manager looked at her. "Mushy?"

"Sometimes they're soft, this time of year." She turned the apple in her hands, feeling it. She wore several rings, and her blue fingernails glittered.

He took out a jackknife and cut an apple in half for her. "Try it," he said. He was not happy. We both saw it.

"Oh, that's all right," she said, "I'll take your word for it. She quickly selected two apples, visited another display briefly, then left the produce section.

I suddenly thought of the famous Sergeant York story, the movie I saw as a kid, Gary Cooper as York capturing all those German soldiers single-handedly by imitating a turkey gobble. "Remember the Sergeant York story?" I said to the manager.

He was staring at the apple halves in his palm; he had been staring at them ever since the woman declined his offer. Now he tossed them into the box of good apples.

"York?" he said. "Sergeant York? Sure. Fooling those Germans with his turkey call."

"The army didn't teach him that," I said.

He took another apple from the display and cut it in half.

"And the army didn't teach Jack to pitch a rock. Listen," I said, "he was much braver doing that than using a gun."

He handed me an apple half. "Tell me if that's soft."

I bit into it. "It's firm, it's fine."

"You know who that woman is? She's a tourist from California."

"Don't let it bother you."

"I don't put out bad apples," he said.

"No, you don't."

"I do the best I can."

"That's all we can do."

"All anybody can do." He looked as if he could use a week's sleep.

I ripped a plastic bag off the roll above us. "Let me have a few of those," I said. "About six." I held the bag open and he put some apples in. "Thanks," I said.

"Well," he took in a breath, let it out, "I guess I'd better get back to work. You take it easy." He picked up the box of remaining apples and carried it off toward a storage room. I watched him. Just before he disappeared through the door, he set down the box, turned, drew himself up stiffly, and brought his hand to his cap in a military salute. For me or for anyone who was out there in his produce section. Holding it there until I realized he wanted it—needed it—returned.

The Roots of
Western
Civilization

They arrived in Athens well past midnight, and Margo
told the taxi driver they wanted an *interesting* hotel.
Their room possessed seven satin pillows on a sway-
back bed whose brass frame, at the head, was a curlicued affair of ecstatic, smiling snakes; mirrors covered two walls; and
while using the shower on their floor, that first morning, they
were casually joined by a man in a long black beard who,
when they passed him on the stairs later, bowed to them in
what appeared to be the robes of an Orthodox priest. He was
followed by a beautiful young boy. Margo whispered to
Thrasher, "Well, it *is* interesting, darling."

Then Nikos Arkanis found them. Spotted Margo in Sintagma Square while Thrasher was off looking for sailing
schedules to the islands. Brushing his palms, laughing, Nikos
said he'd seen her from a colleague's office window—right up
there, he pointed, amazed that such things happen, the large
diamond on his hand exploding with light.

"Wasn't that lucky!" Margo said when Thrasher returned.
"He wants to show us the real Athens."

Nikos said, "The islands will wait for you!" Adding, laughing, "Fags! She told me. How funny. I like them. I don't go

with them but they are, how you say, witty. My tailor is a fag."
Insisting however that Margo and Thrasher leave that hotel,
that whorehouse, it was unthinkable, a bad neighborhood,
personally moving them to a place *he* had for them, cutting
his big Mercedes in and out of traffic with one jeweled finger.
"You like this, Margo? Thrasher? I am a cowboy, this is my
horse! I love America, T–bones, discos!"

He took them to Sebastepolio Street, where his company
kept a suite for visiting salesmen. "You can do everything
here, even cook," he laughed, showing them in. Nikos Arkanis
was short and round and surprisingly quick and smooth as
he moved around the suite, raising blinds in the living room,
the bedroom, so they could see the dark purple furniture better, the mammoth bed, the plastic flowers that his mother had
personally selected. He skipped between the matching velvet
sofas, stroking them. "Is this correct?" he said. He threw open
a cabinet door in the wall–to–wall bookcase to expose a tier
of liquors. He opened another cabinet to point out, giggling,
the "little films" they could show if they felt bored. Thrasher
caught a couple of titles—"Marlene," "Royal Flesh." On the
shelves themselves stood some art books—*Athine, Delphi, The
Monasteries of Greece*—but mainly the shelves held pottery and
bowls of nuts and candies and, in sleek vases, the plastic
flowers that Nikos's mother had personally selected.

In the kitchen he pulled a creamy linen napkin from a
drawer and, deftly as a magician, dropped it on the table; it
landed in the shape of an almost perfect pyramid and displayed an embroidered blue "A." Nikos laughed. "We used to
have restaurants. But they are boring to own, really, so we no
longer conduct that business." He suddenly made for the large
living room window. Across the street, a yellow crane was
hoisting a cement slab up half a dozen stories to a worker
perched on the skeleton of a new construction. The worker
flapped his arms like a bird. Nikos mimicked him. Then

turned around and without embarrassment said, "I am a rich man."

Back in his Mercedes they drove out to the suburbs, to an apartment his family owned, to a house, another house, another apartment in the hills. Nikos Arkanis ushered them in and out of these places as if he were a real estate agent and they were perspective buyers. At each stop he produced drinks, dishes of candy, nuts. "You like this?" he would say, raising blinds, turning on stereos. "Mahogany . . . Persian . . . original!" Margo approved of the furnishings, the rugs, the views. She was having a good time.

"But where do you *live?*" she finally asked.

"In all of them—we get bored easily!"

"No one's ever home, though. I mean, where *is* your family?"

Brushing his palms, he turned to Thrasher, man to man. "Women are all alike. So domestic?"

The Greek was amusing, but Thrasher was getting a sore back. He was tired of this tour, in and out of the purring car, the sweet-smelling rooms. Even the toilets smelled like candy stores.

Nikos said, "Now we must eat. You like steak?"

"Fish!" said Margo. "But not fried."

"And then disco?"

She winked at Thrasher. "Sure—why not?"

"Sure, why not!" Nikos laughed. He picked up a telephone. "I am a businessman," he mugged, "making an appointment." Into the phone, to someone named Andreas, he announced that he was personally bringing two Americans to Piraeus to eat the best fish in Greece.

At the restaurant, Andreas, the owner, lean and nervous in a white shirt, the sleeves rolled up, met them at the door. He greeted Nikos as if years had passed since they'd seen each other. He pretended to scold his old friend, the son of his great friend Stratis Arkanis, for not coming to see him. Two waiters came over and greeted Nikos in much the same way. They also wore white shirts, the sleeves rolled. Their well–lit establishment was meant for serious eating—long tables for large gatherings, families.

Nikos introduced his American friends, then, as if it were his restaurant, led everyone into the kitchen so that Andreas, he said, could show the excellent fish he had. The owner pulled open a large drawer.

"Barbouri," he said proudly.

"Good," Nikos said. "Grill them with a little oil and oregano."

Andreas threw open another drawer to show his best lobsters.

"Very good," Nikos said. "Bring us what we need."

At the head of a long table, Nikos led his guests with his fingers, his fork. He squeezed lemon juice on a tray of oysters and watched them contract. "These are healthy, fresh." He spread roe on his bread and dipped the bread in olive oil before each bite. "Tarama," he said, chewing, "our cavier. The secret is a little onion chopped very small. My mother makes it. Eat, Margo! Fai!" The waiters brought more appetizers, boiled octopus, squid, salad, more wine. Nikos conducted the meal. "I am very hungry tonight for some reason. "By the way," he pointed his fork at Thrasher's thumbless hand, "how did that happen? No—don't tell me," he laughed. "It might be a bad story and scare me. Eat, Margo!"

Afterwards, in the car, Margo tried to hide a yawn, and Nikos said she couldn't be tired, she was too young, eh Thrasher? In the back seat Thrasher grunted. He was full of food and wine; he wanted to take off his boots and lie down on that big bed in the ugly purple suite. The Purple Sweet. "I'll tell you what, Nikos," he said. But Nikos interrupted him. "I have an idea! No disco. My friend Paul was just married. To a nice quiet woman, Helen. They are already bored," he laughed, gunning the engine.

Paul and Helen Stefanos lived in the suburbs in a large new house surrounded by a high fence. Two Doberman Pinschers hurled themselves at the gate, snarling and barking, when Nikos pushed a bell there. "Protection for the lovers," Nikos laughed. Then, waving his arm to take in the house and wooded grounds, "You like this? A gift from the bride's parents." Thrasher could smell fresh-cut lumber and sweet perfume. The dogs continued to snarl and bark.

Margo said, "It's almost eleven, Nikos. Maybe they're sleeping."

"Look at all the lights!" he yelled. "They are too bored to sleep! And I am bored with this barking! Stefanos!"

A voice came out of a speaker in the gate.

"Are you the handsome groom?" Nikos said. "Let us in, Paul, we won't eat you!"

Paul and Helen Stefanos were dressed as if they were going out for the evening, he in a suit and tie, she in a cocktail dress. Their hair, Thrasher noticed, was combed perfectly. But they were not going anywhere, they said to Nikos. "We were waiting for you, of course," Paul said. "Of course!" said Nikos. "To show me the wedding photos!"

Like Andreas, Paul was lean and nervous. No chair, no corner in the big living room seemed to satisfy him. As he talked he moved, straightening pictures on the mantel, a sword on the wall. He gave his guests cognac, his wife brought out candy and nuts even though bowls of sweets and nuts were everywhere. Tables shone with gift silver, gift crystal. Helen Stefanos had a long white neck and an inclination to look sideways toward the floor, as if trying to remember something she ought to do. She said to Margo, "We have been back two weeks from America." Margo said, "I'd love to hear where you went." Nikos broke in, "For the honeymoon they were cowboys! They went to a dude ranch in California!" Paul said, glancing out a window, "I hate those animals, that barking, but what can you do?" Nikos laughed at him, saying to his American friends, "He is too shy to tell us about married life! Paul, please forget the thieving communists. We are here now."

Paul Stefanos flicked a switch and the Beatles issued discretely into the room, singing "Hey Jude." He said, "I hate it loud." Nikos said, "But the photos—show us! Show us how beautiful we are!" He brought forth three stacks of eight-by-ten color prints, each stack almost a foot thick, and placed them before his guests and wife. Nikos, Margo, Helen, and Thrasher sat on the long sofa while he himself looked out a window, straightened something, or looked over Nikos's shoulder as Nikos explained to Margo who was at the wedding. "He was high in the government before the thieves got it . . . and he . . . and he . . . they all used to be in the government before the thieves got it . . . it's filthy . . ." Helen politely continued to place each photo, as she finished her turn with it, on the pile in Thrasher's lap, Thrasher slipping in and out of a doze he couldn't prevent . . .

"Don't you want to get married too, Nikos, and settle down?"

"Sure. As soon as I find a virgin chorus girl . . . someone tall . . . like you . . ."

In the Museum on the Acropolis, Thrasher, his head pounding, studied a hound, whose tail was missing, whose muzzle was half gone, who possessed one complete leg and three stumps. He knew this dog. This long, lean, ribs-showing hound, intent on moving forward. Never mind the missing parts. Look at the dog quickly down the long length of its backbone, and away—and the image in your head will be complete, a dog will be all there.

His head was killing him. The wine and cognac last night, the traffic and construction noises on his walk from the Purple Sweet. His mouth was dry; he could taste chalk, stone, the dust of glory. He looked around at the statues, men and women with perfect private parts and no heads, or if heads, no hands and feet and noses. Someone big and powerful had blown into town and busted ass, made them look bad. And the Athenians were furious, by God. At that moment they were out in the streets in their cars, driving around fast, getting stuck in traffic jams, honking like hell, filling the chalky air with blue exhaust, trying to look good again. Nikos Arkanis was looking good, Paul and Helen were looking good. He wished them a good-looking day today with Margo, who was also looking good. "Darling, are you sure you won't come with us?" He was sure. He said he'd meet her back at the room for dinner. He wanted to see the roots of Western Civilization. See what he'd talked about all those years to classrooms of the sons and daughters of the rich before walking away.

He left the museum and stood, hung over, in the glaring afternoon sun on the Acropolis. Now what? The sun was moving toward Piraeus, but he was moving nowhere. He sat on a fallen stone. He watched the tourists walking slowly over the ruins. They knew what to do. They'd finish up here, then go on to the next attraction, and the next, collecting their snapshots, and then go home.

He bent over to pick up a pebble. A white cat appeared and brushed past his thumbless hand. He showed the cat how he could hold the pebble on his stump. The cat stepped carefully away, among chunks of fallen stone, casting a small shadow where limbs and necks and intelligent eyes had once moved.

Down in the Plaka—old town—Thrasher walked among the backpacking Eurail Pass crowd. He bought a spinach pie at a taverna, for a shot of iron, and ate it walking along. The Plaka, closed to automobiles, was remarkably quiet. His head was better now, but his feet hurt. He should have worn his running shoes instead of his boots. But I am a cowboy, he thought. Where is my horse?

A woman saying "I am a grandmother from Florida" sat on a bench; half a dozen backpackers sat beside her or on the ground. They all had their faces toward the sun, their necks stretched like baby birds. One of the girls held a dog in her lap, a truly ugly rat-faced dog, in Thrasher's view, that was chewing on the loaf of bread in her hand. Her eyes, like everyone else's, were closed. She ripped off a piece of bread for herself and chewed it. The grandmother's expression said she might not move for the rest of her life, she felt that good. Beside her, a boy with long blond hair to his shoulders sat cross-legged like a yogi and ran an emery board across his toenails; another, beside him, played with worry beads.

Thrasher found a travel agency. The *Georgio* was sailing for the islands tomorrow. All right. He started back toward the Purple Sweet, then detoured when he saw a sign for the Central Park. He came to a small wire enclosure that held an elk. The animal had enough room to turn around and that was about it. Thrasher looked at the sticks-and-rags creature, then reached in and touched it. It was real, sure enough. He ran his hand against the grain of its fur, raising dust—the same gritty construction dust that he later blew off the fresh flowers he bought on Vassilissis Street, the same white chalky stuff that he later still wiped off the railing in front of the Purple Sweet building, waiting for Nikos and Margo to finish kissing in the Greek's purring car.

She got out and waved goodbye to Nikos speeding away. Then took a brush from her bag and started fixing her hair. He came up behind her, said, "How are you doing, baby?"

"Thrasher! You . . . you took my breath away."

She ran the brush through her hair, saying Nikos couldn't take them out tonight—some business matters came up—but that was all right—they could relax.

"Shall we go in out of the noise?" he said.

Inside she said, "It's nice being home."

"Home?"

"I mean being back with you. Are the irises for me?"

He handed them to her.

Putting them in a vase, she said, "One man wants to kiss me, another brings me flowers. They must both like me, right?"

"Right."

"Okay then, what's so wrong with that?"

Next morning they packed and took the bus to Sintagma Square. Another bus would deliver them to Piraeus and the *Georgio*. The square was hot, crowded. Thrasher stepped along, wanting to get through the place, swinging his tennis racquet, taking little chops at an imaginary ball in front of him. Margo lagged behind. He found an open space, dropped his bag, and performed an overhead slam against the all-time Greek champion, whoever the piker was. When he turned around to check on Margo she was nowhere in sight.

He waited a few minutes in front of Papa Spirou's—by the first row of tables close to the sidewalk—but still she didn't show. He parked his stuff with a waiter and started to look for her—walking fast, then running. He had on the right shoes for once. He was making a second trip around the Square when he passed a girl looking up from her Michelin guide; she was blowing a pink bubble. He stopped. The bubblegum stopped him, the odor of sugar. "Shooger," as Nikos Arkanis pronounced it, a little wet on the first syllable. "I like lots and lots of shooger, anything sweet, anything." The word, as the old text puts it, made flesh. Fat. Here he was, all warmed up in his running shoes to run a race to find the missing woman, and she wasn't really missing, was she? Tall, fair, friendly Margo Maloney—the closest thing to a virgin chorus girl? Did that fantasy in the Greek's sugary brain attract her? Did it?

The *Georgio* lay in her slip, and Thrasher, on the quay, waited to board. Several backpackers and a few Greek families also waited. The Greeks lived on the islands and were taking back supplies—rubber boots and coils of nylon rope and pieces of copper pipe. The backpackers seemed to be mainly Australians. Two of them, young men, were talking with an English woman about going to South America after they finished with Europe. The amazing thing was, they were telling her, they both worked in Sydney, clerking in banks, but had only recently met in Poland.

The woman said, "I'm going back to Ios. It's lovely there now with the bloody tourists gone. Winston's waiting for me. Winston's my dog." She used a cane to keep her balance; one of her legs wobbled, one arm hung limply at her side. She kept a cigarette in her mouth like a construction worker, exhaling smoke through her nose. She said, "I couldn't travel around like you are. Two bloody years on the go, no thank you. But come visit me in Ios after Crete if you like. I'll be in George's Why Not Pub? You can't miss it."

Thrasher was going to Sikinos, the smallest island he could find on the map. As far as he could tell from the talk around him, nobody else was going there. When the grandmother from Florida came walking along the quay, flanked by the girl with the rat-faced dog and the long-haired boy who had attended his toenails, Thrasher saw a taxi pull up to the quay in a hurry. He saw Margo exit the taxi, followed by a man he didn't recognize. They all five walked toward him, Margo and the grandmother laughing.

Margo, half out of breath, kissed his cheek. "You can't escape me that easily, darling."

The grandmother, wearing a GI jumpsuit and hiker's boots and a big smile, indicated her companions. "We're going to Santorini. This is Pledge and her dog Amy. This is Captain. And I'm Florence," she held out her hand to the Greek who'd arrived with Margo. "Georgio," he said. He wore a white shirt, the sleeves rolled up.

"Georgio works for Nikos," Margo told Thrasher. "After I lost you, darling, I called him and he sent Georgio to help me. Gosh, what a day!"

Georgio said to Florence, "Santorini is my home. You will enjoy yourself."

Pledge, holding her dog, said, "We're going to live in a cave. A friend of ours owns it—a painter. It even has plumbing." She forced open the dog's mouth and shoved a large white tablet down its throat. "Heartworm's all over," she said.

Captain said, "Jackie Onassis used to mule it up Santorini with Lee Radziwill. She had a walkie-talkie and carried on a battle with Ari who stayed back on the yacht."

Margo said to Captain, "You sound like you're from the States."

"I'm from exactly where I'm standing," he said, smiling, his white teeth perfectly even.

Pledge said, "And I'm from everywhere and nowhere, like Amy." She cleaned some milky matter from the dog's eyes and wiped it on her jeans.

Thrasher said, "I'm from the funny papers, myself."

Georgio said, "Well, then. They are ready for you now. They are boarding. Good luck." He shook hands with Margo and Thraser and left in the taxi.

They stood on the rear observation deck. Athens was a cluster of small white boxy shapes in their wake; a bubble of gray sky hung over the city like a muddled thought. Everywhere else the sky was blue.

The sun, going down, laid a rosy path across the sea that led to the *Georgio*. Margo leaned her elbows on the rail and smoked a Players, gazing along the path. Thrasher ate an apple. He was glad he hadn't lost her. He felt ashamed of what he had thought in Sintagma Square, that she had slipped off to take up with Nikos Arkanis, be his tall chorus girl. He also felt pleasantly lightheaded when she took a bite from his apple.

The backpackers were spreading out sleeping bags on deck. One of the bank clerks from Sidney played "Waltzing Matilda" on his harmonica. A bottle of wine was passed. The night grew deep and thick with stars. From somewhere the grandmother laughed, "Yes, by God, long underwear! I come prepared!" Margo whispered, "Where shall we sleep, darling?"

Thrasher found the bursar and paid for a cabin. The attendant made up two bunks and left. While brushing her teeth, Margo used her free hand to unhook Thrasher's belt. The brush still in her mouth, she lay on a bunk and raised her hips so he could pull off her jeans. Sitting up, she pulled his jeans down. She went to the sink and brushed her tongue. Thrasher's balls hung heavy as rocks, yet managed to move in their pouch, around and around. Their turmoil sucked at his brain. She rinsed out her mouth. He began to clean his teeth, tried to concentrate on that, while she helped him out of his shirt. Then she took hers off. He glanced at the tent his shorts had become in front. Now she fished in her bag. The cornmeal. She stood at the sink, naked, rosy, and scrubbed her cheeks. All this time they had said nothing. Thrasher thought, I don't want to think. He looked at her feet and tried to imagine bunions there, horny toenails, warts, clubfoot, gout. Her face a sandpaper of cornmeal, she knelt in front of him and pulled down his shorts, careful about the erection. She licked him once lightly, on the tip, then sprang up and returned to her cheeks. "I honestly do not know," she said, "how people can go without cornmeal."

At the rail next morning Thrasher watched a man row out to them in a small boat. He had three goats in the boat and rowed standing up, pushing the oars. He had come from the island of Folegandros, a good four hundred yards away. When he came alongside, he picked up the goats one by one and delivered them to the sailors reaching down from the hold. He stood on the gunnels of his bobbing boat, straddling it like an acrobat. The Australians watched his performance with Thrasher.

"He's quite lucky," one of them said.

"Lucky?" Thrasher said. "Christ, the man's an athlete!"

"What I meant was," the Australian said, "he's lucky to live over there."

Now an old fishing boat approached with half a dozen men aboard. It came alongside, a few yards fore of the row-boat, and the *Georgio* swung out a crane with lumber, doors, and window frames. Someone on Folegandros was building a house apparently. The man in the rowboat continued to stand on his gunnels, engaged in banter with the men on the fishing boat and with the sailors. When the crane delivered a porcelain tub he let out a mock whoop. When a toilet bowl dangled from the crane his laughter was so great he had to step down from the gunnels lest he lose control of the little craft and capsize. The men on the fishing boat tried to find a place out of sight for the toilet bowl, but it was an awkward thing and would fit nowhere except above the prow . . . like a figurehead with an enormous mouth. They started for home.

The man in the rowboat, laughing and talking to himself, followed them. The *Georgio* revved up her engines for Sikinos.

A wooden dock, one hotel, and perhaps a dozen houses of
white stucco—this was the scene that greeted the Americans.
Only the hotel was available for guests, said the man who
rowed them ashore. Up the road, in the hills, was the village,
he said. Tiny village. He pointed to a couple of cement block
structures in the near distance. "Rooms to let and disco," he
said. "Closed. Open next year maybe." He felt pity, he said, for
the genius who financed them. "The hotel is goot," he said. "I
am Antonio, the assistant."

Antonio was a Greek from Amsterdam who found his way
to Sikinos after World War II and stayed. He wore a black cap
and a maroon sweater and a pair of baggy trousers that once
belonged to a fashionable suit, and he may well have slept, or
half-slept, in these clothes, for he was immediately available
whenever his guests needed something. He was a man with a
cap on his head and a duty. The hotel's owner was away in
Piraeus on business, but the two Americans had Antonio and
Antonio, his watery eyes quickened with responsibility,
watched over them.

He served them his favorite dishes—lukewarm milk and
Nescafe for breakfast, and spaghetti and fish for dinner. He
taught them Good Morning, Good Night, Please, and Thank
You in Greek, and with his fist he struck the ancient television
set in the right place to bring them the basketball game from
Athens. He poured their ouzo and peeled their pomegranates.
His hands had been burned in the war and were scarred the
color of squid. His belly hung grandly over his belt.

But when Margo entered the kitchen, kissed his cheek, and
boiled her own eggs, he suffered. He suffered again when she
did not flavor them with olive oil. Grabbing his ears he would
moan, "No goot, no goot." It confused him that the Americans

wanted to help with cooking, that she did no understand the *taste*. Watching her eat, he made a face full of pity. That she and her man were the only tourists on Sikinos confused him even more. The season—such as it was—was over. What were they doing there now?

"To be with you, Antonio," she said.

"Me?"

"Of course."

"You tell me," he said to Thrasher.

Thrasher took the man's cap off and twirled it on his finger. "You are both crazy."

Waking in the pre-dawn, Thrasher listened to Margo talking to herself. She would ask, "Where am I? Is there snow on the mountains?" She would sing, "Have you ever seen a Cajun when he really got mad? Really got trouble like a daughter gone bad?" And she would answer, whispering, "I hear the sea. I am Margo. And you?" Thrasher would lie beside her, still as the goat who watched him climb toward the old monastery on the tallest peak of the island, and say nothing. Part of him wanted to know more about her; part of him didn't. When she stopped singing, he was sorry. Her voice was soothing. Sometimes he thought of an old man he once saw playing his cello in a bombed-out street, the music so sweetly sad Thrasher didn't move, couldn't move, until someone struck him on the helmet, cursing him.

Mornings he swam in the sea. Margo got up earlier and went off to explore on her own. One morning when he entered the water, which lay silky and flat all the way to the far edge where the sun had come up, the surface in the middle distance suddenly broke, and she appeared and swam toward him. "It's all yours," she said, "and it's divine!" When he climbed to the old sheep pen near the monastery, neither of which was used anymore, and settled himself shirtless on the stone wall, he would study the fields and pastures below for her loping figure and lizardy shadow.

In bed one night, reading her *English-Greek Dialogues*, Margo burst out laughing. "Here's a play for us," she said. Thrasher put down the *Paris Match* he'd found in the closet. She pointed in her book to a list of English sentences under the heading "Between Lovers." She said, "I'll read the first sentence, you take the second, and so on. Ready?"

"Shoot."

"'I would very much like to talk to you—unfortunately I don't know your language well,'" she said.

"'I am a foreigner,'" he said.

"'I would like us to keep company,'" she said, putting her arm around him.

"'Will you be free tomorrow?'" he said.

"'I liked you the first time I saw you.'" She added, "That's true too."

"'I love you,'" he said.

"'I can't find the words to express what I am feeling,'" she said.

"'You have beautiful eyes,'" he said.

"'You have a nice body,'" she said.

"'I like you very much,'" he said.

"'I am absolutely sincere,'" she said.

"'You are very hard,'" he said and she laughed.

"'I am in love,'" she said.

"'I am jealous of you,'" he said.

"'I hate you,'" she said.

"'I would like to know what you feel for me,'" he said.

"'A small present,'" she laughed.

"'I will come to ask your hand from your parents,'" he said.

After a moment she said, "Well, that would certainly shock Doctor Maloney. Then again, maybe not."

"Is your father a good doctor?"

"He used to be."

"What happened?"

"My mother died. Now he flies a lot. He loves to fly his little plane."

Margo took her ink pen and began making "M"s and "T"s
in front of the sentences they'd just read, saying the letters
out loud as she wrote them: "M . . . T . . . M . . . T . . . M . . .
T . . ."

A few days later when an old man from Ios arrived in his
fishing boat, to deliver olive oil, Thrasher and Margo
arranged to go back with him. Antonio stood on the dock,
looking hurt. He said he had been to Ios, had seen the new
hotels, the rooms to let, the disco. He felt pity, he said, for the
Greeks who let that happen. Sikinos, he said confidently,
would never be like Ios. We have no pretty beach, but we
have the sea and sky and the hotel, he said. We have everything. What more did the Americans need?

"But we'll be back," Margo told him

"No," he said, and began to fuss with a loose board on the
dock.

The old man, whose name was Alexander, showed Thrasher
the point of land to steer for, then got out his fishing line and
trolled. The boat's engine sounded like a truck with a shot
muffler. Margo sat in the foredeck wearing one of Thrasher's
flannel shirts and zinc ointment on her nose.

Thrasher's shoulders felt good from helping unload the tins
of oil. And he felt good manning the tiller. It wouldn't be a
bad life, living here, he thought. Get a small boat and deliver
things. Chase fish. Would that work? For how long?

He saw Margo looking at him. He was forty-three. When
she was forty-three he'd be sixty-three.

"You're too young," he said.

She shook her head, she couldn't hear him.

"Too young," he said again. "Too damn young. And spoiled."
She laughed and came toward him.

The old man, hand over hand, was pulling in his line—he
had something. Margo stopped to watch. He brought up a
bunch of seaweed.

Margo sat down beside Thrasher. "What were you saying?"

He looked at her, then at the old man, brown, nut–wrin-
kled, who tended his line as Thrasher's immigrant grandfather
had tended his reins—nothing to it, the horse at the other
end knew where to go, up this side, down the other, the hay-
cutter clacking away behind them, the sweet feed lying in or-
derly, golden rows to be raked up, pitched up on the wagon
later, and then hauled to the barn, forked to the mow. Afterwards he and Thrasher would bathe in the creek, every muscle in their bodies cooled and accounted for. At night, do you
know what they'd do? They'd sleep. God, they would sleep.

"Won't you tell me?"

"Let's be happy."

"Do you want to get married?"

"CAMPINGORSLEEPINGONTHEBEACHISFORBIT"

This was written as one word in white paint on a crum-
bling stone wall on the beach at Ios. There were other notices
scrawled on the windows and doors of places, all closed now,
that seemed to be slipping by minutes into the sand . . .
"CIGARETTES AND CAKE" . . . "THE FAR OUT CAFE" . . . "VALUABLE
LOCK UP" . . . "88 DR. PER PERSON" . . .

They had come down to the beach from their new white
room in the white village that sat on a hill overlooking the
harbor. The braying, honking, wheezing songs of the donkeys
woke them up early, and they walked the mile or so to the
deserted beach. It was November now. The sea was cold but
so beautiful they'd wade out and dive in, leaving the cold
water quickly, tasting the salt on their lips. They would go

back to Paris, they said, and get married there. In the spring. Or maybe in Rome at Christmas! They had lots of time to decide where. Meanwhile, they walked in the hills, following the trails made by donkeys and sheep and goats. When Margo wandered off in her own rhythms and climbed alone to a neighboring peak, he would watch her, wait for her to turn and wave him over, a figure in a far story, a season with a bright name. He *was* crazy and didn't much care.

Only a dozen or so tourists were on the island, Australians and English mainly, and they were quiet—subdued almost—the last of the crowd. They stayed in the village, and they all went to George's Why Not Pub? For the pork chops cooked in red wine by the English girls who had come to Ios as tourists and stayed on to work for George and raise puppies; picking the puppies up between pulls on their fags like babies, cooing to them between stirs of the Special Lentil Soup as if they had no one else in the world—or at least on Ios—to love them. Afterwards they all went to the Kiss Discoteque. There, while the songs changed from one to the next and the colored lights swirled on the ceiling, the English girls invented new drinks with rum and talked about the tourists as if they were locusts or bats.

The English woman Thrasher saw on the quay at Piraeus said the tourists would start to arrive in February, more coming each day until twenty bloody thousand were milling around, and the entire island would turn to them as the dogs in George's turned to you when one of the girls brought out your pork chops. Her own dog, Winston, a blue-eyed mix, lay by her wobbling leg. It was a bloody shame, she said, but there it was, the rent, the groceries.

"You were one of them once," someone said.

"I was rich once too, wasn't I?"

"You've still got more than the rest of us."

The woman turned to Thrasher and said fiercely, "Did you hear that bloody rot?"

He picked her up and carried her to the other end of the bar. When he put her down she said, "I once loved a boy from California named Harry Lust. A surfer. Years after I had my stroke. He didn't mind at all. Said it made me different. You're not from California?"

Tonight was someone's birthday, and a cake, its candles lit, was brought to the floor. The music became louder. Margo danced around the girl holding the cake; several other dancers followed Margo, forming a circle, including the crippled woman and Thrasher and Winston. Suddenly the music stopped.

"Where is she?" someone said. "Where's Lyla?"

"Lyla!"

"Come now, luv, don't be frightened!"

"She's still at George's!"

"No—no one's there. We've locked up."

"Lyla!"

"Oh dear, what a pity."

"Well, let's blow them out for her!"

"Isn't that bad luck?"

"Better bad luck than none at all!"

"Lyla!"

"Lyla!"

Thrasher and Margo continued to walk on the deserted beach. When they returned to the village, they took showers and made love and ate at George's. They listened to the talk about Lyla. Some said she went to Santorini, others said to Crete, to Mikonos, to Turkey. It was like her, they said, to pick up and just leave. But no one saw her leave, did they? Was anything wrong? No. Wasn't she happy? Of course. Ah, who knows.

"I've seen enough of Ios, Margo."

"Let's cruise."

They inquired in the harbor about the *Georgio*—about any ship going back to Piraeus. Soon, they were told. The schedule varies now, they were told. They found different paths to take them to the beach, but they never stayed long for fear a ship would come and leave without them. Then the rains came and drove them to their room, to sit wrapped in blankets, to sit in long silences. They took turns going to the window to gaze at the grainy sea. They read old mysteries that smelled of mildew, that were missing pages, that suddenly produced the dried carcass of a roach.

Looking up from his book, Thrasher would see Margo's eyes fill with tears. "If it's not this waiting," he would say, "what is it? Tell me."

"You don't know anything about it," she finally said.

"Maybe I do."

"You don't. Leave me alone."

He made a speech. He said their adventure, their affair, had almost nothing to do with them. They were an accident. They had simply found each other in the Luxembourg Gardens at a moment when they could no longer tolerate being alone with their fears.

She said, "What the hell did that mean?"

"For Christ's sake, Margo."

"What are you trying to say?"

"Get someone your own age."

"You think I'm waiting for Nikos, don't you? You don't trust me. That's why you hang around all the time!"

He hurled his book against the wall and left. He stood on the cobbled path in the rain and fought to control himself. A man came along driving a donkey up from the harbor; the donkey carried cement blocks, and the man struck the beast with a switch and cursed it for not moving fast enough.

Thrasher shivered. It occurred to him that he really was mad. Margo appeared. She had Thrasher's coat for him. She screamed at him to make the man stop beating his donkey. Hearing her scream, the man stopped. The three of them looked at each other as if they had been called together to solve a difficult problem in a totally unsuitable setting. The crippled English woman hobbled by with Winston and snickered.

When the weather cleared and a yacht sailed into the harbor, Thrasher was not surprised to see Nikos Arkanis, all in white, like a jolly ice cream man, standing on her gleaming deck.

"I was bored," the Greek said.

Margo was breathless, renewed.

"You rescued us, Nikos!"

Brushing his palms he laughed. "I am Greek. Besides, I am hiding, eh Georgio?" Georgio, his sleeves rolled up, smoked a cigarette and looked at the sky. More bad weather ahead, he said. Suddenly angry, Nikos said, "It is such a joke, this new government. They understand nothing important. Under the old government when I was called to serve in the Army, they left me alone, of course. They knew I have work to do. But my time to serve is not finished. I have one or two months left. Can you see me shooting a rifle? Driving a truck? I don't even have a uniform!"

Georgio said something in Greek.

"Yes, my tailor will make me one. Very funny," Nikos told him, and dismissed this ugly military subject. He had come to see his American friends! Show them the *Ariana!*

"How are Paul and Helen?" Margo asked.

"Married!" Nikos said, and they both laughed, leading the way, arms linked and glasses held high—the gracious host and his polished, charming, renewed guest. Thrasher jumped ship. Georgio, seeing him go, said, "You will be back?" Thrasher shouted, "Why not!"

He sat in George's with the English woman and Winston. She told him about Harry Lust and her parents. "They thought he wanted my money. He did of course, but he also earned it." She lit up a cigarette. "For years Mother claimed that her mother had had an affair with Paderewski and bore him a son. All very secret. She was proud of that, Mother was. But my affair with a surfer, oh no. As for my father, he kept furtively looking at Harry's eyes. Oh yes, I could tell."

"His eyes?" said Thrasher.

"They were heavily lidded, you see, and my father kept looking at them. But saying nothing, not one word. Harry's thick eyelids and beautiful dark round face—oh, I knew what was going on. A famous Polish pianist was perfectly all right, wasn't it, really a feather in one's cap—but a surfer who might indeed be Japanese? Oh no. Well, I showed them, didn't I? I gave Harry Lust everything. Everything. And then I told him, Go away, Harry—and come back, if you like, when it's all spent. I'll be right here." Thrasher drank his beer.

"That's what I told him," she said.

When Thrasher returned to the harbor the yacht was gone and it was raining again.

Next morning they still were not back. The sea was worse. In the post office he shouted, "How the hell can I get off this God damned island!" Shoulders shrugged. The sea was bad. No boats today, no boats tomorrow. Look at the sky.

"But Margo sailed. *He* sailed!"

The shoulders shrugged.

In George's a black deckhand, grinning, told him, "The *Ios* is sailing tomorrow."

"Is that true?"

"Yes, of course. We have our orders. For Crete."

In the morning Thrasher found the captain of the *Ios* on his haunches under a black slicker cleaning fish beside his ship.

"You sail today?" The captain looked up all smiles. "Nice fish," he said.

"Yes, nice fish. You sail today?"

"Not big. But fresh. Fresh is good." The captain ripped out entrails with his forefinger.

"I am told you go to Crete," Thrasher said. There was an airport on Crete. He could fly the hell out of there.

"Yes!" the captain sang out, happy over his fish.

"Today?"

"Yes!"

"What time, today, do you sail for Crete?"

"No!" the captain sang, as happily as he'd said yes.

"Santorini?" There was an airport there too.

"Next year!" The captain gave Thrasher a happy smile, holding up a fish. "Not big. But fresh. Fresh is good."

Two days later, the *Ios* took Thrasher to Santorini. At the top of the long climb up from the harbor he saw them. Laughing, brushing his palms, Nikos said, "We wondered when you would catch us!" He held out his hand, but Thrasher was looking at Margo who looked lovely. She was flushed, radiant, and she was smiling, she couldn't help it, darling, poor darling.

Thrasher felt light and heavy at the same time, and as though he were watching them, himself included, from a short distance away; and what he understood from their expressions was that a joke had been introduced and one of them wasn't getting it.

"You should have been with us, darling, those *waves*, I thought we were going to sink!" She kissed his cheek.

"Swells," Nikos corrected her.

"We pitched and rolled, it was worse than our crossing from Brindisi, remember?"

He remembered. It seemed years ago. Jokes ago.

"But *nobody* got sick. The *Ariana*'s a wonderful boat!"

Nikos said, "We are not here. We are over there," he indicated the opposite side of the island. "I do not like it down there," dismissing the main harbor, "everyone can watch us."

Margo took Thrasher's arm. "We were just going out for a short ride, and then we couldn't get back. That's really what happened."

"It was easier to come to Santorini," Nikos said. "Besides, Georgio was lonely for his island, poor boy."

In part of his head Thrasher was preparing a speech: Airport . . . I'm leaving . . . with or without you. In another part he was foolishly happy to see her.

"I'm so glad you're all right," she said.

Mint. She smelled like mint.

They rode in a taxi to an area on Santorini call Kanakari, where Georgio's family lived on a farm. There was no village, just farms.

Georgio welcomed them. He shook Thrasher's hand. "I am very happy to see you," he said. "We have been waiting." Georgio looked like a man who had come through a successful operation and was relieved and grateful to be alive. Thrasher envied him.

His mother came out of the house carrying a pail and a knife. She was a large woman with untroubled eyes. When she shook Thrasher's hand she hummed and glanced at the sky. "Your size impresses her," Georgio said. His mother then said something to Nikos and they laughed. Georgio said, "She asked Nikos if he wanted to gather basil from the garden. This is a joke, you understand." The woman gave the pail and knife to Margo, who said, "But I know what to do!" Nikos followed her, calling out, "I will be the assistant!"

"Come," Georgio said to Thrasher, "I will show you around."

They walked through a ravine that leveled off into fields. In the near distance Georgio's father was working a mule, and chating, "Delaxo–de . . . de–de–delaxo . . ."

"He is singing. It's for the mule," Georgio said.

"What does it mean?"

Georgio shrugged. "He is encouraging the mule. And warning him to take care." The son looked around. "My father—his name is Kosmas—he was born on Santorini and has never left it. He sings to his mule every day, the same song, and never tires of it. When I was younger, I thought, I must get away from this. The same land, same sky, my heart was in a cage. We have no word in Greek for 'too much.' 'Very much' yes. And 'very, very, very much'—as many verys as you want. But you can never have too much of anything, either of pleasure or of pain. When I was younger and confused I felt that I had too much of Santorini."

They climbed a rise to a weedy orchard from which they could see the *Ariana*. She lay at anchor a hundred yards out where the sea, smooth as paint on a floor, changed from light green to blue. They said nothing. Georgio then led Thrasher down the other side of the rise to an old tomato factory, which was now used to keep pigs. They stopped at a gate to the cellar, and several pigs came over. "It's a good place for them," Georgio said. "We know where they are. We also hunt in here. For birds." Then he led Thrasher down a path to the seashore.

Coming toward them were three young women in white dresses.

"My sisters," Georgio said. "Sometimes I dream they can fly."

" . . . maroóli . . . radíkia . . . bakalyáros . . . poolákia . . ." Georgio's mother named the dishes on the table as Thrasher pointed at them—the greens, the salted fish, the little birds. She held Margo's long smooth fingers in her big round hands and rolled her eyes in mock envy. Georgio's sisters blushed in the new white dresses that Nikos had bought for them.

"Like in a marriage," Nikos said, appraising the sisters.

"Three beautiful brides," said Margo.

"No, no, the girls who *serve* the bride," he said.

"But who is the bride?" she said.

"Who?" he laughed. "Who? Ah, that is the mystery."

He sat at one end of the long table, Kosmas at the other. The old man, like his son, was small and wiry, and they both, standing or sitting, bent slightly forwards as if they had injured their backs. In the face they were strong, handsome, and wore thick mustaches. Georgio sat at his father's right and seemed very happy to be there. During the meal neither one spoke much; when they did it was mainly to each other in quiet asides. Nikos did the talking. This was his party. He joked with the daughters and made them giggle and blush. He bantered with Georgio's mother. She told him he needed a wife. (Translating this remark for Margo and Thrasher, Nikos feigned modesty and horror.) He replied that he was waiting for the correct girl. "Someone like Margo," he said, laughing, picking up her hand and patting it. "But someone who eats!" he said. "Look how skinny American girls are! Eat, Margo! Fai! Fai! Make Georgio's mother happy! Look, I give you a lesson." He ripped off a piece of bread, soaked it in his salad oil, and said, "Open." He fed it to her. Then dreamily licked his fingers.

When he and Georgio and the Americans were leaving to spend the night on board the *Ariana*, he stuffed two large dracma notes in Kosmas's shirt pocket, and roared as if he knew something no one else did.

"You are my conscience," Nikos said to Georgio, and playfully slapped his cheek.

The four of them sat around a teak table on the afterdeck drinking champagne. It was early evening. In the amber light they all looked flushed, as though they had been swimming or running. The *Ariana's* generators quietly hummed. The crew, after helping Nikos and his party get aboard and get settled, had disappeared.

"Yes, my conscience," said Nikos. "Which is why you can't leave me."

Georgio stood up and moved to the railing. He lit a cigarette. Nikos laughed. "Enough," he said. "We won't discuss it. We are boring our guests. Georgio, what shall we do?"

Georgio said nothing.

"Anyone for bridge?" Margo said.

"Bridge?" Nikos made a face. "Paul and Helen play bridge."

"I wasn't serious, Nikos."

"I have an idea," he said, getting up. He went below deck and returned with a walnut-colored box shaped like a coffin. "I have a hobby. I collect fans. Georgio," he said, "is this a good idea?"

At the railing Georgio smoked.

Nikos opened the box and took out his fans, laying them on the teak table, naming them: Japanese fans made of eagle feathers; dolls' fans one or two inches long; fans commemorating balloon flights; mandarin fans; mourning fans; flag, hide, and rubber fans.

"Look," he said, "the baby-skin fan here. The skin is high quality, the best. A good surface for inks, watercolors, and so forth. This quality skin comes from very young animals, very young. In fact it is obtained before they are born, do you believe it? By killing the mother. It is very thin, very delicate, and very—what is the word?—supple."

The fan he held up had an ink drawing of a loon resting by some reeds. He opened another baby-skin fan. It bore a pastel watercolor of Eve on her knees before Adam; she held a snake in one hand and Adam's erect penis in the other.

Nikos suddenly seemed bored. "Georgio, please," he said, putting the fans back in the box, "let us have more champagne. And more English cheese."

Georgio went below deck to fetch it.

"He is a philosopher," Nikos said. "You know why? Because he comes from Santorini and is poor. The poor from Santorini make very good philosophers and very good"—he searched for the word he wanted, found it and said it quickly, biting it off—"servants." He brushed his palms lightly together as if crumbs or dust were on them. "Well," he said, "what did you think of my collection, Margo?"

"Delicate."

"You think so? And you, Thrasher?"

"The same."

Nikos laughed. "Delicate," he said. "Like Santorini. Margo, tell him what you learned, that Santorini is a sleeping volcano."

She kissed Thrasher's cheek, and whispered, "I missed you."

"You didn't mind where the skin comes from?" said Nikos. "I saw your face. I think I'm beginning to know you."

Georgio returned with champagne and a tray of cheese and fruit.

"Look at his long face," said Nikos. "What did I tell you, a philosopher. Georgio, what are your thoughts?"

Georgio lit a cigarette and turned to the sea. Then he said something in Greek.

Clapping his hands, laughing, Nikos said, "The sea will be rough, so what?"

"Very rough," Georgio warned, looking at them.

Nikos shrugged. "Why do I have a crew?"

Georgio spoke to him in Greek. Nikos replied in Greek, angry. Then he cut a piece of cheese and stuck the knife, straight up, in the teak table.

Smoking his cigarette Georgio returned to the sea. The amber light was leaving them, draining off to the west. Great masses of rich blues and grays were following it. The *Ariana* rocked easily. No one spoke for a while, only the seabirds made noise, diving inland, soaring out, crying.

Thrasher looked at Margo who was looking at the first star. He looked at Nikos who was pinching the piece of cheese in his hand and glancing back and forth between Georgio and the great expanse of water off the starboard bow. We make a pretty picture, Thrasher thought. We could be on a poster in the travel bureaus. Come to romantic Santorini, the sleeping volcano. Come drink French champagne and eat English cheese on a Greek yacht.

Nikos broke the silence. "If it's too rough—we fly back to Athens! Eh, Margo? So what!"

She laughed recklessly. "So what!" She included Thrasher in the carefree moment, holding out her hand to him. "Eh, darling?" He took her hand. Let's get out of here, baby. Now. But he sat there, a lump, it occurred to him, on a log.

"You like Greece, Margo?"

"You know I do, Nikos."

"But not Athens."

"Less than the islands."

"You like the mountains."

"I love the mountains."

"We should go to Switzerland and visit my parents. My father I am sure is going crazy with nothing to do." Nikos looked at Georgio. "Some people hate Athens. Like Georgio here, our philosopher. You hate Athens, Georgio."

The other said nothing.

"He wants to come home, he tells me. Isn't that so, Georgio?"

"Yes."

"You see?" Nikos said to Margo as if he had been cruelly betrayed.

He brooded, pinching his cheese. Finally he threw it overboard, past Georgio's gaze.

"Georgio is thirty years old, an old man now. He wants to retire and *think.*" Nikos drained his glass and refilled it. He poured more champagne in Margo's glass, spilling some.

"Thrasher," he said aggressively, "how old are you? Do you want to retire? And *think?*"

Thrasher said nothing. He let go of Margo's hand.

Nikos said, "I am one year older than Georgio. Should I retire, Margo?"

"That's up to you, Nikos."

"Of course! Here," he handed her glass to her. "Drink to me—to us!"

After hesitating she took a sip. She looked at Thrasher—her expression said, What can I do, darling, he's crazy.

"You and I, Margo, we act. We leave the thinking to—to other people." Nikos leaned closer to her. Thrasher could smell him. He smelled like the perfume in his toilets.

Margo's left hand rested on the table and Nikos began stroking her fingers. "You know what I am thinking?" he said. "I am thinking that Georgio's mother is right. Yes, very right."

Margo laughed. "You sound too serious now."

"Do I sound serious, Georgio? You know about serious talk, tell me."

Georgio spoke sharply in Greek. Nikos continued to regard the fingers he stroked as if they were things he just that moment discovered.

He said, "I want to get married."

Thrasher felt blood thudding in his ears. He started to get up. Georgio's arm stopped him. Then, leaning close, Georgio said, "Margo. Those little birds we ate today, poolákia, you re-member how we caught them?"

She nodded, looking puzzled. Thrasher felt dizzy.

Georgio said, "We went in the old tomato factory. We went at night when the birds were asleep in their nests. You remember?"

She nodded again.

"We went very quietly," Georgio said. "We took care not to excite the pigs."

Nikos said in a low voice, "We don't want to hear this." He continued to regard Margo's fingers, stroking them, enjoying them. "Did you hear me?" he said to her.

Margo shook her head.

"We carried torches," Georgio said. "At the right moment we shined them in the birds' eyes, blinding them. Then we reached in the nests—"

Nikos slapped Georgio's face. He was on his feet. He had hold of Margo's hand, bending her fingers back. She was still seated, crying, "Please, Nikos—let go—" The two Greeks were shouting at each other. Thrasher and Georgio had stood up at the same moment and, in the confusion, briefly embraced. Nikos was jockeying back and forth behind Margo, using her as a shield. Georgio reached him first and groaned. Thrasher saw the knife enter Georgio's palm and stopped to watch the man whirl around and around with the blade in his flesh. Then the box of fans fell off the table, onto Thrasher's toe.

The next day they stood in the Athens airport, in the main terminal under the big departures board. Madrid . . . London . . . New York . . . Rome . . . Los Angeles . . . Paris . . . Thrasher was thinking about Georgio, his hand wrapped, leading them off the yacht . . . walking with them over his father's fields.

The incident on the *Ariana* had embarrassed him deeply, he said, but finally it was comical. He saw them to a hotel and instructed the clerk to help them with the airlines in the morning. He was all right, he told Thrasher. No bones were broken, nothing, just fat. What happened was comical really and a good thing. He wished them good luck and left them, a smiling man.

Now they watched the names of cities spin in their slots on the big board, stopping at new combinations. People came and looked at the board with them, waiting for the spinning to stop. The air smelled like kerosene. A man holding a poodle in his arms like a baby said to his woman companion, "What did I tell you? Eighty-two years old and his lips, his nose, are beautiful. Did you see?" The woman pointed up at the board and said, "Look, we're just going to make it, Jesus Christ."

Thrasher and Margo finally rented a car. Following signs to Delphi, they passed a chicken factory whose front gate bore the name APOLLO; above the name a huge rooster stood in full crow, its red comb running, streaking the bird pink. Farther on they saw clusters of blue bee boxes on the green mountainsides—toy blocks, Thrasher thought, left out by a big kid. At Delphi they overheard a guide try Spanish and English before she found that German was what made her audience smile and nod in front of the Rock of Sibyl.

In the theatre, Margo said, "Where are we, Thrasher? Where are we really?"

"The last row."

"Are you very mad at me?"

"Mad?" Was he mad? "No."

"Maybe you should be."

"I'm just a tourist here. Like you."

Her eyes were red and sore-looking. She hadn't slept much the previous night either.

"Let's go see the stadium," he said.

Two Japanese girls in jogging suits were racing from the stadium's far end, toward them. Their suits said "U.S.A." across the front. At the finish they giggled, found their cameras, and took each other's picture.

Thrasher always felt good standing in the sun on a field used for sports. He especially loved those first few warm days in April, getting loose, stretching, shagging fly balls and smelling the grass again after waiting all winter for it. You could stand out there for hours and not lose track of things. And when you went up to hit, your hands were sweating good, the bat feeling so sweet, you knew where you were, and you knew what was next.

He took Margo's hand and walked over to the Japanese girls and asked if they would do him a favor. Would they take a picture? Of him and his friend? They giggled and said, "Sure."

"The wonderful word *sure*," he said.

"Can we send it to you?"

"No, no. Just take it."

Something
Special

We had to do something special over the Fourth. Lenny, Eddie Z., and the Solak twins would be turning sixty that month. Plus Walter and Junior, the twins, were retiring early from Ford. So why not a big gathering at Uncle Komo's place up north at the lake? All our kids and their kids, everybody. We hadn't had a real get-together in ages, it seemed, what with people going off here and there to do their things.

Tanya and I got busy. We were the ones to organize everything since I am married to Eddie Z. and Tanya is married to Walter. Lenny's Gloria would have been right there with us on this, God rest her soul, but like Tanya said she was with us in spirit. What a grand, generous girl that Gloria was. Anyway, counting all the kids and spouses and grandkids we had a mob lined up. Three days of great food, music, dancing, swimming, fishing, and sleeping out under the stars. Plus fireworks on the Fourth itself. Just like in the old days. Uncle Komo said he would make a big pot of *bigos*, the authentic stuff. He said he couldn't wait. That was Uncle Komo for you—eighty-seven and still full of life.

The only one we couldn't reach was Lenny. Ever since Gloria passed away, he had become a kind of wild card, following one scheme or another and disappearing for a while. But nothing like this. When four weeks went by and still no sign of him, Tanya and I began to be concerned. Finally I said to Eddie, "Okay, Mr. A.I.P., let's see what you can do about finding Lenny." He moaned. He said, "Amber, I am a car dealer. I am long past detective work, as you know." He also mentioned his foot problem and his back problem. I did not point out how neither of these problems ever kept him from jumping up to go chase pheasants with Bubbles our pointer. I just said, "Then maybe I will ask my mother to find Lenny July." My mother, who is Jade, to this day enjoys giving Eddie the business when she can. "Though she is seventy-four," I said, "she is still tough as a horse, as you know. She will be happy to turn over minding the Tip Tap to Curly for a couple of days and locate Lenny for us. Jade is always dependable in an emergency, busy as she is."

So Eddie put an announcement on his work machine— "Eddie Z.'s Antique Autos is on vacation. Leave a message." Then he changed into his shoes with the steel supports, packed his kit, and went to find Lenny. This was the Eddie Z. who could give me primo goose bumps.

His first rule, I could never forget, was: "A good private investigator is always undercover, and should possess the necessary skills to make the cover stick." Therefore at the A.I.P. Academy (the letters meant nothing, on purpose), Eddie, who was the founder, director, and only instructor, taught—besides Surveillance, Clues, and Self-Defense—barbering, plumbing, carpentry, cooking (short order), small animal grooming, and the Bible. He himself either had a license or had done serious reading in each of these areas. To really get the goods on a subject, Eddie felt, you did not just follow him. You cut his hair. Or his dog's hair. Or you unstopped his plugged toilet. Or you fed the rat a fluffy pancake. Or you sat behind him in church and prayed with him. Then you nailed the son of a b.

Eddie was so deeply committed to camouflage that every year he changed the Academy's location. First he's in a drafty, cold warehouse loft, then in a former funeral home (that moved to a larger building—boy, there is a good business). Then Eddie took over the offices of an optometrist who was in prison for tax evasion. Then he sets up in a corrugated tin shed on the premises of a septic tank concern—"We Dig Tanks" was its motto. Eddie, as he liked to say, kept loose. Interested parties who saw his ad in the back pages of certain publications (as my mother and I did) were advised to query a P.O. box. Eddie would then send these prospective students an application form.

A.I.P. applicants had to be at least twenty-one and have U.S. citizenship. You could not be a convicted felon, hold political office, or weigh more than 300 pounds. (This last stipulation was added to the brochure because of DeWayne DuPage—if that was his real name—a student who could not fit behind the wheel of a regular car.) Eddie asked for a recent photo ("not a glamorized studio portrait") and a letter of recommendation from one of the following: family dentist, minister (or priest or rabbi), former teacher, local grocer. The letter writer needed to say only that he knew you for at least one year and that you seemed honest. If that was all the letter *did* say, then Eddie, knowing how people blabbed, would take it as a pretty good sign that that was all the writer *could* say. To Eddie this was a plus. Because, as he explained at our first in-the-flesh meeting, what he looked for in an applicant was somebody who was almost a nobody: a plain, gray type whose face maybe even his dentist, minister, etc., had trouble recalling.

My mother said to me at this first meeting, for everybody to hear, "You ever been called a plain, gray type, Amber?"

I said, "Never."

"Me neither," she said. "So I guess we have wasted our valuable time."

Eddie said, "Hold on, there are always exceptions to prove the rule. I meant that *in general* your plain Sears Roebuck type will often surprise you and turn out relentless as a Rottweiler."

I think that was where Jade and Eddie's special relationship, let us say, began. Anyway, the course at A.I.P. was divided into two equal parts totaling eight weeks. First came the correspondence segment, during which Eddie gave us a number of assignments. The one most challenging to me, personally, was "The Mask." You are on a job and suddenly, to protect your true business, you have to pretend you are a hard-of-hearing foreigner ("nationality your choice") who is only taking pictures of cloud formations, spiders, or city skylines. If someone starts asking you nosey questions, you have to use vague hand language and throw in a few artistic/scientific terms in broken English. Boy, you have to be a good actor. He also asked us to learn how to breathe through a plastic straw ("always carry one") while submerged in a body of water, if that should become necessary. And so on. This was followed by the "on campus" segment. We all came to wherever the Academy was then located and learned how to drive nails, tail a live subject, unplug a toilet, discern pertinent dirt from common trash, administer pepper spray from a device hidden in the cheek pouch, and so on.

When Eddie first opened A.I.P.'s doors, me and Jade and the obese DeWayne DuPage were his only students. DeWayne right off wanted nothing to do with a pepper spray device in his mouth, or with bending over anybody's damn toilet. "And I never did try to breathe through any plastic straw under water—I just wrote you I did because look at me," he said to Eddie at that initial meeting. In the school where Eddie had received his private investigator's diploma, someone like DeWayne would not have been accepted, and you can bet Eddie would have refused him too if DeWayne's application photo had gone below the neck. In any case, there we were, staring at each other, because Eddie was stumped. Then my mother, who is a bartender and experienced in quarrelsome patrons, said, "Hand him back his money and tell him where to go. If Amber and me could submerge ourselves, so could he."

"I'd only float," DeWayne said.

"Don't give me that," my mother said, "you could hold a rock."

"Thin people don't know anything about it," DeWayne said, and his eyes welled up.

"Oh my god," said my mother, "he's going to cry."

"So what if I do," DeWayne said.

"Well, don't," my mother told him. "Me and Amber can't stand it." She opened her purse and took out her brass knuckles. She put them on. "I see the snot of self-pity on a man, all I want to do is break his nose," she said. A few days later DeWayne DuPage left on his own. No one was surprised.

Well, I see I have got somewhat off my subject, which is the whereabouts of Lenny July, and Eddie Z. in pursuit. So it's a Missing Person job, one of the most difficult, and not exactly Eddie's special line. Divorce and Employee Theft are more up his alley. Anyway, he was busy all day checking out the nooks and crannies in Detroit where Lenny was known to "find refreshment." That was how Lenny liked to describe his visits to the library, the Institute of Art, and other such quiet places. Eddie also checked with the Board of Education, because Lenny was on the substitute teacher list. He learned that Lenny had subbed a dozen times before Christmas but not since.

"What did you find at the house?" I asked.

He said it was closed up tight as a nut, but nothing he couldn't open. He went in and found the place clean, everything ship-shape, not one fishy sign. Which of course might make any other investigator suspicious, because normally men are not so neat. But Lenny was. And it was not a fussy kind of neat. He just naturally kept his life simple. Eddie said the fridge (which was one of his favorite sources for clues) contained exactly two cans of Vernor's Ginger Ale, one package of Bird's-Eye frozen spinach, and a box of grape popsicles.

"In other words, the exact opposite of Jade's fridge," he said.

"Is that a relevant observation, Eddie?"

"I counted seven jars of kosher dill pickles in there the last time we went over. Why can't the woman finish a jar of pickles before she buys another one? I won't mention all the stuff with mold growing on it."

"So what next regarding Lenny?"

"His personal toilet articles were missing. Likewise the pickup. He has taken a trip. He wants to brush his teeth and shave."

"And?"

"I'm thinking, Amber."

I was thinking too. I made a phone call to Tanya. "We should have a meeting over here," I said. "Eddie will cook hamburgs on the porch."

So we gathered on the porch—Tanya and me and our husbands, plus Walter's brother Junior, your classic confirmed bachelor. (Although the woman who might have been tempted to try and change his mind is hard to imagine.) It was early April when nights in Detroit can be cold, but this was a nice one. You could smell the grass getting green again. I love that, especially after smelling the various solutions and lacquers in the shop all day. Anyway, to start things off I said everyone present had known Lenny a long, long time. In my case it was for the thirty-two years I had been hitched to Eddie. Tanya knew him almost as long. Eddie and the twins grew up with him.

"You guys were like brothers to Lenny," I said.

"Hey, Amber," Eddie laughed, "you make it sound like Lenny's kicked the bucket. He spends a lot of time with his books, but he's still a tough guy."

"Lenny's very tough, that's for sure," said Walter. "Hey, remember when we sat on him in the cinders behind the trash burner at school? How it took all of us to hold him down?"

"My god," said Tanya. "Why did you do such a thing?"

"We had to," said Walter. "We had to explain something to him. He didn't know what a bastard really was. He thought almost anybody could be a bastard, even Sister Hedwig when she whacked us. But we spelled everything out."

"Is that right?" I said to Eddie.

"Yeah," he shrugged. "We were kids. Nine, ten, somewhere in there."

Junior, who seemed to be elsewhere, like always, suddenly said, "Yeah, we sure did. We said, Lenny, you're the only true bastard in the whole neighborhood." Junior laughed.

Tanya, whose tongue can be sharp, said, "Junior, are you an animal?"

He blinked. "Aw, come on, Tanya." But he looked at his hands. She'd got him pretty good. Tanya and I operate Bette's Hair & Nails. There is no Bette, it's just a name we thought up years ago after I decided not to pursue detective work and instead went into a business where I could make better money. Also, personally, I did not care to do a lot of divorce work, which seemed to be an investigator's bread and butter. Eddie said he hated to see me take my brand new A.I.P. diploma and rust away in a beauty parlor. I said, "It's nothing against you, Eddie." But all the same he was hurt because we were sweet on each other by this time, and now what? he wanted to know. I said we would just have to see. Well, that hurt his pride even more, and the upshot was he moved A.I.P.'s location and wouldn't tell me the new location. I had to use my detective skills to find him.

Anyway, there we were on our back porch watching him fix the meat. He likes to mix onions and garlic in the patties.

I said, "We can't have a big party at Uncle Komo's without Lenny, it's that simple."

"It's only April fifth," Walter said. "We got time. We got three months, Amber."

"Time flies," Tanya said.

"Where can he be?" I said.

"South," Eddie said. "I think he went south for the winter and just isn't back yet. Didn't we have a crummy winter this year?"

"That is not like Lenny," I said.

"What *is* like Lenny?" he said. "The moon?"

I said, "Are you getting sore, Eddie?"

He said, "No, I am fixing the meat."

"Did he tell anybody anything?" Walter said.

"Does he ever tell anybody anything?" Junior said. "I mean, what's wrong with the guy?"

"What's wrong with *you*, Junior?" Tanya said. "Does something have to be wrong with a guy who doesn't shoot off his mouth to everybody what his plans are?"

"I didn't mean anything was *wrong* with him, like wrong wrong," Junior said. "I only meant, you know, why is he so hard to find once in a while? Like, are *we* hard to find?"

"He's a quiet guy," I said. "A nice, sweet, quiet guy. Who cares about people."

"Exactly your type," Eddie said.

Junior thought this was really funny. So did Eddie. When they stopped laughing, Eddie put on the meat. Flames shot up.

We were all quiet a minute, watching the fire. Then Tanya said, "Besides, he has suffered a great loss. Do I need to remind anybody what a beautiful, beautiful couple Lenny and Gloria were?" She looked off at the sky, which was sprinkled with stars. Just mentioning Gloria's name could bring tears to your eyes, especially if you had stars to look at. After a while, Tanya cleared her throat, and said, "I still can't get over you three big palookas beating up on him and telling him what you did. The more I think about it the more it makes me ashamed for you, it really does."

Eddie, Walter, and Junior glanced at each other. Finally, Eddie said, "We didn't beat him up, Tanya. In fact, *he* was the one always taking pokes at us—right, guys?"

"That's exactly right," said Junior.

But Walter said, "Though it's basically true what you say, Eddie, I have to admit we egged him on a little hard about that sometimes."

Tanya looked at her husband. "Walter, why am I only learning this now, after all these years?"

He looked back at her. Walter Solak, like his brother, was a big palooka, as Tanya said. Give them a football to throw and catch or sit them down across from each other at a table to Indian wrestle or ask them to move something heavy for you and they are all smiles and ready to begin. I don't mean to hint that they are strictly in the strong backs/weak minds category—certainly Walter isn't—but if you asked ten people what are the Solak twins like, nine would say something pretty close to what I just said. Walter and Junior both started at Ford right after high school, went into the Service, then came back to Ford. Now, thanks to Walter's good planning, they were getting out early. Not all that early, but as Walter said a few extra years were a few extra years. They would have more time now to spend up north, fishing and so forth, and to supplement their pensions until Social Security clicked in, they would paint houses, repair furnaces, and do maintenance work for the parish. Junior also got a disability check from the Army for some accident with a forklift that gave him that gimp knee. He and Walter spent their Service time load-

ing and unloading trucks, so they never had to shoot anybody or be shot at, unlike Lenny. My clever Eddie got excused
from all that because of his foot and back problems.

Anyway, Walter looked at Tanya after she asked him why
was she only now hearing about the poor treatment Lenny
got from them as a young boy, and you could see he was
thinking. You could see in his eyes he was latched on to
something important, that maybe hurt. I guess what I'm trying to say is I give Walter a lot of credit. Of all those guys who
hung out together, he was the only one who took Lenny's advice about using the G.I. Bill to improve his mind. Going
nights to the community college in Highland Park, Walter was
able to get off the line at Ford and into supervision. It is my
personal opinion that Lenny was also a large influence in
Walter's thinking that he and Junior could retire early and be
their own bosses. Walter even began to sound a little like
Lenny. "What is your life worth?" you heard him say, which is
a typical Lenny quote. Lenny had things pared down, stream-
lined. No extra do-dads to clutter up his surroundings. I
should say his and Gloria's surroundings. They were a perfect
match. They were a lot like one of those big sailboats that go
past Uncle Komo's place on their way toward Canada, and
you're standing on the shore watching, a little envious, wondering how in all that wind and choppy water something can
work so nice, so smooth.

"I wonder," I said to Eddie, "if some of Gloria's former music
pupils might have info. You know how Lenny and Gloria
doted on those poor kids."

"This is an item on my list, Amber, but with a very big
question mark. Look how long she has been gone."

"Not long as far as I'm concerned," said Tanya.

"A subject's history, Eddie," I reminded him. "Chapter One
in the handbook."

"As I say, that particular item is on my list."

"Hey," said Junior, "how does it feel getting back in the gumshoe racket, Eddie?"

"I am not getting back in," he said. "I am trying to keep peace in the family." He flipped over the meat like he was mad at it.

"Oh, is that right?" I said. "Here I thought you were concerned about Lenny's whereabouts like the rest of his friends."

"Amber," he said, "don't start."

"What is she starting, Eddie?" said Tanya.

"I am a dealer in classic cars," he said. "I had five messages on my machine today that I cannot follow up because I am hanging out in libraries and museums and poking around in the house of a man who is following his spirit somewhere in the sun."

"Oh," Tanya said, her eyes popped open, "I *see.*"

"When you went off today, Eddie," I said, "I was so proud of you. I had goose bumps. Now I am learning a few things that make me feel bad."

"For god's sake, Amber," he said.

"Ganging up on Lenny and telling him he was a bastard. He was nine years old," I said.

"It makes me sick," Tanya said.

"What is nine?" Eddie said. "It's nothing!"

I said, "It could be everything, Eddie."

"Okay, okay," he said, "calm down, the both of you, and tell me what is a person who has no legal father? Is it not a bastard!"

"A bastard who isn't even proud of his Polish name," Junior said.

"Junior," Tanya looked at him, "you are pathetic."

"Tell me why he goes by July and not Lipiec?" Junior said.

Walter said, "That was Angie's decision, Junior."

Tanya said, "And they are the same, are they not? Doesn't Lipiec mean July?"

"Our mother didn't change our name," said Junior.

Nobody said anything. Junior was being so dumb there wasn't anything we *could* say. I think we were all starting to feel funny about this conversation. For one thing, it was no secret that Lenny's mother Angie Lipiec had him out of wedlock, and then died soon after, and that Uncle Komo raised him. All of us knew that about Lenny. It was one of those things you learned about a person and it was like the color of his eyes or like the songs he sang when he really felt happy or like his dreams, good or bad. It was part of why he was your friend.

I went inside the house. Tanya followed me. She said she'd help set the table. We were doing that, and dishing out the coleslaw and stuff, her saying Junior's name under her breath, when Walter came in. I don't know how two twins can look and act so much alike and be so different. But it wasn't just Junior who had turned the evening sour. Junior was Junior. Not a bad guy, really, which was what Walter was trying to tell us. "I have heard that song for thirty years," Tanya said. "Would you please change the record?"

I stopped them. I'd had enough. I said, "Junior has his good qualities. It isn't him. Personally, I don't know what it is, exactly." And I didn't. I was thinking of how Lenny had grown up without a mother, and then of how much Gloria and Lenny loved each other. How they never got upset over things people should not let bother them. How they were always taking those disadvantaged kids up north to Uncle Komo's place and showing them a good time. How Uncle Komo always treated them like his own. How Uncle Komo had had only Angie and how she had had only Lenny, and now that was the end of the line. I couldn't follow where I was going for sure. Was it that Eddie and I and Walter and Tanya had half a dozen kids and that many grandkids already, and Gloria and Lenny had none? I didn't know. I was shaking. I wanted to tell Eddie how I felt. How I really felt. And how precious time was. Now. Just the two of us. I was so excited when he came in with the burgers, I dropped two big plates. I stood surrounded by the broken pieces not knowing if I would cry or shout. He looked odd, like a waiter or a janitor, definitely someone in the wrong place. He said, "Amber, Amber, Amber." He went tip-toeing around the broken plates, balancing the tray of meat as if it mattered so much, saying my name and saying he would take care of it, he would take care of everything, sounding like just anybody.

Somewhere
Geese Are Flying

At a café near the Métro St. Michel, sitting outside, Thrasher watches the evening show going by. The Africans hawking their leather goods, moving from café to café as if sleepwalking, bewitched, their faces revealing nothing, their beckoning black arms offering the same string of purses, the same possums hanging from the same black branch—the backpackers among them weaving in and out, Americans, pioneers, eating Italian heroes, ices, their eyes wide open, eager to discover something—the couples close together, a hand casually in the partner's rear pocket, palming a cheek, keeping the hand warm, the other hand a fist at the mouth, warm breath being blown into it—the street wet, glistening, reflecting hot colors—the odors of perfume and tobacco and cooked meat gathering . . .

Thrasher blows breath into his own hands, finishes his cognac, and leaves. He crosses the Quai St. Michel in the middle, a taxi shrieking its horn at him, and walks along the river toward Notre Dame.

In a corner of his brain he can hear something good. Ducks, geese. This time of year? This late? Stopping, leaning on the parapet, he looks at the Seine. After a while he sees himself running across a golf course behind his daughter's retriever. Sweet, blessed fresh air! He gulps it, hogs it down. His brain spins and his legs tremble. What is he doing? Suddenly the dog stops—it whirls around, foam flying from its lips, and gives Thrasher a look that says the same thing, or worse, "Who are you?" It is thirty degrees, more snow is promised, and a lone figure far out on the fairway—a crazy—approaches his ball. It is four o'clock on a gray, brittle afternoon on the prairie, dusk is gathering, and the figure swings his club. The sound to Thrasher is that of a slap against flesh . . .

Barbara is standing in the driveway, home from the office, when he returns the dog. They look at each other a long time. She seems smaller, more precise. She has dyed the delicate gray wings out of her hair, and he wants to rub there, rub them visible again.

"Why are you here, Thrasher?"

Her voice is more precise too, it almost has corners, a frame around it.

"Because I couldn't answer your question . . ."

So he is back in the States. In a motel with a pink heron perched on the roof. And a record cold is predicted for the prairie. He pours a shot of Jack Daniels. He exchanges stares with the white-faced cattle on the motel's calendar, the prize feeders. Then he goes out, to wait for his daughter on the path that Barbara has directed him to, down a slope behind the school, a pasture beyond. Two horses nose each other, exhaling doilies of breath in their manes. What will she say? What will *he* say? His mind can produce nothing. I've got a pink heron on my roof, Francine. Or is it a flamingo? No jokes, Dad, please. How would you like to come to Scotland with me? We could climb in the Cuillins, the sky's the color of apricots there—

Then he saw her. Tall, slim, dragging her bookbag down the slope as if she were pulling a sled. Coat unbuttoned, whistling, glancing back at the bookbag—yes, she *was* pretending to pull a sled! Thrasher's throat tried to close up on him.

He coughed.

She cocked her head, squinting. Then she stopped.

"Francine," he said.

She didn't move. Her eyes were bright blue startled things rimmed with black. Mascara?

"Guess who?" he said. "The monster from the deep lagoon."

"Dad!"

They were hugging and Thrasher was thinking he wasn't there, he was up in a tree, that tree over there, holding on, tired, any second now he'd let go, have to—his throat was closed up good now, no hope for it—she was so big . . .

He held her hand. They were talking. What did they *say*?

Sociology, she was just in sociology thinking, God this is so boring.

You've got winter here, Francine, winter, lord.

Have you seen Ralph?

Yes, we ran, I jogged, he's . . .

I got him a cat. Stanley. Stanley's a girl, we didn't know.

You're so big. You're—you're going to catch cold. Is school . . . ?

I hate it, except for—so you're back.

So he was back. For Christmas, yes. And one night, wrapping presents on the dining room table, Francine ordered them not to come in, to go make themselves scarce. Barbara took him downstairs to the basement room she'd fixed up—carpeting, sofa, a TV—yes, it is nice, he said. She pointed to a clock on the wall between two round mirrors.

"The last time my parents were here," she said, "Dad built that for me. You can hear the second hand click off the seconds if you sit quietly."

They sat on the sofa and listened.

"Yes," he said, "I can hear it."

"It runs on a common flashlight battery. For a year."

"Your father always was good at, you know . . ." He trailed off.

A long silence gathered between them, pricked by the clock.

"It's supposed to be a sunflower," Barbara said.

"Yes . . . yes, I can see that. It's very good."

"He worked on it all one afternoon. He was so proud of the petals."

"The petals?"

"Those sticks." Barbara pointed to the clock.

"Yes," he said, "I see, they were a delicate job."

"It's balsa wood. He gave it two coats of stain."

They watched the second hand and listened to it click.

"Whenever he visits relatives these days," Barbara said, "he builds them a clock."

Thrasher reached back to remember his former father-in-law, the bald suntanned head, thin white mustache. He knew where the fish were, said he could smell a trout, proved it, never came home empty-handed. Clocks?

"We thought about joining them in Arizona for the holidays. But I can't get away," Barbara said.

"Arizona?" Thrasher said.

"They've left Michigan. They're old. The Arizona weather is kinder to them."

"How are they?"

"Mother still yells at him like she did. She just doesn't realize what she sounds like. He teases her about it, I do too, but she doesn't get what we're trying to tell her. Of course if we told her how really awful she sounds, and how it hurts Dad, it would crush her."

And one night he and Barbara drove into town for a drink after Francine and her date went off to the school dance. They talked about how she'd grown, how grown-*up* she looked in high heels, her new dress—how her laugh made the room warmer, lighter, how it promised to return, Thrasher said, after circling a few stars in the sky.

They were excited, talked easily, at times quickly, together, and smiled remembering how self-conscious her date was, Kenny—tall, skinny, couldn't get his tie right and Barbara fixed it for him.

Thrasher said, "Those hands and feet! Kid'll grow another foot, two—that's how you tell, like with a pup, the hands and feet."

Barbara said, "He's a nice boy, not a dog, Thrasher. And he rides a bike. Races, you wouldn't think so, thin as he is. Francine rides too, we both do. Did she tell you she's planning to *build* a bike next summer?"

"She's something," Thrasher said.

"She's a very confident young woman. Much more than I was at her age. Gee, when I was sixteen," Barbara shook her head, smiling, "I think I ruined every sweater I owned."

"Fighting?"

"No, Thrasher," she said with mock patience, "perspiration. The nervous kind, the worst kind."

"The sweet sweat of youth."

"Shall we have another?" She held up her glass. "Another drink, I mean?"

The chubby waitress brought their drinks over.

"You folks got all your Christmas shopping done yet?" the waitress said.

"Yes," they said.

"*I* want Santa to bring me a set of snow tires!" she said and burst out with a raw throaty laugh that followed her all the way back to the bar.

"Cheers," Barbara whispered, touching his glass with hers.

"*Na zdrowie,*" Thrasher said.

"I know what!" she said suddenly. "Let's take Ralph for a walk on the golf course. He'll love it."

They crossed a field where pumpkins had grown—here and there one rolled up in the moonlight, frosty, mottled white, a clown lifting his head from a nap—and entered the golf course. They let Ralph go free. The turf was frozen, spiky, and their boots made a sound like a small fire starting. They walked without speaking. From time to time Ralph came racing back, brushed one or the other's legs, and sped off again. Climbing a knoll struck white with moonlight and weather, Thrasher fancied he was stepping on a mammoth eyeball and stepped softly. In the distance, all around them, timber reached for the sky.

"I'm finished with guilt," Barbara said and her voice made him whirl around, not what she said but the sweet noise of it—for a second or two he thought she was singing a song. Then her meaning, like an echo, came through and he thought, Yes . . . of course . . . you should be. And he felt happy for her. For both of them.

But as they walked along and he thought more about it, he wanted to see guilt, see it all by itself, a thing you *could* be finished with like a dirty rag, a rag stained with human grease. The best he could do was imagine a pile of sharp stones in the road, boulders, a huge pile, a mountain, bearing a crude hand-lettered sign on top: GUILT. You couldn't go around the mountain of course, that wouldn't be earning your freedom. You had to climb over it, over all the sharp edges. Years and years it might take, but finally you're over it. Now what? Do you fall down on your hands and knees in gratitude, thanksgiving? Hell yes. And while you're down there, catching your breath, maybe starting to hum a little, smiling to yourself—I mean, you did it!—might you also be tempted to pick up that small pebble over there, yes that one, just to take along for a souvenir?

I mean—if you can shrug off a sense of guilt at will—

Thrasher broke into a jog. "Come on, Barbara!" He didn't want to think about guilt, not even play with it, he wanted to hog air, move, feel the heart earn its keep!

"How do you feel?"

"Fine!" she said.

They jogged side by side around a sand trap and up to a snow-covered green—a gorgeous piece of china, a giant discus—over the green, down around another sand trap, and out on the fairway.

"I saw a guy out here the other day whacking a ball! Can you believe it?"

"Yes! It's the curse of the prairie . . . people go mad . . . perfectly normal one minute . . . playing golf on ice and snow the next. Whew! I've got to take a break."

"You know," he said, winded himself, "you're not bad for a middle-aged lady."

"I'm not, am I." She looked around. "Now where's Ralph?"

Thrasher whistled.

"Here, Ralph!" she called.

"He'll come."

"Little devil better. He's been known—"

"There he is."

Ralph came running up and Barbara tried to put the leash on him, but when she commanded him to sit he'd bow down on his front legs, then leap away as she approached.

"Rascal wants to play," she said. "Now behave, you! He's been to the pound twice since Thanksgiving."

"You don't sound like you mean it when you give a command."

"Ralph!" she said, stern.

But the dog only played harder to get.

"He got hit by a car too. Not hurt though. Ralph, *please*."

Thrasher said, "Sit!" and the dog, after hesitating, sat. Barbara put the leash on.

"We'll walk now," she told him, "nicely."

Thrasher had to laugh.

"What's so funny?"

"Oh, nothing. I just feel good."

"You were laughing at me."

"Because you're so sweet."

"You think I can't be tough?"

"I *know* you can be tough."

"I can be tough about other things than a divorce, if that's what—" She stopped.

They'd reached another green and were standing in the middle of it. They stood there a while without speaking. The divorce, Thrasher thought. Let it die and leave nothing behind, no will, no rags . . .

"How about that way?" he finally suggested. "Toward that bridge?"

"I'd rather go home. Come home with me, Thrasher."

Home, Thrasher thinks, crossing the Seine toward the Cathedral. You know what Frost said—home was where, when you had to go there, they had to take you in. Home rimes with poem and poem with apple, or close enough. A pomme a day, you're the pomme of my eye, the forbidden fruit. He is approaching the Place du Parvis now and *parvis*, he thinks, comes to us from the word *paradise*. Of course. And there's the great façade of Our Lady and I am in paradise among the late tourists popping their flashbulbs. Is there presently a janitor with a rural eye in one of the great twin towers, seeing us as the first fireflies of the season? Or the last? Or maybe they don't have fireflies in France, only us poppers standing in paradise. To my left is the Hôtel-Dieu for the lame, behind me is the Préfecture de Police for the blame, to my right a little green we can call the Garden, and straight ahead, fixed in stone, balanced, cast with kings, angels, saints, birds, monsters and flowers, with the wise and foolish, the good and the damned, with a God–Child and His Virgin Mother, sure of its beginning, middle, and end, straight ahead, no joke, no playing around, no money down, no easy payments, straight ahead on the main concourse is The Story.

—I mean, if you can shrug off a sense of guilt at will, what in the world else will be true?

Her room had a bed he didn't know and a bookcase and chest of drawers he did. He sat on the strange bed, at the foot, and gazed toward the books, waiting for her. She had told him to go on in, she'd be just a minute. They had come back from the golf course and, in the kitchen, still in their coats, she leaning against the counter, he against the door (the dog lapping noisily at his water dish between them), they looked at each other. Finally she said, "Well?" Then she took off her coat and went into the next room and he could hear her climbing the stairs. "Ralph can come up too," she called back.

Thrasher now turned from the books to the dog who lay flat out, panting quietly across the threshold—and then she stepped over him.

"You're still dressed," she said, rubbing lotion on her hands, the stretch marks from Francine the same delicate, pearly trails running above and below her tan line.

She tossed the extra pillows off the bed and got under the quilt.

"Thrasher?"

He turned. She was looking at the ceiling.

"I'm pretty nervous, Thrasher, I wish you'd hurry up."

He undressed and got in beside her, close, closer, slid one arm under her shoulders, the other around the backs of her cool legs, pulling her tight to him. He moved his nose back and forth in her cowlick.

She said, "I'm going to kiss you now, Thrasher. Hold still."

"I can't."

"Sure you can. One, two, three—stop."

She kissed him a quick peck on the lips.

"You still wiggle around like a big fish, you know that?"

He moved his nose to one of her ears.

"Can you feel my heartbeat?" she said.

He gave her a sudden big hug.

"Oh God—whew!—I'm not a tackling dummy!"

"Just getting warm," he said. "I'm nervous too."

"I think you cracked a rib."

"Ribs don't do much."

"Thrasher?"

"What?"

"I'm ready."

So he was back in the States, in a strange but good bed, his palm smeared with blood, afraid. He'd been dreaming of running with the dog again, cleaning out his lungs, getting in shape, real shape, eight or ten miles worth at a clip. But first, in the dream, he was lying in a vast field of timothy, thinking about the run, savoring it, and also regarding the sky, for the sky had said—a voice up there had said—*You are almost home.* Then he was waking up, he could hear someone in the distance preparing a tub, could hear Barbara call to Francine, "It's time, Sunshine . . . it's time . . ."—and Thrasher, leaving the field of timothy, about to go run, felt warm, felt ready. Then the thing happened on his face—struck his face, clawed it once quickly and was gone. His eye burst into flame. He covered the fire with his hands and cried out, "The cat! Take it away!"

Leaving the Place du Parvis, Thrasher walks up the dark Rue du Cloître–Notre Dame toward the Pont St. Louis. It's not a street he likes. Though it's deserted now, big buses are often parked there, the customers collected in knots on the sidewalk, the guides switching from German to Spanish to English to explain the symbolism of the serpent under the Virgin's foot or what time lunch is. But the other way around the Cathedral to the bridge, through the pretty Square Jean XXIII, is closed at this hour. Thrasher goes to the Square to read sometimes. In the afternoon babies and small children are brought there by mothers and grandmothers. He's gotten to know a few by sight—in particular a chunky little girl and her grandmother who always take the same bench and discuss the grandmother's dreams. Because they speak slowly Thrasher can follow them well enough to know that the woman has a recurring dream in which, like an angel, she flies a lot, around the Eiffel Tower, up and down the Seine, and somewhere in the suburbs where, during the war, she raised chickens for German officers. Telling her granddaughter about it, she shakes her head no, no, no, she doesn't want to, but what can she do? She lights a cigarette and sits back wearily on the bench. "I am fatigued from it!" she says in French. The three or four times that Thrasher has witnessed this scene, the little girl has responded that these adventures are good for her grandmother's appetite and complexion. The chunky girl reminds him of Orson Welles. The woman on the other hand is slim, fine-boned, and certainly must have been beautiful forty years ago.

Standing on the Pont St. Louis now, gazing down at the Seine, Thrasher remembers that one time she covered her face with her scarf and held it there until her cigarette burned her fingers.

"Anyway, what do you *do?*"

They were all three at the kitchen table. He was sipping coffee with one hand, holding an ice cube in a washrag under his eye with the other. And his daughter, who was so much older than the daughter he saw the last time, whose position in the universe—she had let him see—she was learning to protect with sudden laughter and could do all right with it, was now giving him another view of her: regarding him as hard as she could, as hard as those fragile eyes could bear to look at anyone who might hurt her, she wanted to know something he owed her, no joking around.

"Well," he began, "I travel to names on the map to see what they look like. I try to go by bicycle if I can. Once I rode across Montana on a bike and slept in Deadman's Basin, which looked like a place plenty of men and women had died in, although I didn't see any that night, dead or alive. The sky, Francine, was wide open and full of stars, and you could smell sage everywhere. Made me hungry for a pork roast."

Thrasher looked at his daughter hoping she would smile.

"What else do you do?" she said, cool as a cop with a clipboard.

"Well, I do a lot of that, camping out and getting hungry. Except up in Canada. I didn't have the right gear and it was very cold. Had to abandon my bike up there too. But I caught some nice fish in Alberta, near a place called Henry House, not far from Pocahontas. Henry House—sounds like something from a kid's book, doesn't it?"

"All by yourself you do this?" Still cool.

"Pretty much."

"But don't you have friends?" Ah, she was warming up a little.

"You meet people, sure."

"I mean *friends.*"

"No."

"I can't believe it," she said.

Was he lying to her? "Can't believe what?"

"Everything."

"Hold on now."

"You do next to nothing and have no friends. You enjoy that?" That foolishness, did she mean?

"I work when I can—seasonal jobs, canning, farming. I'm learning things, Francine."

"Like what, though?"

"Oh, that I might like to start a fish farm. Raise trout from fry. I know how to do it, from working in hatcheries out West."

"Where would you do it?"

"Maybe"—he glanced at her sidelong over the washrag— "around here some place, the great prairie."

Her eyes narrowed a notch.

He said, "It would be fun, don't you think, raising fish?"

Barbara said, "Don't rub your eye. Here, let me see it again. Oh, it's much better. But another dab of this cream, I think. Hold still."

"He can't," Francine said as if to herself.

"There," Barbara said, "you'll live."

Thrasher looked at his daughter. What *could* he tell her about his—his time away? That he'd been trying to understand a few simple things. What would that mean to her? *She* was trying to understand a few complicated things. He shook his head. Look, baby, I'm stuck for words—can't you see that? Your old man's tongue-tied. The cat just missed his eye but got his tongue. Stanley, you ugly bastard. But I'm here, I love you, and I want to see more of you before . . . before you grow up. Grow up? Before you *leave* us, Francine, the three of us. I want to come back!

But Thrasher could say none of this. Instead, his armpits wet, he said, "Would you tell me more about school?"

"School?" she said with contempt.

"Is it really so bad?"

Rolling her eyes, "Yes."

"Yes," he agreed, suddenly tired, "I suppose it is . . ."

"You got out," she said, looking at him hard.

He knew that was coming. If the teacher hates school, why can't the student? He nodded. "But—" But what?

She sighed heavily, and said, as if reciting a prepared speech, "Sociology is boring, a waste. I do not believe in judging people as groups despite what Mr. Phipps says. I believe in brotherhood but that's another story. Composition for the College Bound, no comment, just ugh. Spanish is fine. Of course you can put up with a lot when you love the language. Modern Dance is good for my body and American Literary Masterpieces, you'll be glad to hear, has helped me to like Robert Frost. I'm the only one in the class who does."

They were quiet for a while. Then Francine said to her mother, "Tell him our favorite sentence from Dr. Marty."

Barbara said, "Dr. Marty is the principal. He writes a monthly newsletter for parents. In one of them, under something called 'Parent Support Group,' he wrote: 'Besides sharing concerns, parents will have an opportunity to practice facilitative communications and to use a decision-making model for problem situations.'"

"Basically though," Francine looked her father in the eye, "I hate school and can't wait to get out and start living my life. You can understand that."

Thrasher's not alone on the bridge, he now sees. A nun—a nun?—no, a man in a long coat, a small tent, stands near the far end, almost on the Île itself. He lifts a bottle to his mouth. Mr. Flood? Having a nightcap under the stars, sir?

It's late. Though Thrasher is tired, whipped, he doesn't want to go back to his hotel. He wishes he had a bottle too. One sits in his room ten minutes away, a nice Margaux, but he wants one here, now, on the Pont St. Louis, between La Cité and the Île St. Louis, in February or March of this year, this unusually warm season. A bottle, if he could choose, of Polish vodka, yes, the bull on the label, the golden straw inside, cheers, *salud*, health, *na zdrowie!*

He's walking toward the man now. The man hugging his bottle looks up slowly, suspicious, an old man—Lord no, a man about his own age—a man wrapped in three or four coats, furry brownish weasel face, eyes floating in egg white, runny, mouth sinking into his head, no luck, no tit, the man's had nothing, no sunny childhood, kicked from the womb by a startled mad hag who crawled off and never looked back. A bum. A clochard. Thrasher can smell the river water that's lapped at his skin without washing away anything.

He holds out a ten-franc piece. The man's eyes fry, congeal, and his collapsed lips separate, the hole smiles. The man takes the money. Thrasher points to the bottle.

So he was back without being back, splitting wood for their Christmas Eve fire, moved in without being in, out from under the heron anyway, the staring beef, in the yard with Ralph watching, snow on the ground and more falling, big sudden stars of it, Barbara and Francine off in the car, dropping off presents here and there, friends they'd made, a white Yule, Bing, Rudolph, and Barbara said he could stay a while, let's not plan anything now, they shook hands (shook hands!) after coming apart, I did miss fucking you Thrasher, straight from the shoulder, no theatrics, sweet but not soppy, Francine knocking on their door after the dance, I'm home, I'm sober, the light laugher (protection? because he was there? careful Thrasher), a match being struck, a slight odor of tobacco smoke, her own door closing, she has one a day Barbara told him, a Camel, your brand Thrasher, she's a lot like you, likes you too, you can see that can't you, can see I can't do anything that's not in our best interests, we've become—I hate to say—like sisters, but I like our life, my life, still we had all those years, good years, tender, corny, they get in your bones, mine anyway (mine too!), that's why I wrote, my bones wrote, curious, middle-aged, don't you think about getting older, getting a few things straight?

Yes!

Bringing the axe down hard, clean, a good split. Smell that red oak.

He'll build a splendid fire, ice the champagne—no, first take a walk, come on Ralph, put one foot in front of the other, stick out his tongue and snare a few snowflakes, eat the stars, those intricate feathers, tail feathers Ralph, pay attention, from a rare bird that flies only once in a blue arctic moon, during the mating season when his quickened heart, and hers, beat so rapidly the results can be seen as far away as your little plot on the prairie.

The bum on the bridge, mumbling, wiggling shit-colored fingers, wants a cigarette. Thrasher gives him one and takes another pull on the sour bottle—the skin housing his mouth drawing tight, puckering. Rhubarb juice in there? Or some exotic disease that will claim all his teeth?

It's starting to blow a bit, witch tails on the Seine, and here comes the rain. Be gentle.

"You know," he says to the bum, "I've often wondered about you fellows."

The bum puts up his collars, grunts for the bottle. Opens his hole, pours, ahhh, belches *baarawwk!*

"We all wonder, sir. We see you sleeping on a hot air vent in the sidewalk, broad daylight, having a steam and a sprawl, relaxed, oblivious to the daily bump and grind, rosy-nosed, snoring perhaps, and we wonder."

Thrasher accepts the bottle for his turn at it. He remembers sharing a bottle of beer with his father, at lunch on the job site, a swig or two before biting into those thick roast beef sandwiches his mother packed, the apple pie, good whole-some fare, coffee with Pet Milk afterwards, maybe a snooze in the back of the truck, head resting on a stack of sweet white-pine two-by-fours . . .

He pulls at the sour wine, wipes his mouth—

"Yes sir, my man, we wonder. And what we wonder—some of us—is this: what do you think of us as we hustle past in our clean cottons and polyesters, underarms protected, un-sightly nostril hairs removed?"

He hands the bottle back, or starts to—his companion wants him to hold it a minute while he unbuttons and has a pee. Not so easy, two or three pairs of pants. There. Ahh . . . throat graveling satisfaction, steam rising, laughing as he sprays the bridge, one hand pointing up in the rain, "Dieu . . ."

"Yes, I see. You're both having a leak, you and the Almighty. So *that's* what you think of us, is it? Wonderful!"

Baarawwk!

"Excellent!"

His companion is ready for a drink now, the job's done, a thirst created. But what's this, the bottle's almost empty! The man shakes his head sadly, drinks, measures the level, regards Thrasher (wants an opinion? sympathy?), quickly takes an-other drink, then offers Thrasher what's left. The sludge.

"You are too kind, sir." Thrasher lifts the bottle above his head, "A toast. To God's kidneys!" He downs the stuff . . . rhubarb leavings, stringy, awful. He spits.

The bum, appraising the empty bottle, broods. Gives it a final, fruitless suck. Bah! Seems to be sinking farther into his tent, mouth first. Hunched. Mumbling. No luck, no tit.

Thrasher lights a cigarette.

"My good fellow," he says at last, his shriveled mouth–skin making speech difficult, "I have an idea! Not far from here"—he points—"lies a surprise that"—he spits again—"that I suspect will follow your noble number admirably. Come."

His companion isn't sure. The eyes floating forlorn.

"But of course," Thrasher urges him, pointing, lifting a phantom bottle to his lips, smacking them, "of course!"

Back from his walk with Ralph, Thrasher laid wood in the fireplace then went to work in the kitchen, celery, carrots, onions, garlic, breadcrumbs for the stuffing. Barbara and Francine weren't home yet. Mincing, chopping, I should call my mother, he thought. But what would I say? She'll cry and ask me why and I won't want to talk about it, and what kind of a Christmas is that for her? She'll say Barbara is so sweet. I'll say I know. No, first she'll say where *are* you? At Barbara's I'll say. At Barbara's?! She'll be confused . . . she'll be having a drink . . . my brother and his family just came in . . . everyone ebullient . . . her stuffing, her bread smell wonderful . . . Are you *living* there? Are you getting back together? Oh son. *Then* she'll start to cry. And that sweet Francine, she'll say, I feel so sorry for her. The truth is, Mom, I came home to ask Barbara to take me back. We've decided for now not to decide anything. We shook hands on it. Meantime I'm careful, watching my step, the old temper, the Polish half. Meantime I run with the dog and help in the kitchen. Meantime I've slept in her bed and you're right, she is sweet, sweet as ever. Meantime, ah meantime . . .

No, he'll go see her after the holidays, not so much pressure then.

Thrasher's companion, they discover, has a name, Claude, and as they approach the Hôtel Jeanne d'Arc on the Rue Jarente—dark now, even the little café closed up—Claude begins to sing in the rain, or croak, or croak-and-wheeze; in any case he smells the bottle that Thrasher has promised and repromised half a dozen times during their journey, and his spirits are high, the weasel face, the runny eyes almost shine with health and adventure. A couple of times he's tried to throw a friendly arm around Thrasher's shoulders, but standing a good foot shorter and wrapped in all those bulky clothes his arm only bounced off Thrasher's back.

At the hotel door his *beeg Anglais* friend quiets him down.

"My concierge, sir, who is also the owner of this establishment, is a Yugoslav lady with very white skin and flaming red hair piled up in a tidy cone. Moreover she comes from a fine family in Ljubljana. She would get a pimple if she saw you."

Inside, however, the coast is clear and Thrasher leads him up the stairs. It's warm in the hotel. The madame does not like *zima*, the cold. On the third floor, halfway, Claude's furry face, Thrasher sees, begins to pale where it can and the flaps of skin around his mouth-hole flutter in and out for air. Thrasher takes off his coat and indicates that Claude should do the same; but when Claude does—reluctantly, and only one of his valuable coats—Thrasher is sorry. A rich new odor assaults the warm Yugoslav keep, an animal days-ripe in the hateful trap, a stink to make the duke think twice about crossing the swamp and taking his rightful castle.

They stop for Claude again on the fifth floor, his runny eyes at the brink of losing their yolks. Thrasher whispers, "Don't die here, sir, please, the maids in the morning, their sensibilities, you understand. Yes, that's it, breathe slowly, accept the fear, go with it . . ."

On the sixth floor finally, Thrasher shakes his companion's clammy hand. "We're home, boy!" In the room he decides against suggesting that Claude remove another coat, settles him in a chair, opens the window. At the closet he gets the Bordeaux he's promised.

"A gift from an angel," he says, bringing it to Claude, show-ing him the label. Chateau–Margaux, seventy–four. A decent year, I think. You agree?"

Claude's eyes achieve a confused light, his tongue appears at the hole like a freshly skinned mouse. He really hasn't recovered from the climb yet, but he's working at it, working at it.

"Ah, a respectable pop," Thrasher says, pulling the cork. "I suppose we should let it breathe a bit, all that loving care in-side . . . then again—" He takes a slug. "Umm, not quite up to the sass yours had, but it'll do. Have at it, pal."

Claude receives the bottle with trembling hands as if it were a brand new thing—no, much more—a brand new life, bright and shiny with good teeth, no aches, nothing broken or cracked anywhere, a life promising beauty, dignity. His eyes begin to overflow.

"Damn you, Claude, this isn't the time for that." Thrasher puts a hand on the bottle and urges the man to drink. "Come on, fella. No theatrics. Wet your whistle. Enjoy."

Closing his eyes the bum drinks.

Thrasher moves away, toward the window, "Thata boy." He sucks in fresh air, gesturing to Claude to keep the bottle, have all he wants, take his time—and lighting a cigarette Thrasher looks out over the rain–glazed rooftops, there, in that direc-tion, west . . .

Barbara and Francine were setting the Christmas table and laughing about someone named Rick the Stick who had writ-ten a love letter to someone named Charlotte. Somehow the editors of the school paper got hold of the letter, thought it was a parody, printed it, and Rick the Stick's ears, which stuck out *any*way, were crimson all week. In the dining room, reporting this story among the sounds of silver and dinner-ware being handled, Francine laughed until she cried.

"Is my mascara running, Mother?"

"No, darling."

Thrasher tended the fire, red oak and hickory, and the room was expanding—he could feel the white walls moving back giving him space, the Lake Superior shoreline hanging over the sofa winding for miles toward summer, *into* summer, a deep brilliant blue, and Thrasher could smell it and smell the pine timber and the rich loam he left his tracks in, and if anyone came along right then and said, Thrasher, it's only that little tree hung with tinsel and balls you smell, he'd pick the fellow up and shake him to show he had a few screws loose—of course he could smell that timber!

And in that full mood he got out the champagne. Snow was falling past the window in fat flakes. They met at the table, laughing, beaming. The table shone with candles, china, snowlight, the glazed turkey steaming, giblet gravy, a floating galaxy of hearts and gizzards, the rich reds and yellows of fresh cranberries and buttered yams bursting their jackets, startling green asparagus spears! He raised his glass. He felt large. Any second now he believed his cheeks would crack from the clownish smile they bore. In part of his brain he stepped quickly aside, had to, he was dancing, in an orchard somewhere, whooping it up, he needed room—he held Barbara in one arm, Francine in the other, smelling apple blossoms in their hair!—and he moved closer to them to accommodate this vision. He hugged them now, spilling champagne, groaning the great good feeling that was filling his face, his chest. He wanted to pick them up, carry them off. He raised his glass again, but nothing would come out, no words. All he wanted was a simple phrase or two, here's to us, to more, much more. Anything. Lord. Somebody, help me out. He looked at them. They were waiting. Don't be afraid. Then his mouth opened and he couldn't stop, he said he wanted to come back, for good, the three of them, be together again, we can do it, don't cry, look I'm carving the turkey, it's easy, out comes the stuffing, on go the yams, the berries, these little hearts and gizzards, everything, look! And working fast he piled each plate high with the rich colors of their feast, the reds and yellows and greens, piled them higher with seconds, thirds, the creamy white meat, the nutty dark, pouring more gravy, more stars, they needed all the help they could get, he was saying, they had a long, long way to go, when Barbara put her hand on his arm.

Claude sits in his chair, head fallen back, snoring. The bottle's protected in his arms. Thrasher looks at the man. The party's over. It's time for the man to go.

"Get out," Thrasher says.

But the man continues to snore. Thrasher feels weak and light and unable to move. He wants to hear Francine and Barbara in the next room, hear them talking, he wants to go to them, take their hands.

"Look," he says, "we're alive!"

But all he hears is a man snoring.

Thrasher looks at the man, at a man who understands the beauty of sleep. Finally Thrasher goes over to him. He frees the bottle from his arms. Then he picks him up and carries him to the bed. The man continues to snore, undisturbed. Lucky man. Thrasher takes the wine and leaves.

Outside the sky is a wide bruise, but the rain has stopped. Thrasher walks, pausing now and then to drink from the bottle, stepping aside as the garbage trucks begin to come out and swallow lettuce leaves and baby shoes and the brown arrangements of bone. His legs feel stiff, as if they are all bone. He turns at the Rue de Turenne, again at the Rue des Francs-Bourgeois. He comes to the Place des Vosges, the oldest square in Paris. "Ah," he says, "the seventeenth century. Order, elegance . . ." The gate is locked. Through the bars he sees Louis XIII astride a white stone horse. Now the moon appears, turning the monument, turning everything brighter. Thrasher moves along the fence, gripping the bars as he goes. His knuckles look blue, don't they. Never mind, he wants to be in there. He wants to walk across the grass, which is against the rules. The park guards during the day keep you off it, wag a finger, speak firmly, it's not correct—dapper little soldiers, estimable women, round and round and round they stroll, keeping an eye on the likes of Thrasher—as they should!—look at him now, prowling the square, stinking, he's a bad character—*peau de vache!*—skin of a cow!—

He drinks from the bottle, wipes his chin on his sleeve. His sleeve? This is not his sleeve. Nor his coat. It's the bum's coat. No wonder he's stinking.

He looks through the bars. Tell me, Louis, doesn't your ass get sore just sitting there? No? And the birdshit on your nose? No problem either? Of course not. It's a nice life you've got, symmetrical, the houses around all alike, you at the center, children at your feet, their pretty mothers, the old folks respectable, dozing, wrapped up like babies, balance, yes.

His eyes close. He sees her standing in a field of virgin prairie, gathering the wind in her hair . . . and he getting up from his bed in the dorm and walking to her window, standing there under the harvest moon, waiting beside the brilliant ivy. He has not spoken to her yet. For weeks he has watched her take her seat, watched her write her words in a blue notebook, watched her leave. Now the beaming professor has ushered them all out to the field at the edge of town, and he is watching her there too, following her, until she turns in that turning wind and says, "Listen." He looks up. Somewhere geese are flying. Under the wide, plum-colored swirls of sky he knows it. He can hear them at the edges of his heartbeat. He can smell them . . . marsh-ripe, fish-breathed, feather-wet

. . . and suddenly he knows he must go there, where the blues and specklebellies are, where the Giant Canadas are.

The street is silvery, moon–sweet, and calling *wah, wahaa*, calling *ha-lonk, ha-lonk*, he starts out, slowly . . . and slowly sinks to his knees. He'd like to climb this fence and sit on the horse with Louis but, sad to say, he is bone–tired. Tail–dragging whipped. Skunked. But surely he thinks about things, his mind isn't gone, is it? About getting older? Getting a few things straight? Hold still, Thrasher, I'm going to kiss you now.

A Million Dollar Story

"All you need is a sleeping bag, a good one—there's nothing worse than being cold. Some coffee. Some wire too. You don't want to sleep on the floor of an empty box car if you can help it. Especially if the cars on either side are full—you get a kind of corrugated jolt. So I string up a hammock. And read. I love it. Trouble? Oh, once a bull stuck a big gun in my face. A train cop had been stabbed, and somebody said a blond guy did it. So the bull spots me and my hair in the yard—which are the only bad places, the yards, you don't want to hang around them, especially in the east, in Minneapolis you get three years, man, if they catch you there—so he spots me, this bull, this is up in Canada, B.C., shoves the piece in my choppers, and then puts the cuffs on. He really threw the first one on—they know how to hurt you if they want to. I said, Oh, man, you don't have to do that, I'm just hitching a ride. After this is cleared up I'll buy you breakfast. So he put the second cuff on easier, he was an okay guy. Later, when they saw I was clean, this same bull even drives me out to a spot where I can catch the train I want. No, I haven't had any trouble. But I always have money in my shoe, a wallet full of credit cards. Those Canadian cops, for example, they looked at my driver's license, my plastic, they said this isn't you. But you could tell from the sound of their voices they were a little confused. I said, Look, I like trains, I hate all other kinds of travel except walking. And that's true. I like making a fire in a boxcar at night and slipping along under the stars, warming my personal engine. One night I'm on this long, long train and we curl around a big bend and it's like some goofy constellation came down—I mean, there's a fire in every boxcar! Top that one. Or this: You know how they piggyback engines? They're empty of course, so that's where I ride when I get the chance, in one of those, right up where the engineer sits, my arm resting on the window ledge like a man who's just made a major purchase. I'd go nuts if I couldn't hop trains. And I'll tell you this: I sleep like a baby, inside or out. Here's a funny thing that happened: I'm in an open gondola one night and this *grit* is blowing in my face. What's happened to standards? I say to myself. Can't they sweep these honeys off anymore?"

That was not the end of his monologue. But I had finished my ice cream and cake, Margaret's daughter was home pacing the floor (Margaret had given me several eye signals in the last ten minutes), and, in fact, I was tired. Parties are not what they once were for me. So when the train-hopper paused at the end of his next anecdote (the grit flying in his face was cement, which coated his hair and the beard he then wore, giving him a ghostly appearance, which got him a lot of very strange looks from the patrons in a café he stopped at for breakfast, and which later, when he went to use the john, hardened on his head and face as he tried to wash it off) we left the party. In the car Margaret said, "You could tell he was a salesman the minute he opened his mouth. What a line."

"The train-hopper?"

"Train-hopper, my foot. He sells computers in Eugene."

Margaret is the skeptical sort. When I first met her she disliked me, did not trust me on sight.

"Well," I said, "he was the most interesting person there, whatever he does."

"Millicent is probably half out of her mind." Millicent is Margaret's daughter. She is fifteen. If Margaret is not home by nine o'clock, Millicent turns on every light in the house, both TVs, the radio, and paces from the kitchen to the dining room to the living room to the family room at the far end of the house and back again, over and over, working her mouth into a tight bunch and giving her mother holy hell the second she steps in the door. If I am there, Millicent stomps into her bedroom and lets fly from behind her fish tank until Margaret goes in to pacify her. Two years ago Margaret left Millicent with Margaret's father for a couple of weeks. He died suddenly. Millicent has never forgiven her mother for leaving her, as she says, "with a dead man."

Tonight I was going to my own place. Margaret was not happy about this, but I needed a breather. I wanted to wake up in the morning and hear birds and surf, not barking Welsh corgis and a hair dryer. I wanted to sit down to breakfast at a table not littered with cat tracks and the dribbles of careless youth. Millicent eats first, at the same time she feeds her animals. She places their dishes on the floor snug by her chair, though Lavender the cat hates it down there. Millicent must be finished with breakfast and putting her makeup on and drying her hair by seven in order to catch the school bus. I am inviting trouble if I arrive in the kitchen before Millicent's rhythm is completed. It would help matters considerably if the table were larger. It's an antique table that Margaret is very fond of, but it seats only two with any comfort. When I first began staying overnight there, Millicent took her egg and Cheerios in the family room and ate while drying her hair and watching television. But lately she has switched to the kitchen, taking the chair I have been using. The other chair is directly under a pot of ivy hanging from the ceiling. If I use that chair I have curlicues of ivy in my face. Margaret can sit there because she is shorter than I am. So is Millicent. But that chair, Millicent points out, is in a corner, next to the rocking chair, and there is not room on the floor for the animals' dishes. Thus I time my shower to end around seven. When I come out Margaret is in the rocking chair with her toes crossed having her coffee and reading Ann Landers or making her daily list. She has unusual feet but the prettiest penmanship of anyone I've ever known.

People who leave food on their plates are lonely. They want to let their host—or themselves—know that they've been there. This is me—this uneaten flower of scrambled egg, this crown of radish bearing my teeth marks. They leave food on their plates in case they come back from a fruitless adventure and require some affection. Speak to me, O Leftover. Lend me thy juice.

This is a fancy I had (along with, perhaps, a touch of self-pity) when Honey came back the last time. She came back for a week to heal her blisters, pick up some things; then she went off again, to walk in the Utah desert. She can walk fifteen miles a day. To look at her you wouldn't think she'd care to walk around the block. She's lean of course, lean everywhere except in her face, and there, in the cheeks, she's likely to put you in mind of fresh apricots, at least she does me. Her eyes are a hard blue, and her mouth, when you look straight down on it, will give you wings. Honey is not a good name for her. It's too frivolous, too chummy, not complicated enough. No, to look at her you'd believe at once that a walk, in her opinion, was a waste of time. I call her Mrs. Richards. Or—when we are hot—Big Sharp Delpha.

I work at the library in town, part-time. I've been in semi-retirement about a year now, thanks to the state lottery

Honey and I won. We won it four years ago, though at times it feels like ten or a hundred. We opted for the monthly-payment-for-life plan rather than the lump sum. Right away we said, okay, this is not going to change anything. It was a Friday night. We put Memphis Minnie on, Washboard Sam, Merline Johnson. I wore my straw hat. Honey climbed up on the refrigerator with a broom and, crossing her legs at the ankles, strumming her fingers over the handle, sang out, "Too late, Daddy, your baby's in prison now . . ." while I beat time on the toaster, the pepper grinder, and her pearly knees with a wooden spoon. She sang "Digging My Potatoes" and "King Size Papa" and "Has Anybody Seen My Pigmeat on the Line," and the more she tried to sound down and dirty the more she sounded like a no-nonsense kindergarten teacher tipsy on half a glass of sherry. She was not a schoolteacher—except for two years in the Peace Corps—but she looked and sounded like one to me. Dressed up in heels or wet and shiny in the shower she made me feel like this: that if I was good, after lunch she'd read me a story, help me get sleepy, as I lay on my rug for a nap. But on that Friday night when we celebrated our jackpot, she sang, "Daddy, you may never see my smilin' face again, but you must always remember that I have been your friend . . ." And later, in bed, both of us whipped from all the jumping and rolling around, she said, "Henry? What are we going to do? I'm afraid." I repeated what we'd said earlier, that nothing was going to change. Nothing that mattered, I said. I felt strong.

Well, you get tired of certain places, certain human failings, when you know you can pick up and go. We left Detroit two months later. I had had it with my boss at the racetrack, a man who ate breakfast at noon and started off with two vodka martinis on the rocks. His liver was his own business; what I didn't like were his cracks about where and how we

lived. Even before we won the lottery he said almost daily—
always in a jokey way—why in hell didn't I buy some decent
clothes and move out to Birmingham and give Honey a nice
backyard to raise some kids in, or at least some turnips if I
liked greens so much. Birmingham was the suburb where he
lived. He also had several choice remarks to make about the
old Studebaker I drove. His idea of the good life was a house
with tall white plantation pillars and three and a half baths, a
regulation pool table in the rec room and a brace of Chryslers
in the driveway that never got more than a year old. He
traded them in every spring, on his birthday. His real name
was Buddy Snipes, but he'd changed it years ago to Marlowe
Kincaid. He wore a thin mustache. All of his front teeth were
capped, and he'd had an operation on his ears that brought
them closer to his head. He told me all this one day over a
long lunch. He said his daddy had just died in a home where
he'd put him, and he felt like talking if I didn't mind. He said
I could call him Buddy. He said no one would know it was his
real name. Lucinda didn't even know, he said. Lucinda was his
wife. She sold real estate and was taller than Buddy, and the
reason she didn't know his real name, he said, was she
wouldn't understand.

Every Wednesday a black barber downtown named Julius
trimmed Buddy's mustache and clipped around his ears and
doused him with a cologne called Fifth Avenue. Then Buddy
broke his fast at Mister Kelly's, a saloon across from Tiger Stadium where the weekly meeting of the Detroit Sports Writers
and Broadcasters was held. I'd go with him. It was part of my
job to buy drinks for the media, be one of the boys, so they
didn't forget us out there at the track. The truth is I was not
unhappy in my work. I like trotters. For one thing they take
me back, in a comforting way, to those county fairs I couldn't
get enough of as a kid. For another I like the old guys who
drive them. They sit there in the sulky as if time and speed,

the whole modern conflagration, were a lot of nothing. But after Honey and I won the lottery, Buddy dropped his jokey tone and asked what was I trying to prove. I said nothing. He said, Then damn it all, Henry, get with it, get smart. He said that his daddy came up north from a wormy Arkansas shack, from pissing in the dirt, and made something out of himself, and I could do the same now that I had no excuse, by, one, buying another coat and tie and, two, moving to where nice folks lived. I was thirty-seven years old. I was in love with Honey, and we *liked* old neighborhoods, liked a good mix. So I said to hell with it. Summer was coming and summer in the Motor City can be sticky and, except for the trotters and the Tigers, graceless; but we could find horses and baseball anywhere, we said, and aimed the Studebaker west.

If you like rain and are inclined to put your feet up on a porch railing and look for meaning or at least interesting patterns in the way it falls and suddenly slants and bounces on things like tricycles left out and leaves and turned-over flowerpots, then Oregon may be the place for you. To arrive here, as we did, you get on the old Lincoln Highway as soon as you can and stay with it until a road you can't pass up comes along. You give the Mississippi a long look. You eat Amish food family-style in Iowa, marveling that the restaurant's owner once played for the Yankees. In South Dakota you step, half on purpose, in a mound of fresh buffalo dung, and then you poke around Montana and almost buy an old hotel because the bear-claw tubs are big enough for two and the view beyond a certain window is so wide and deep you find you have to hold on to something or the distance will take you for keeps before you're ready, even though, in a way, you *are* ready. You walk around and around that hotel as if you were tracing sun-dogs fallen from the sky, and your circle keeps getting larger until you are three or four miles away from the front door looking back at it from a field of shifting wheat. One of you asks, "Should we do it?" and after a minute the other asks the same. You are the hotel's only guests. Mainly railroad people stay there, and a few people like you who hate freeways and Holiday Inns and McDonald's, but over the course of a year not many. The bar and the dining room are what keep the place going. The locals drink there most afternoons and often stay to eat Dorothy's butterfly pork chops or baby beef liver and onions at round oak tables under a big ceiling fan. Dorothy runs the one-woman kitchen and her sister Kate runs the front desk and bar. They say, "We saw you coming a mile up the road!" Dorothy has just pulled a lemon meringue pie from the oven.

But you can't decide about the hotel because you've got a motion going. You're sliding—down through Anaconda and Wisdom into Idaho, and though there's fishing on the Salmon River like you've never had before, you keep sliding down, in a zig-zag giddy ride as though the car were on ice, through Helper and Devil's Garden and Shivwits and Carp (visit the Lost City Museum!), and you slip into Las Vegas, into a casino at six on a Sunday morning for one turn at the wheel, just one, and you win thirty dollars, thirty pieces of silver, and you scram, fast, and then you skirt the bombing range, cut through Death Valley, sliding hard now, taking the smallest roads you can find, only they keep getting bigger, wider, and finally you're at the freeway. And your ears start to ring.

"It happened so fast."

"We can go back, try another way?"

But you don't. You get on the thing in order to get away from wherever you are as quickly as possible. After several hours one of you suddenly sees this perfectly round, perfectly white moon, like a mammoth Alka-Seltzer, hovering just above the ocean—

"Look at the moon!"

"That's not the moon," the other says. "That's the sun. We're in L.A."

Your hands feel like meat hooks on the wheel.

What's the point in reporting this numbness? I'd rather tell how and where Honey sniffs a muskmelon to see if it's ripe, how she knows exactly where to scratch my back when I yelp like a dog under the covers. Margaret once said, "I think your wife needs professional help." That was in the beginning of course, and uncharacteristic of Margaret. Normally she is a lady. And under other circumstances I think she would like Honey, for if nothing else they have that one remarkable fact in common: they both taught school in Africa. When I sat in our local library listening to Margaret's impassioned syllables about her time in Zimbabwe, about "how at least one revolution is trying to work"—when I watched her ears turn cherry red with anger and frustration during the question-and-answer period as first Mrs. Snaw, the dentist's wife, and then someone in a pea-green pill box hat worried Margaret's theme into a squall of stock phrases about the threat of world communism, etc.—when I could no longer stay quiet and interrupted these women to ask if our speaker would tell us something about the lovely dress and earrings she wore, surely they were the work of the admirable people she had lived among—when, then, she responded, easing gracefully and with tact back to the main business of her theme (darting suspicious glances at me from time to time)—when, in short, all of this happened on an evening of fierce humidity and rain, Margaret and I shook damp hands, and drank a cup of the library's sweet punch together, and agreed to have lunch one day, even though, as she said later, she did not trust me for an instant.

Why?

Because I was the library's janitor, and janitors do not ask questions about women's dresses.

"Hmmmm," I said, thinking this was an odd comment, especially in view of her egalitarian politics.

"What are you really doing here?"

"Having lunch with you."

She sighed heavily, and poked at her halibut.

"All right," I said. I told her that I spent most of my day thinking. I had come to Oregon so I could do that, and look at the ocean. Maybe I would buy a sailboat to go with my yachting cap. I was married, but hadn't seen my wife in six months, and then only for a week. Honey was a walker, I said. Also, I said, I believe she is giving communal living in the Southwest a serious try. She likes the out-of-doors. Edward Abbey is her favorite author. She has a degree in education from the University of Michigan and can do fifty pushups from her toes but is not what you would call muscular. She has, as she herself would say, a lot of nervous energy. She would also say she is a late bloomer. We met at the racetrack—her uncle Orly owned some trotters and she helped him train them. She likes horses well enough but what she really likes, above everything else, she hasn't discovered yet. She knows it's out there, though, this great object. She is five-foot-nine, a Leo, a lapsed Catholic, half Irish and half an amalgam of you-name-it, and ten years younger than me. I'll be forty-two in August. You will be interested to know, I said to Margaret, that Honey spent two years in Africa, teaching in the Peace Corps. This was before I met her. I met her on St. Patrick's Day. She likes snakes, by the way, but psychology, self-help books, fried food—these things bore her. Her hair turns auburn in the sun. She has tiny freckles on her nose. Four years ago we won slightly over a million dollars in the Michigan lottery. Three or four, it's hard to remember.

Margaret, I noticed, looked as though she had swallowed something sour and was doing her best to ignore it. We sat there a few moments without speaking. Finally she placed her fork on the table, dabbed her lips, and said she had an appointment.

Living in a small seaside town you forget a lot and, paradoxically, remember a lot. What you forget are the big chunks that go in the middle. The little pieces around the edges are what suddenly surprise you. They surface like driftwood, like shells and jellyfish, they are brilliant and want to mean something. "I'm a *good* woman," Margaret once cried out in her soft bed under a skylight dizzy with stars. Who could begin to understand the full range, the body of that opinion? I held her close. I wanted to reassure her. Of course she was a good woman, whatever that means, and it means a lot, I know, but what, finally, could you do with it? I don't mean to sound cynical or morose or uncaring. We had roasted a fine chicken; we had had a lovely walk on the beach; we had brought our bodies one to the other and popped extravagantly at the same moment. Now in the aftermath she was expressing—suddenly—what sounded like part of a difficult history. And I? I was recalling a scene, years before, in which I had rounded third and was determined to get home. A girl named Joyce Dudzek was leaping in the stands. She had long blonde hair and buck teeth and her father, an usher in our church, tooted his trumpet after I crossed the plate. Oh yes, that did happen. And so did this: lying down in those long-ago gardens, sucking tomatoes, rolling peas, moon white, straight from the pod.

Margaret's garden is large and lush and colorful, but to name the great variety of flowering and edible stuff that grows there is somehow beside the point. As I see it, the point is this: among the lath and string and climbing vines, among the neat valleys and small green explosions, her hair in a bun, she is intent and precise as a bee. She has a small tool in one hand, a curl of root in the other, she is on her knees, her glasses have ridden out to the edge of her elegant nose, and she is pink with sun, humming.

Her husband was a captain in the Army. He was killed in Vietnam. "We were college sweethearts," Margaret said on one occasion. On another she said, "We met our last year at Washington. Neither of us had dated much. We were serious and shy and I don't remember if he even proposed. At the wedding I wept, and couldn't see, and twisted my ankle. I think, if he lived, we would not be married now, we had so little in common."

One thing they never did was go dancing. Margaret likes to dance. She likes to fix herself up—high heels, seamed hose, a peach-colored silk dress—and drive over to Eugene, to a cowboy bar we found. We dance to Hank Williams and Webb Pierce and when the band takes a break we put quarters in the jukebox and dance to Patsy Cline and Tammy Wynette. I have purchased proper tack for these nights, a Stetson and a pair of Tony Lama boots, and I know "I'm Walkin' the Floor Over You," by the great Ernest Tubb, by heart. The silk dress Margaret wears belonged to her mother. It has padded shoulders, a tight waist, and it falls sleekly to her knees. Margaret has pretty legs and very nice breasts and when she puts this dress on and moves through the bar's blue and red lights, she's a shimmering knockout, a perfect reproduction from the '40s. She keeps her glasses in her purse and her eyes sparkle. "Tell me how I look," she whispers in my neck.

Margaret's parents are also dead. Her mother preceded her father by a dozen years, and he never remarried. He spent his days in the drugstore he owned, chewing horehound cough drops, pacing the floor; at night he studied the stock market,

growing richer. He had never taken Margaret's mother dancing, never taken her anywhere except to his mother's house
for boiled chicken on Sunday. "He was not a bad man," Margaret says, "only dull. A Baptist. And yet he bought her a
wonderful piano—a Steinway—and would sit for hours while
she played. After she died he would tell me, 'Your mother was
a great musician.' She was not even mediocre, poor thing. He
got old very quickly. Near the end he believed he had taken
her on the train to San Francisco, to hear Paderewski."

Following Margaret's example, I now make a daily list. Usually it starts off with some sweet I wake up wanting—an
apple pie, a brownie. Today it also says, "Climb on roof—find
leak." During the night rain fell basso profundo, and I heard a
steady drip, a timpano, near the vicinity of Honey's sewing
machine. Why didn't she take that with her? And her saddle?
Her mountain climbing gear? Every thirty days (this also appears on my list) I send her half of the monthly check. In the
beginning of our separation I would also enclose a note,
telling her, for example, how many sea lions I had spotted recently, if a whale came by, how the "Ems" were shaping up.
The "Ems" are the Eugene Emeralds. One night I dreamt I was
an "Em." It was one of those dreams in which the details were
so sharp I could smell the infield grass, the chalk on the base-
lines. In high school I had been a pitcher, a pretty good one. I
had entertained serious notions of playing professionally
until, my senior year, I developed a chronic sore arm. Too
many curve balls too young. The end. But in this dream I had
made, if not the majors, at least the Northwest League. And I
was on the field! Except they had me playing a new position.
They had me playing fourth base. What a long, long throw I
had to make over to first!
    But now I just send Honey the check.

Margaret's dreams always wake her up, and then she can never get back to sleep. She lies there and worries, she says. About everything—pollution, world hunger, Millicent's sullen phase, whether she can find someone in Eugene who can repair her antique grandfather clock or if she'll have to haul it up to Portland. Finally she gets out of bed and scrubs and waxes the kitchen floor, fingers through jelly jars full of screws and buttons and things she can't even recognize looking for God knows what. It'll be four A.M. by this time. Lavender sits on the window ledge outside and looks at her. His expression is always angry, accusing. Margaret wants to open the window and let the cat in, but she is afraid to. Afraid to approach the window, that is, because Lavender might have a rat under his paws. At moments like this she hates the cat. Hates her house, her garden, the town, the ocean, the dead fish that wash up, and most of all the image of her father pacing the floor, worrying about his investments.

The Saturday following the birthday party Margaret and I had a date to drive up to Canby—trotters were running at the Clackamas County Fairgrounds. When I got to the house Millicent was sprinkling confectioners' sugar on a plate of pancakes. She wore a button on her bib overalls that declared "FUCK ART—LET'S DANCE" and looked disgusted with the world. She said, "She's outside. I'm surprised you didn't see her." I went back outside and found Margaret sitting in her biggest fir tree. A ladder stood against the trunk.

"I walked right past here a minute ago," I said. "Why didn't you say something?"

She sat on her branch, gazing up into the tree. Finally she said, "I have needles in my hair and my hands are sticky with pitch, but all in all I feel pretty good."

"Is anything wrong?"

"I haven't done this since I was a kid!"

Just then her neighbor came over from next door, where he had been pruning his roses. We'd waved earlier when I turned into Margaret's driveway.

"I spotted you at breakfast," he said to Margaret. "At first I thought you might've been a bear. I know something about bears."

"You know Mr. MacKenzie, Henry," Margaret said.

"Oh sure, I know this young fella," MacKenzie said. "You're at the library. You've got Skinny Dickerson's old job."

"How are your roses?" I said.

"Fair. Just fair. How's the weather up here?" he asked Margaret.

"Fine!" she said. "I can see three sailboats!"

We looked at Margaret for a while. Her hair was gathered loosely in back with a piece of string, and her profile, white against the green tree, reminded me of the figurehead on a ship in San Francisco; I used to pay two dollars to walk on that ship. She'd hauled Chinese laborers and gold, and looking up at Margaret I realized something: that I walked on her polished decks and climbed her lookout every time I quit another job. As if she could take me anywhere.

"Yes sir," I heard MacKenzie say, "I spent an entire night in a tree because of that bear."

"A bear?" Margaret said.

"You bet. It was down on the Rogue River, near Zane Grey's place. She was an old sow with cubs. You don't argue with a sow with cubs."

We agreed that that was so.

He plucked a twig from the ground and studied it. Then he told us he'd caught a six-foot sturgeon on the Rogue, and while beaching the fish—which was not easy in a canoe—the bear surprised him. He threw his bait at her, and high-tailed it up the tree, with the sturgeon. And like he said, he had to spend the night up there.

"Oh, Mr. MacKenzie, what a wonderful story!" Margaret said. "Were you frightened?"

He must not have heard her, for he said, "Well, that happened almost sixty years ago. Before I started on the railroad. Before I met Violet even." He let go a little laugh. "She never did believe me. She called it my all-night whopper." He studied his twig. "You know," he said, "I was thinking of that big ice storm we had—you know the one I mean—limbs down all over the place, electricity out, couldn't drive anywhere—and you and your daughter came over for popcorn. We made it in the fireplace, remember that? Wasn't that the berries?"

I could barely hear her say, "Yes, it was."

"Heck," he said, "I was retired. I didn't have no place I had to be. Those were the days all right." He gave his twig a last look and tossed it away. He said he'd see us later, he had to go fight with his roses some more.

The front door opened and Millicent stepped out, hands on hips. Staring more or less straight ahead, she shifted her weight violently from one foot to the other, back and forth, throwing a little heel-stomp into it, as if she were both rendering fury and practicing a new movement, a variation on the flamenco perhaps, for the dance her button declared she was keen on. After several minutes of this, during which her mouth gathered in a bunch, she blurted, "In Zimbabwe you acted like my mother!" Then she returned inside, slamming the door.

I found MacKenzie's twig and scratched among the fallen fir needles with it.

"Are you coming down by and by?" I said.

"I don't think I'll ever come down."

I climbed the ladder and sat beside her on the limb. We looked at our dangling feet. She eased off her loafers so that they clung to the tips of her toes. Holding on to them that way, she said, "I miss Violet. She was the most cheerful person on this street. In this whole town. She would come outside in a floppy hat and whistle songs like "Good Night, Irene" and "On Top of Old Smoky" in an upbeat tempo. Some days when I felt low, when I had no more antique spoons and forks to polish and hide under the sweaters in my cedar box, I'd go out and putter in the garden just to hear her whistling."

After a while Margaret let her shoes drop to the ground. I kicked mine off too and we adjusted our positions on the limb. I sat against the trunk and she leaned back against my chest. We watched the sailboats. One was tacking on a perfect parallel with the line where sea and sky came together, the other two, one behind the other, seemed to be making a circle. Margaret told me about waking up from a dream that morning—"I never get to the end of them, Henry!"—and washing and waxing her kitchen floor for the second time in a week. I said my dreams almost always ended, and described my game with the "Ems" when I played fourth base. She laughed at the part where my best throw bounced over to first on the tenth or eleventh dribble, then she laughed harder, making me laugh with her, and we nearly lost our balance. When we settled down again she said, "Maybe that computer salesman really does hop trains." "What made you think of him?" "I don't know," she said. "Climbing up here, I guess. Wondering how far this tree could take me." We never did go watch the trotters that day. I don't remember exactly what we did instead, pulled a few weeds in her garden, repaired a loose rung on the ladder, things like that.

A Week in
South Dakota

He was a labor organizer from Dallas, had beautiful black curly hair and painted her toenails. She was sixteen. A month after she met him she suspected, vaguely, that she was pregnant. Two months later she lay in bed one morning listening to a crow squawk and knew it. Since then she's been trying to catch up.

The marriage lasted six years. She began to dislike him, feel sorry for him, maybe even hate him, after a year. The second child, another son, was an accident. "If he had only let me breathe," she said. "Given me room." He taught her, tried to teach her, everything. How to dress, to cook. "He cleaned the house. He picked out my clothes. One day he came home—I was stirring something at the stove—and kissed me on the neck from behind. I turned around and slapped him. The next morning, after he left for work, I packed a suitcase, dressed the boys, and drove home."

Home was Oklahoma, the farm. Her father was dead. Her five sisters, her brother—all scattered. But her mother was there, and she was there, twenty-two years old, two sons, no money. Her husband showed up on her birthday with a big stuffed animal. She told him she was getting a divorce. He left and came back and she said no to everything; then he told the boys they were dead to him. She never saw him again.

"He'd do things like this: we'd be eating dinner, the four of us, and suddenly he'd drop his fork, fall on his knees, and in front of the boys tell me how much he loved me. He'd grab my hand and wouldn't let go. He'd be crying. Or he'd want to set my hair . . . put it up in curlers."

After the divorce she decided to go to college. She took a test at a teacher's college in Oklahoma and was admitted. While she was away her mother watched the boys. "Funny how things turn out, me being a teacher now . . ."

In the fourth grade no one liked her. One day at recess the teacher took her inside and gave her a spanking for fighting. All of her classmates crowded up to the windows to watch. Each time Mrs. Birdsong brought her hand down the children cheered. On the last day of school the children filed past Mrs. Birdsong's desk to say good-bye. Mrs. Birdsong hugged each one. When Lyda's turn came the teacher simply said, "Good-bye, Lyda, have a pleasant summer."

Her second husband farmed for a while. But he didn't like farming and the place didn't do very well, so he quit and took welding jobs. "He said he got lonely sitting on a tractor way out in the fields."

Lyda *likes* being by herself—at least some of the time. Probably her best memories are of sitting all day by the creek when she was a kid . . . just watching the shadows on the water. After a while she'd rub her green apple, sprinkle salt on it, and lie back and watch the sky, her lips puckering. One time, lying in a field, she found herself listening with great pleasure to a cow chewing grass. "It sounded so good I couldn't hardly stand it. I got down on my hands and knees and took a mouthful—and chewed and chewed, trying not to spit, but finally I had to it was so bitter. Then I got sick as a calf."

At ten she was given a book with fifty music lessons in it for the piano. After you learned a lesson you got a silver star to paste next to it. She never got past lesson 4, but she did like lesson 3, and she still remembered the little verse:

> Running away to the ocean
> is the river,
> Nobody tells him he shouldn't be running a–
> way at all.

The motorcycles, their tubes chopped, circled in front of the house. Lyda's mother was practicing Revelations for her sermon on Sunday. She was a pumpkin–plump woman with apple cheeks. Across the room Lyda was wondering why she just didn't keep driving that Friday afternoon two years ago when Cricket, the lonely farmer, sat waiting in the Methodist rectory, cracking his knuckles. She was a hundred miles into Texas when she pulled over to the side of the road. She smoked four cigarettes before she turned back toward Oklahoma, toward the rectory where he sat or stood or paced—probably sat—waiting for his redheaded lady teacher.

The motorcycles stopped. Her mother rolled her eyes over the Bible, humming, "Yes, Jesus Loves Me" while tapping her slipper. Lyda followed a varicose vein in her mother's leg. It was a road on a map that led nowhere. She had wanted to stop the car beside a wheat field—the wheat field in Kansas where she ran last June and lay down. It was very hot and the earth was like beach sand. On her knees she took off her blouse, then she lay back, moving her hands in circles in the sand. She was all alone. She loved her sisters and brother and mother; she loved her boys. She loved her husband too, but not the same way. She loved him at night when she could close her eyes, just touching his skin. She loved his skin, and she loved his being a welder. All the men she met at college—

teachers mainly—were soft and dull and took forever to get to a simple point. Cricket was dull too but he was not stupid. He didn't pretend to be an expert on everything—and he was hard, firm. If she had to choose between intelligence and physical strength, she would choose the physical. At least you could close your eyes and think you had everything, and get lost in that, and sleep.

Her mother stopped humming. She closed the Bible, smoothed her dress, and laid the book in her lap. Then she said, "Do you recall that time I requested prayer for you, Lyda?" Lyda smiled. She was twelve when her mother warned her that's what she'd do if Lyda didn't quit skipping church. Lyda didn't believe her mother would do it, would ask the entire congregation to pray for her wayward daughter. But she did. "Yes, I remember," Lyda said, still smiling, wishing she could go back to being twelve again, tall and skinny and fixing her red ponytail in the hall mirror and free. "I remember it well . . . and I wish I could go back there and have you embarrass me all over again. I wish that right now more than anything."

Then Lyda excused herself and went outside and stood on the porch. One of the boys who had been riding his motorcycle up and down the hill near their house lay beside his bike in the yard, stabbing a screwdriver into the ground. Lyda said, "If you would drive me to South Dakota, I'd give you a kiss you'd remember." But she didn't say it loud enough for him to hear; she barely heard it herself, already trying hard to imagine what would happen when she got there.

She turned to go back in the house and saw her mother standing in the doorway, her eyes behind her thick glasses wet and large as the brown pebbles she once saved from the creek.

In Rapid City, in the shadows of the Black Hills, I watched a drunk Indian slide to a sitting position in a doorway in the saloon and gun shop district. His skinny ankles were blue. A fat woman came by with a thin, old man, and they looked at the drunk Indian, looked again, then stopped. The woman said something. The man cackled and scratched his crotch. Mumbling angry sounds, the woman walked away, and her thin companion, now in a coughing fit, followed, spitting every third or fourth step.

I went back to the hotel. The elevator boy was talking to the woman who had had the operation. "They quit when they took out half my stomach," she told him. Her red lipstick had got on her teeth, and she was wearing a white dress like the dress a young girl wears to her First Communion.

"That's what they do all right," the elevator boy nodded.

"Did you see the square dancers?" she asked me.

"No, I didn't."

"Oh, they're so sweet. So young-acting and happy. I wish them every good fortune, but most of all health. If you don't have your health, life is mean and hateful. I know." Then she smiled, showing the red lipstick on her teeth.

"You and your wife having a nice time?"

I said we were.

The boy stopped the elevator and let her off. When he closed the door he shook his head and made a little whistle. He had a fresh haircut but still wore the black pointed shoes. "Yup," he said, "that's what they do all right."

The lights were all on in the room. Lyda was in the tub, drinking bourbon and reading the Creeley book. She had a towel wrapped around her head.

"How are you doing?" I said.

"Fine. I like this man's poetry. 'Ballad of the Despairing Husband'—I like that one a lot." She set the book on the toilet and hugged her knees. "You have a nice walk?"

"I saw a drunk Indian."

"That all?" she laughed.

"And the woman who'd had the operation."

"The poor soul."

"She changed her dress. And the elevator boy got a haircut."

"You *are* observant." She put her head on her knees and smiled. "I was thinking. You know that couple we saw yesterday taking movies of the buffalo herd? I wonder what they thought of us?"

"They didn't know us."

"Now don't tell me you never think about people you don't know. And what they might think of you. Besides, they *did* take our picture."

"We were between them and the herd, an accident."

"We were two good-looking people, that's why, and you know it." She laughed away the subject and stood up. "Wipe my back?"

I dried her back, then we sat on the bed drinking bourbon.

"You want to know why my breasts are like this?"

"They're lovely," I told her.

"I had them fixed in Kansas City. I went to a doctor who also fixes the faces of kids who get burned or hurt in car accidents. We all sat in the waiting room together—the woman who wanted to be beautiful and the ugly unlucky children and their sad, smiling mothers." She poured more bourbon in her glass. "My sister in Denver advised me never to tell you— she said it would ruin the atmosphere." Lyda laughed. "That was her word, 'atmosphere.' I think she meant 'everything.'"

I told her they were lovely again.

"I just couldn't stand them all fallen down like they were."

"You did the right thing."

"You don't believe that."

I said I did.

She laughed and called me a poor liar. "But it's nice to hear, anyway."

We drank more bourbon, then turned off the lights and I listened to the air-conditioner until I fell asleep.

In the morning, going down, the elevator boy asked us, "Hear all the commotion last night?"

We hadn't.

"The lady in 502 jumped out the window. Had about six police in uniforms plus a detective up in the room till about an hour ago. I told them, 'Sure she acted funny, always talking about her operations and things.'"

He shook his head and whistled. "I saw her too, just before they picked her up. Looked like a pile of fancy hankerchiefs."

Out on the highway we were almost to Nebraska before we said much. She told me she was joining a tour to England during her Christmas break and would look up all the places I had told her about. She'd never been farther east than Kansas City and now she was going to Europe; she thought that was appropriate to the way she lived. And then she thought of something funny. Just before school was out Cricket had decided to take up archery. "I think he saw one of the books about England I had lying around." Now didn't I think that was funny—a welder from Oklahoma coming home every night and shooting arrows into a bale of straw in his cowboy boots and overalls?